Terence Faherty

Die Dreaming

WORLDWIDE.

TORONTO • NEW YORK • LONDON
AMSTERDAM • PARIS • SYDNEY • HAMBURG
STOCKHOLM • ATHENS • TOKYO • MILAN
MADRID • WARSAW • BUDAPEST • AUCKLAND

DIE DREAMING

A Worldwide Mystery/July 1996

First published by St. Martin's Press, Incorporated.

ISBN 0-373-26207-8

Printed in U.S.A.

For Reagan Arthur

A TIP

It was a part of Boston where the big, outdated apartment buildings along Beacon were a front for quiet, little neighborhoods of winding streets lined with old trees and slightly newer cars parked bumper to bumper against granite curbs. I drove slowly along a street called Pickett, looking for an unoccupied stretch of granite. I found one halfway up the hill that Pickett climbed and parallel parked on my first try, centering myself in the space the way true Bostonians do, by alternately tapping the bumpers of the cars behind and in front of me.

I climbed out of the delivery car, a small, square sedan whose paint had weathered down to the primer, and then leaned back inside to retrieve the reason for my visit to Pickett Street, a case of Budweiser, cold. Then I started down the hill on a sidewalk that was itself a series of small hills and valleys. As I walked, I noted a brass plate the size of my heel inset in the concrete of the path. It was shaped like a bell and bore the name of the company that had laid the walk in some forgotten year. This design was one of hundreds that dotted the sidewalks of Boston. Not for the first time, I thought that it would be fun to travel around the old city, making rubbings of these plates the way less whimsical collectors rub tombstones and church brasses.

I stopped at 31 Pickett Street, a two-story brick house that leaned stubbornly against the slope of the hill. I shifted my load to open the wood-and-wire gate and then followed a path of bare earth that led me between 31 and its near neighbor. As I walked this narrow alleyway, I was surprised to hear voices coming from a side window. I'd made regular deliveries to the little house, and I'd never known the owner, Mr. O'Reilly, to have a visitor.

The backyard was small and thick with the uneven and intensely green grass of early spring. The back porch consisted entirely of two wooden steps. Standing at the bottom, I raised my left foot to the top step and balanced the case of beer on my knee. Then I leaned across the carton and knocked on the back door.

The man who answered the door was not Mr. O'Reilly. He was a tall man with wispy white hair and merry eyes. He wore trousers and a well-filled vest of the same dark gray, a white dress shirt, and a black bow tie. A watch chain hung across the front of his vest. It was decorated with a gold St. Christopher medal.

"Just the gent we've been hoping to see," the man said.

He opened the door wide and stood back out of my way. I carried the beer into a tiny kitchen whose air was thick with cigar smoke. The old man left his post by the door and performed a similar service at the refrigerator. I bent to slide the case onto an empty rack.

As I straightened, the man handed me a folded bill. A ten.

"The change is yours," he said.

"Where is Mr. O'Reilly?" I asked.

"If we're to discuss metaphysics, we'd better have a beer." He nodded toward the still open refrigerator.

I pulled out two cans and handed him one. He opened it and raised it to the height of his twinkling eyes. "Happy Days," he said. "Or maybe the toast should be to the dear departed. Terry O'Reilly is dead. We just got back from burying him."

I started to say that I was sorry, but that sentiment seemed at odds with my host's high spirits. I took a sip of beer instead.

We listened to sounds of laughter coming from the room beyond. "How old are you, son?" the smiling man asked.

"Twenty-eight."

"You're too young, then, to take death so seriously. I'm a damn sight closer to joining Terry than you are, but I'm not about to let it get me down. That's the snare Terry stepped into."

"Are you a relative?" I asked.

"Me? No. Terry only had distant relatives, too distant to come to his funeral. A lot of his old friends are distant, too, having crossed over to the other side, but there were still enough of us on hand to do right by him today."

He raised his beer can in another salute and drank. With his free hand, he extracted a square of paper from the pocket of his vest. He handed the paper to me.

On it was written: "To die well is to die dreaming."

"What is this?" I asked as I handed the paper back.

"It's Terry's suicide note. That's what the police think. It surely was the last thing he wrote down before he shot himself. This is just a copy, of course."

"What does it mean?"

"Ah, well, that's an interesting question. You've years ahead of you to work it out, I hope."

He watched me drink and then said, "You've delivered here before, I take it."

"Yes," I said.

"Did old Terry ever tip you?"

"No."

"You keep this then," he said, handing me back the slip of paper. "It's a long overdue tip for you. A tip from the grave."

BOOK ONE

ONE

I DON'T KNOW what made me do it. Place the phony ad, I mean. The reunion committee certainly hadn't pressed me for one. They would have been happy to dismiss me with a brief reference. Keane, Owen J.; Occupation: various; Spouse: none; Children: none; Hobbies: drinking too much and hiding away in mystery stories. In place of those true but unsatisfying facts, I composed a new reality, a quarter page ad in bold type: "Owen Keane Detective Agency. Unanswerable questions discreetly answered." And water walked across, I should have added.

But I'm getting ahead of myself. It was March 1978. I was living in Boston, near Cleveland Circle, not far from Boston College, where I'd been an undergraduate some years before. I was working as a clerk in a liquor store on Beacon Street, a place called Nab's. I worked behind the counter some days, but mostly I stocked shelves and made deliveries. Not much of a job, I sometimes thought, for someone with a bachelor's degree in English literature. But then I'd factor in the credit hours I'd compiled toward a master's in theology, and it would all start to make more sense.

I also thought from time to time that a liquor store was the last place a solitary drinker like me should be working. But that wasn't really true. The absolutely worst job for this solitary drinker would have been in a mystery bookstore. The shelves and shelves of bottles that surrounded me at work were, after all, just bottles. I was fond of their numbing, pacifying contents, but I'd never mistaken it for a way of life or a way of plumbing life's secrets. I'd made that mistake about solving mysteries, however, and it had cost me a shot at the priesthood and other things I'd come to value as much or more than my lost religion.

I got back to my apartment building about ten that night, back to its formal stone entryway that smelled of pigeon droppings, its largely ornamental cage elevator, its marble steps that changed to creaking wood one flight above the lobby, and its metal apartment doors hand painted to look like wood (no two exactly the same, I'd determined). Back to my own dark apartment with its tasteful decor of books and old newspapers and the discarded packaging of take-out meals.

On this particular evening, I arrived home with a meatball sandwich, a cold quart of Miller High-Life, and the mail I'd collected from my lobby box. It was really mail for a change, as it contained something other than bills and solicitations. There was a long white business envelope from a New York law firm—Ohlman, Ohlman, and Pulsifer—that would contain, I knew, a letter from my old friend Harry. There was also a less prosperous looking blue envelope that bore the marks of a long journey. It had been forwarded from two of my previous addresses, and the hand stamps and labels that obscured the original address gave it the air of a well-travelled trunk. It's return address was intact, though: OLSHS (Our Lady of Sorrows High School, I deciphered as I read) Class of 1968 Reunion Committee, followed by a street I didn't know and a city I knew fairly well, Trenton, New Jersey, my hometown.

I settled into my Salvation Army recliner, whose movements scattered fragments of foam padding around my apartment floor, like bits of yellow cartilage working free of old joints. I opened the beer, the sandwich, and the white envelope, in that order. Harry's letter was the product of a busy man trying, unsuccessfully, to be chatty. Mary, his wife and my lost love, was fine. Work was fine. Their new town house in some recently laid-out New Jersey suburb was especially fine. Harry then got around to the point. Had I made up my mind about the research job with his family's firm that he'd offered me some months back? If not, why the hell not? Sincerely, et cetera, et cetera.

The contents of the blue envelope were equally predictable for an experienced deducer like myself. It contained a photocopied invitation for my tenth high school reunion, to be held in late May. Tucked in the bottom of the envelope, almost as an afterthought, was the fatal notification that the committee was selling advertising space in the reunion program.

I knew, sitting there with my half-empty beer bottle in one hand and the invitation in the other, staring into the darkness beyond my reading lamp, that I would attend the reunion. I had yet to actually make the decision, but I knew I'd go. Just as I knew I'd turn down Harry's offer of a job, though I was still pretending to consider it. I recognized that offer for what it was, a thinly disguised attempt to redeem me, and I wanted no part of it. So whatever attracted me to the reunion, it wasn't the promise of redemption. What, then?

That I hadn't stayed in touch with my high school classmates was certainly part of the reunion's attraction for me. I'd lived away from Trenton for the most part since going off to college, and I no longer had family there. So I felt confident, in my beery, unreflecting way, that the Lady of Sorrows crowd could know nothing of my failure in a midwestern seminary and the long slide since. The reunion seemed to me a way to reestablish contact with a time before the big failure that had divided my life into two barely related parts. The flimsy, impersonal invitation gave me a chance to be the other Keane again, the one before the fall. That desire might also explain the phony detective agency I whipped up out of beer foam and regrets. The ad I now designed on the back of Harry's envelope was both a joke on myself and a nod to my earlier self. It was a future the lost Keane would have taken by the hand, smiling.

When I'd completed my ad, I searched the apartment until I found an envelope and a stamp. Then I took my assembled reply out into the night, carrying the last of the Millers along for company. There was a mailbox on one edge of the ongoing mêlée that was Cleveland Circle. I stood watching the noisy traffic for a time, its patterns making less sense to me than usual. Then I dropped the letter into the box.

It should have occurred to me that my fascination with mysteries and detectives had led to the very failure I was trying now to forget. That I'd gotten myself mixed up by seeing the big questions of this life as puzzles that I could solve. If I'd made that connection, I would have avoided the earlier, dangerous Keane and saved us both a lot of trouble.

TWO

THAT'S HOW I happened to be driving to Trenton in late May in my trusty Volkswagen Karmann-Ghia. I didn't often drive anywhere, so I would have enjoyed this exception even if the weather had been hot and humid or rainy. But as the day was especially fine—the clear, bright spring holding off summer until the last possible moment—it felt like a vacation just to be shifting the Ghia's tired gears again. To head south, I first had to drive west through Massachusetts, past towns and small cities so carefully delineated by rivers and green hills that it seemed as though nature had laid itself out to conform to municipal boundaries. As I drove, I was conscious of returning to the starting point of my wanderings, of swimming back upstream, mentally jumping rocks and rapids in search of quieter water. I was certainly reversing the journey that had taken me from Our Lady of Sorrows to Boston College ten years earlier. Westward from Boston on the Mass Pike with its pilgrim-hat signs and crazy drivers. Then south into Connecticut through Manchester and Hartford, Waterbury and Danbury. From there into New York state and a detour that would carry me well around New York City, where Harry Ohlman sat at a desk dreaming about his lost clarinet, a symbol of college dreams that had held up no better than mine. A change of interstates at Brewster took me southwest to the Hudson and the massive Tappan Zee Bridge. Then I was into the clutter and traffic of my own home state.

Once safely in New Jersey, I left the beaten path, the New York to Philly corridor around which most of Jersey's millions lived and sold each other things. I headed west for the Delaware River and then south on a winding two-lane that ran along it. Eventually, I began seeing towns I recognized: Stockton, Lambertville, Titusville, Washington's Crossing. The next stop would have been Trenton, if I'd stuck with the river road.

I turned east instead on a new interstate, I-95, that ran through Trenton's northern suburbs. This highway crossed Route 1, which I took south for a few miles to a Howard Johnson Motor Lodge.

I would never have thought of the motel as a stopping place, if it hadn't been mentioned on the reunion invitation. The manager, a balding black man with a wide gap between his front teeth, asked what had brought me to Trenton while he searched for my reservation in a rotary file.

When I told him, he nodded. "We've got a lot of you Lady of Sorrows people staying here," he said. "On account of the special rate."

"What's the connection?" I asked. "I can't remember any Howard Johnsons in our class."

He laughed politely. "There is no connection. We work all the reunions we hear about. It's good for business."

The place needed every trick its management could pull. The main building was a white brick box set at an angle to the busy highway. My single was on the ground floor, its door opening directly onto the parking lot. I thought as I entered it that the room fit the mood of the weekend perfectly. It surely hadn't been redecorated since my senior year at Our Lady.

The bed-sitting-room was a rectangle walled in textured plaster and carpeted in a thinning orange shag. The door barely cleared the foot of the double bed, which was fitted out in approximately the rug's shade of orange, the fringe along the edge of the bedspread showing random gaps like an old comb. A half circle of gray Formica bolted to the wall served as a night stand. Above it hung a reading light with a shade that looked like a Japanese lantern executed in pebbled plastic. The headboard of the bed was white, as was the dresser, which was on my left as I entered. To my right was the doorway to a tiny bath, whose counter was fashioned of the same gray Formica as the night stand. On closer inspection, I found that it was really white Formica inset with thousands of tiny metal flakes like a high-priced bowling ball.

Going from the soft, clear light of the late afternoon into that orange room had a predictable effect on my high spirits. Dur-

ing my long drive, I'd been genuinely looking forward to my
reunion. The time I'd spent at Our Lady seemed, when seen
across the wreckage of the intervening decade, four golden
years. I'd been in, or on the edge of, the right group. I'd known
the movers and shakers of my class, the team captains, the
honor students, the class officers. Most of them had belonged
to a single informal society with an irreverent name: the Sorrowers. The Sorrowers had been *the* exclusive clique at Our
Lady of Sorrows, as known for their parties and practical jokes
as they had been for their academic achievements. I wanted to
see how these special people were faring in the world. More
than that, I wanted to know that they were doing well.

That desire had been part of the anticipation I'd felt on my
drive. Now, as I sat on the bed looking at my reflection in the
white-framed mirror over the dresser, I began to wish I'd made
my inquiries over the phone. My detective agency joke, created primarily to entertain the Sorrowers, no longer seemed
very funny. I analyzed this phenomenon and decided that there
were two distinct problems. One was that my real life was more
laughable than my gag career and therefore undercut it. The
other problem was that I was stone cold sober, which was the
wrong way to appreciate the subtleties of the Keane sense of
humor. Fortunately, I could do something about that. I rum-
maged in my bag for a going away present from Nab's, a pint
bottle of J & B. There was a glass tumbler in the bathroom,
wearing a paper doily as a hat. I discarded this decoration and
half filled the glass with scotch, which I cut with tap water fresh
from the Delaware. The old world meeting the new in micro-
cosm. Then I took my seat again on the bed.

Sure enough, after a few sips of warm scotch the young man
in the mirror began to look more presentable. Not much different than he had on graduation day, surely. Almost as thin,
brown hair shorter certainly but its numbers more or less intact. There were no scarlet letters or brands or obvious scars to
give away what I had or hadn't done with my ten years. I would
slip into the old crowd without notice.

THREE

AT SIX THIRTY I set out for the big event. By accident or subconscious design, I was dressed for the silly part I'd written for myself, in a gray double-breasted suit I'd picked up cheap when vests came into style. I could have passed for Nick Charles from an old thirties movie, except for the detail of my tie. I'd chosen one that had haunted my closets since high school, a wide, violet-and-purple statement that would not have looked out of place tied to the aerial of a psychedelic van. The combination of the suit and tie made me look like a detective as I might have pictured one in 1968. Be true to your school days.

The reunion was being held at a hall connected to the Lawrenceville firehouse, Lawrenceville being a middle-class bedroom community for crumbling Trenton. The weather had gone downhill while I'd sipped scotch and studied my reflection in the mirror. I now drove under a low, overcast sky, the Ghia's windows rolled up tight against the cool, damp air. I made two stops on the way, the first at a convenience store where I bought a pack of cigarettes and a disposable lighter. I could quit again later.

My second stop was at Our Lady of Sorrows High School itself. I left the Ghia in the parking lot, intending to walk around the place, but the first drops of rain cut short my tour. I settled for staring at the sprawling school, all additions and wings with no real center, trying to recapture the feeling of the place. After a moment, I gave it up. The feelings I was straining to recall were tied to people, not a pile of bricks, and there were no people here.

THE LAWRENCEVILLE firehouse hall was new and neutral, its interior an overlit combination of beige cinder block and matching linoleum. Standing in the doorway, I could see twenty or more tables arranged around a wooden dance floor. A few streamers in Our Lady's gold and blue dangled from the ceiling, and a small flower arrangement in the same colors had been placed on each table. A good-size crowd had already gathered around the tables, and I scanned it nervously for faces I knew.

I certainly recognized the woman behind the reception table, and even came up with a name, Carol.

"Remember me?" I asked as I stepped up to her station.

"No, but the tie looks familiar. Only kidding. It's Owen something, right?"

"Keane," I said.

"That's correct." For a prize, she handed me a name tag and a shock. Some creative mind had gotten the idea of putting copies of our yearbook photos on the tags. There I was, smiling out at the world like a farmer at the state fair, with eyes so wide they were crying out to be poked. The picture dispelled the illusion I'd talked myself into back at the Howard Johnson, the idea that the events of the past ten years hadn't left a visible mark. In memory, that face in the motel mirror seemed dark and dazed.

I folded the name tag and buried it in my pocket. They could guess.

Three steps into the room I was blocked by two women who looked enough alike to have been twins.

"Bev, you here, too?" said the one I remembered as Nancy somebody. "God, they're letting anyone in."

"Not true. They just stopped Ricky Gerow at the door." The speaker exploded in laughter at her own joke, while her audience sobered visibly.

"That's not funny," Nancy said.

The pair then moved on, leaving me to wonder why the idea of stopping Ricky Gerow at the door would be either funny or offensive. Nothing came to me, not even a very clear memory of Gerow's face. I decided that I needed some brain lubrication.

The bar had been set up in a far corner of the room. I made for it, nodding at familiar faces along the way. I squeezed in next to a tall blonde and waved down a harried bartender. "Scotch, please," I said.

"Hello, Owen," the blonde said. Our noses almost brushed as I turned, so I took a quick step backward. The golden hair cascaded from her head in one of those feathery arrangements popularized by Farah Fawcett. The woman beneath it would have been slightly overdressed if the rest of us had been wearing tuxedos. Her blue sequined dress was strapless, and it shimmered as though lit from within. Against the trappings, it took me a second or so to place the face. It shouldn't have. The blue eyes were two sizes too big, and they were still outdistanced by the smile. Her old nickname, Teeth, came back to me first then her name.

"Maureen," I said.

She rewarded me with a hug that drew stares from our neighbors at the bar. "Is that a tie you're wearing or a slipcover?" She laughed in my ear. "Don't run out of here without talking to me." She picked up a tall drink from the bar and hurried off.

A second bartender, a fellow graduate named Frank, came by in time to watch her go. "How long has she been a blonde?" he asked.

"Not long enough," I said. I was already sucking the ice in my first drink. I ordered another. "What are you doing on the wrong side of the bar?"

"Helping the help," Frank said. "I'm catering this lavish affair." He handed me a bright yellow business card. It made me wish I'd designed one for my phantom detective agency. Something dignified, with an eye in the center.

"Where's your program?" Frank asked.

I told him I'd forgotten to pick one up.

"Get one," he said. "It's the only way you can spot the insurance salesmen."

I thanked him for the advice and stepped straight into one of the Crupe twins, armed with pictures of his kids. I like children, especially in still photographs, but after a few minutes I needed a cigarette. I excused myself and moved to an empty corner.

While I was patting my pockets for my lighter, a quiet voice next to me said, "Having problems?"

The speaker was Ann Quinn, the first person whose name had come forward voluntarily. It wasn't a name that had figured prominently in my daydreams about the reunion. I hadn't dreamt that large. As I looked at her now, it occurred to me that this one moment could justify the whole expedition. Ann had been the famous beauty of our class. I'd firmly believed that every male of our year had a crush on her, for which certainly I'd needed no more evidence than the torch I carried myself.

Sometime during my school career, someone had told me that the leaders in any high school class were the people who just happened to mature early, the physical adults surrounded by gangly children. I'd thought immediately of Ann when I'd heard that, understanding for the first time her quintessential attraction. Not the prettiest girl at Our Lady, far from the most outgoing, not even the sexiest by the primitive measures of high school, Ann had been the most complete. A person who had gracefully achieved the goal toward which the rest of us had been awkwardly groping.

"Some detective," she said. "Can't find a match."

"I'm improving," I said. "Used to be I couldn't find the cigarettes."

Ann looked at me reprovingly, a look I often seemed to inspire. Whatever mechanism had matured her ahead of the rest of us was still at work. Tiny lines flanked her full lips and fanned out from the corners of her blue eyes. Those eyes were smaller than Maureen McCary's, but they made up for it by being much deeper, eyes you could high dive into. The long, fine brown hair, parted in the middle and curled slightly at her temples, was exactly the same as I remembered it, as was her pale, almost translucent skin. Her small teeth were whiter still, I noted as she smiled at me.

"Owen," Ann said. "Are you really a private detective? I can't believe it."

"Doesn't seem too likely to me either, at the moment."

She took my right hand and examined it. "You haven't duked anyone out with this recently."

"You've been watching too many old movies," I told her.

"So has your tailor."

Ann's attire was more up-to-date, a golden brown dress of simple lines made of some silk-like synthetic. "Who are you sitting with for dinner?" she asked.

"You?" I asked back.

"If we can squeeze in somewhere."

I was still raising my jaw—mentally, at least—when Maureen McCary trotted up. "Come on you two," she said. "We've saved you seats."

I didn't react fast enough to suit her, so she took hold of my left forearm and tugged me into motion. Ann Quinn fell into step on my right, slipping her arm lightly under mine.

The tie hadn't been such a bad choice after all.

FOUR

UNTIL THE MOMENT Maureen found us, I'd been wondering where the old crowd was hiding. The Sorrowers, I mean, the movers and shakers I mentioned earlier. Maureen led us to the quartet of tables the Sorrowers had staked out with handbags and suit coats. We made the trip via the bar, where I collected yet another drink, so my belated reunion with the Sorrowers was a moment of hazy emotion. I hugged relative strangers and shook hands and said, "You look great," over and over, by which I meant unchanged. They looked prosperous and happy, too, which pleased me. I could have gone home to Boston at that moment perfectly content. I should have, in fact.

Before I'd regained my equilibrium, it was time to sit down to dinner. I was surprised to find that Ann and I had been seated at McCary's own table. Ann had been a genuine member of the clique and therefore deserved the honor. Perhaps, I thought, my temporary association with her had won it for me. Or perhaps I'd been a full-fledged Sorrower all along and not known it.

The tables were round, but when McCary chose her seat at ours she seemed to be identifying its head. The broad theatricality of her movements reminded me that she had been the lead in our senior class play. To McCary's left sat her bored date, identified to us briefly as Roland, a name that went well with his white, three-piece suit and dark, open-collared shirt. To his left was Lucy Criscollo, our class valedictorian, and Mary Kay Ellis-Humphrey, who had been editor of *The Guardian,* our school paper. If McCary's seat was the head of the table, I was at the foot, more or less opposite her. Ann settled in quietly next to me. The last two seats were taken by Bill Pearson, once captain of Our Lady's football team, and his wife Patty, who tried unsuccessfully to engage Ann in small talk.

I was identifying everyone by their old, Lady of Sorrows achievements. I soon learned of their recent ones, as bits of autobiography flew back and forth across the table. McCary was now an actress and appeared irregularly in commercials and in New York soaps. Criscollo worked as a public defender somewhere in Delaware. Ellis-Humphrey was still a journalist, now with the *Newark Star Ledger*. Pearson was an associate professor of history at a state college near the shore, where his wife also taught.

Unlike the others, Ann Quinn seemed reluctant to talk about herself. She sat listening politely, asking pertinent questions and giving nothing away. Part of her old attraction had been a natural aloofness, I remembered now as I listened to her parry questions from Mary Kay and the others. The nickname Inaccessible Ann came to mind, but I wasn't exactly sure if it was an old memory or a scotch-inspired insight.

When Mary Kay tired of interviewing Quinn, she turned to me. She'd always worn glasses, the current pair large rose-coloured ovals that dwarfed her small features and made it hard for me to read her eyes. She was wearing a plain, brown business suit whose pockets sagged from years of carrying notebooks and pencils. I busied myself with my salad, poking around for bits of lettuce in the sea of creamy Italian dressing before me. This clever ruse did me no good.

"So, Owen," Mary Kay began, "what are you doing now?"

The band hired for the evening had decided to serenade us during dinner, and the resulting noise divided our table into three or four separate conversations. This made my confession easier. "I'm in the retail liquor industry in Boston," I said. In it and supporting it.

"What happened to the Owen Keane Detective Agency?" Ann asked from the left flank. I could barely hear her voice above the opening bars of an old Association hit.

"That was just a joke," I said.

And not a very funny one I judged from the way Ann abruptly pushed her salad away. I thought she was going to ask me who the joke had been on, but instead she just said, "Why?"

Mary Kay saved me from that imponderable by shifting the subject slightly. "I remember you always carrying a mystery novel around," she said. "Did I get you started on those or did you do it to me? I'm really hooked now."

We then discussed her favorite author, Agatha Christie, for a time. Ann drifted into a conversation with the Pearsons. I gave Mary Kay a recommendation I'd once received, telling her to try Dorothy Sayers and Margery Allingham. When we'd exhausted detective fiction, Mary Kay told me about her husband, who had refused to be dragged to the reunion, and their two children. By the time I'd been briefed on her entire hyphenated family, our entrées were being cleared away, and I thought it would be safe to turn again to Ann.

She was looking at me a little less severely. "Let's dance," she said. "If I'm here when the dessert arrives, I'll eat it." When I hesitated, she smiled. "Relax. This group's never heard of disco."

I gave the bar a last, longing glance and followed Ann onto the dance floor. The band was playing "Lighter Shade of Pale," an echo of dead prom nights. We blended into the other dancers easily. Ann had a weightlessness in my arms that relaxed me completely. I inclined my head a little to enjoy the fragrance of her hair.

Without preamble, Ann said, "You've been in love since I saw you last."

"I'm always falling in love with someone," I said, giving her fair warning.

"I mean you've been in love once. For real."

"How can you tell?"

"There are signs."

"Don't tell me *you* have a detective agency."

I felt her stiffen ever so slightly. I would have kicked myself if I hadn't been preoccupied with keeping time.

After a moment, Ann asked, "Who was she?"

"Someone I met in college."

"What happened?"

A million things, but the last event summed up the others. "She married someone else."

Maureen McCary breezed across the dance floor at that moment, the dancers parting before her like a trained ensemble. She paused momentarily near my free ear. "The next slow one's mine," she whispered. I was so jaded by the evening's successes that I didn't even blink.

When McCary had disappeared again, I asked Ann, "How about you?"

"How about me what?" she asked, playing dumb.

I ignored the hint. "Any great loves in your life?"

The music stopped, ending our dance and, I thought, our conversation. But on our walk back to the table, Ann said, "There's been nothing like that." She picked up her bag from her chair. "I'll see you later," she said.

Years later, I decided she meant. I spent the next two hours drinking and mingling. The name-remembering portion of my brain had came unstuck, and I rattled off the most elaborate Polish and Italian tongue twisters with ease. Marvelous thing, scotch.

I was thinking of calling it a night when Maureen McCary came shimmering out of the misty heather. "What happened to our slow dance?" she asked.

All the dances were slow now, the band's fatigue coinciding perfectly with a mood of parting that was settling over the gathering, Maureen led me to a quiet corner of the dance floor. When I'd made this same circuit earlier in the evening, Ann Quinn had seemed as ethereal as the music we'd moved to. McCary was the opposite, so concrete a presence that she almost seemed rooted to the hardwood. She kept me at arm's length, and the sequins of her dress felt like tiny armor plates beneath my hand as I struggled to align us with the beat. My other hand held hers, her thumb stroking mine in a twitchy motion.

"Is something wrong?" I asked. "You seem uncomfortable."

She moved a little closer. "I need your help," she whispered. "Professionally, I mean."

Now we were both uncomfortable. "Maureen," I started to say.

"I'm being blackmailed, Owen," she said in a rush. "Just when things are starting to click for me. I don't know what to do."

I'd had a lot to drink, but not enough for me to consider leading McCary on. "Look, Maureen," I said. "If you're talking about that ad in the program, that was just a joke. I'm not a detective." I was prepared to be as honest as I had to be to get off McCary's hook. I was ready to tell her how I dusted bottles at Nab's and how much I was paid every hour.

She never gave me the chance. "Are you still my friend? That's what I need now. I need help. I need advice."

A little bit of the latter came to mind immediately. "Call the police."

"No!" Her fierce whisper rang in my ear like a shout. "That would be like calling the *Trentonian*. I've got to keep this quiet, don't you see? I'll lose everything I've worked for if I don't. Promise me that you won't call the police whatever happens, Owen. Promise."

"I promise," I said.

She'd gone from rigid to extremely pliant while we'd argued. Now she lay against me as though she was close to fainting. Her head rested on my shoulder, and I saw the dark world around us through a cloud of yellow hair.

None of that improved my dancing or my thinking. "Tell me about it," I said.

"I did something stupid years ago. Something bad. Don't ask me what. Not here. Just tell me you'll help me. You're the only one who can."

"Why me?"

She was making small movements like suppressed sobs. After a moment, she said, "The person doing this is someone we both know. Someone from the old group."

"A Sorrower?"

"I think so. I'm sure of it. Whoever it is hates me. I'm scared."

She pushed herself away and ran a hand over her face. "I can't go around looking like this," she said. "The group is getting together at David Radici's later. We can talk there. Thank you, Owen.''

She leaned forward and kissed me. Not hard, but long, a lingering dry softness.

Then she was gone.

FIVE

DAVID RADICI found me before I'd gathered enough of my scattered wits to leave the dance floor. Radici had been evolving into something resembling a hippie when I'd last seen him at Our Lady of Sorrows. That hadn't exactly made him stand out in the late sixties. It was novel, however, that he was still playing the part of a flower child ten years later. Living the life of one, I should say, to give him the benefit of the doubt. I deduced his constancy to the old ideals from the way he was dressed, in a well-worn sports coat over T-shirt and jeans.

"Keane," he said in greeting, "another longhair gone Republican."

The same could not be said of him. Hair radiated in long, curly waves from his head, forming a foil for his narrow, clean shaven face. He wore round wire-rimmed glasses and a grin that grew wider as I watched.

Radici put his hand on my arm. To steady himself, I thought. Then I realized he'd done it to steady me. "You okay, Keane?" he asked.

Maureen McCary's confidences should have sobered me. Instead they'd made me suddenly conscious of how unsober I was. "I'll be fine when I wake up," I said.

Radici laughed at that. "I don't think you're going to enjoy waking up at all. You'd better switch to Maxwell House." He handed me a sheet of paper. "Directions to my place. I'm having a reunion survivors party. Sorrowers only."

"Seems I've heard about it," I said. I gave Radici's map some serious study. The notations appeared to be in Chinese.

"You need a ride out there?" he asked.

I was working up a clever reply when my place in the conversation was taken by Ann Quinn. "I'll look after him," she said.

Radici's grin grew an inch on each side. "I'll have to remember to drink more in the future," he said. He then hurried off, waving a map at another lucky Sorrower.

I turned to look at Ann. I would have been surprised to see her again, if I'd still been capable of surprise. She'd borne the rigors of the reunion well. Remarkably well. She was now looking very much as she had at Our Lady, the worry lines eradicated by the dim lighting or my dimmed senses. I could almost see her again in a plaid skirt and navy blazer, clutching a stack of books protectively against her chest. I think I *was* seeing her that way, until she gently shook my arm.

"Owen," she said. "You've had enough old times for one evening."

"Early Times," I said, naming a bourbon instead of a scotch in my eagerness to be witty.

"Why don't you skip the party?"

That idea sounded so good to me that I knew at once to check for my ulterior motive. One wasn't hard to find. I wanted to steer clear of Maureen McCary and her mystery. I wanted to sober up and sneak back to Boston with my memories of the reunion and the Sorrowers intact.

Ironically, it was Ann Quinn, the person encouraging me to get out, who made me stay. Ann had been disappointed somehow by my phony ad. I knew she had been without exactly understanding why. I didn't want to disappoint her further by running out on an old friend.

"I have to go," I said. "Don't worry about me. I'll be fine."

"Maybe someday." She took the map from me. "Come on, then."

Scattered hugging had broken out in what remained of the reunion crowd. We moved through small, emotional groups, hearing over and over the admonition to "stay in touch."

We stopped at a closet guarded by a sleepy old lady in a shiny black dress that rustled as she stood up to retrieve Ann's raincoat.

Ann looked back toward the banquet room. "Most of these people won't see each other again until the next reunion," she said. "Why pretend otherwise?"

"It isn't a pretense," I said as I struggled to help her on with her coat. "It's a heartfelt wish. They just won't remember it in the morning."

I was trying to be profound, a problem I have when I've been drinking, but I succeeded only in producing the first laugh I'd heard from Ann in a long time.

It had rained in earnest sometime during the evening. We walked arm in arm through a maze of puddles, each one lit unromantically by a reflection of security lights. I tried to stop at the Ghia, but Ann tugged me onward. "I'll drive," she said. "You navigate. With any luck, we'll end up in Cleveland."

David's place turned out to be well north of the city, in Hopewell Township. We followed the map he'd given us until we saw the man himself, standing in the middle of the road under an umbrella. He was waving a flashlight toward what looked to be an overgrown field, but was actually his front yard. Three or four cars were lined up in the driveway. Ann pulled off into the weeds.

Radici's wife, Libby, had been a year behind us in school, which made her even more a child of the late sixties than her hippie husband. I'd spotted her briefly back at the firehouse, where she'd seemed uncomfortable in her regulation dress. She greeted us now on the front porch, smiling away in sweatshirt and jeans.

Libby's outfit had set the dress code for her guests. A discarded jacket and tie hung on the inside knob of the front door, and a small pile of wet shoes had collected in front of the burning logs in the living room fireplace. Ann added hers to the assortment and then tugged on my tie.

"We're giving this thing a Viking funeral," she said. She pulled the tie free of my collar and tossed it onto the fire. The tie's violet and purple clashed one last time with their surroundings before the yellows and oranges of the fire consumed them, sending thick smoke up the flue.

"I think you've just violated some EPA regulations," I said.

"Around here who's going to notice?"

I wasn't sure whether she was referring to New Jersey in general or just the Radicis' living room, which was already hazy with smoke, cigarette mostly. One of Simon and Garfunkel's albums was playing on the stereo, a complex-looking system that was a probably worth more than all the furniture in the room. The decor was eclectic and secondhand: an overstuffed sofa, fringed at the bottom like the bed in my motel room, two matched armchairs, an ancient radio cabinet that contained the bar, and bookcases made of plastic milk crates and unpainted lumber. A framed poster over the fireplace advertized a Monet exhibition in Chicago.

I liked the room. It could have been a big college dorm room from ten years earlier. It certainly fit David and Libby, two people who seemed stubbornly fixed in time. Our host had come in from the street and was now busy passing out drinks. He started to offer me a beer, thought better of it, and handed me a Coke instead. I looked around for McCary, but there was no sign of her. That was a relief, of course, but I still felt the sharp point of her mystery hanging over my head. I tried to sidle out from under it by telling myself that she would find me when she wanted me.

The half dozen people in the living room were only a subset of the Sorrowers who had attended the reunion. I wondered what the odds were that Maureen McCary's blackmailer was with me now. And what was she being blackmailed about anyway?

"Tune in tomorrow," I said aloud.

"What?" Ann asked.

"Nothing."

Lucy Criscollo, assistant district attorney, was sharing the sofa with Mary Kay Ellis-Humphrey, the Agatha Christie admirer. Bill Pearson sat cross-legged on the tired carpet in the center of the room.

"Where's Patty?" Ann asked him.

"I dropped her at her folks," he said. "She was bushed."

Mark Plesniak, the president of our class, came out of the kitchen carrying a tray of potato chips and pretzels. He was another longhair gone bad, or in Mark's particular case, bald. Almost bald, anyway. A handful of golden hair was arranged artfully across the top of his head. The healthier growth around his ears was darker, almost brown, and oily. He'd balanced his hair deficit a little with heavy sideburns and a well-trimmed cowboy moustache.

I hadn't had a chance to speak with Plesniak at the reunion, so my greeting now was unduly enthusiastic. I called out the campaign slogan that had scandalized the nuns at Our Lady: "The Spirit of Che lives in Mark Plesniak!"

"What?" he asked, startled. His reddened eyes achieved a remarkable blankness. Then the old synapses fired. "Oh yeah, I remember. Those were crazy days."

He banged me on the shoulder as he passed, scattering chips at my feet. Mary Kay helped me pick them up on her way to the kitchen.

Ann had settled in on a hooked rug near the fire. She caught my eye and patted the spot next to her. As soon as I sat down, she stretched out at a right angle to me and rested her head on my leg. She was asleep before I'd finished my soda.

Simon and Garfunkel wrapped up their set. Their place on the turntable was taken by a Beatles album, *Magical Mystery Tour*. The music had to compete with Plesniak, who was describing his position at a local bank with a modesty that was undercut by his booming delivery. Plesniak's principal audience was his near neighbor on the sofa, Lucy Criscollo, but everybody seemed to be listening. It would have been hard not to.

"Don't let my title fool you," Plesniak was saying. "Banks pay in titles." He was balanced on one arm of the sofa, not far from me. I briefly considered moving closer to the stereo, but Ann was definitely settled.

Criscollo was eyeing Plesniak as though she was thinking of tipping him from his perch. Lucy still had her remarkable high school figure: almost matronly breasts on a tall, bony frame. The contrast was heightened by her dress, a light-weight gray knit that clung to her like a second skin. She wore her black hair long with bangs cut straight across her forehead an inch above her heavy eyebrows. The rest of her features were also dark and severe, eyes so brown they were almost black and a profile that had always reminded me of Basil Rathbone, hero of my favorite detective movies.

"Our class revolutionary," Criscollo said. "Now Assistant Vice President of Mortage Loans."

"The spirit of Che!" Plesniak said, holding his beer can aloft.

"The spirit of Chase, you mean," Criscollo said. "Chase Manhattan."

"New Jersey National," Plesniak countered happily. It was impossible to tell if he didn't get her sarcasm or just didn't give a damn.

Lucy ignored him. "What happened to our social consciences? That's what I'd like to know."

"Mine's out back on blocks," Radici said.

Plesniak was suddenly snapping his fingers. "This reminds me of a movie I saw a year or two back. It was about a bunch of old friends getting together after a wedding or something. I can't remember the name."

"Our Days," Radici said.

"Old Days," his wife corrected.

"Right," Plesniak said, awarding the pint to Libby. "Great flick. Sitting here with you guys reminds me of that."

"I saw it," Lucy said. "The dialogue was better."

Mary Kay appeared in the kitchen doorway. "So were the people," she said. "Richer anyway. No offence guys, but I didn't see any Porsches outside."

Radici took time out from rolling a joint to giggle.

"Mine's parked next to my social conscience."

"A Porsche is a substitute for a social conscience," Lucy said. "We're none of us rolling in money. Except maybe for Teeth. Where is Maureen, anyway?"

"She promised she'd be here," Libby said. "She's probably still signing autographs."

"A lot of the gang isn't here yet," her husband observed, looking around the room. "This is just the first wave."

The members of that wave looked around at each other for no particular reason. I looked around, too, and happened to spot an unsmoked cigarette in my shirt pocket, the cigarette I'd been trying to light when Ann had found me before dinner. She was still an impediment to the project, as her head was resting very near the pocket of my pants containing my lighter. The solution to this dilemma arrived in the form of a joint that was being passed around the room. I lit my cigarette from its burning tip, and then held the joint out to Ellis-Humphrey, who came back into the room to take it from me.

Meanwhile, Assistant Vice President Plesniak was getting cold without the spotlight. "I meant that this moment reminded me of the movie. A bunch of old radicals sitting around, comparing careers and wondering where the old ideals went."

"Were you wondering that, Bill?" Ellis-Humphrey asked.

Pearson looked genuinely startled. "What?" he asked. He waved the proffered joint away. "Sorry. I guess I've been tuned out."

I was going to ask him his secret, but Criscollo reclaimed the floor. "I thought those people in the movie were a pretty phony bunch of radicals," she said. "Sipping their wine and thinking how noble life had been before income taxes. Remembering how they'd stormed the barricades in school when all they'd really done was give their baby-sitters a bad time."

"It was more than that," Radici said. He was suddenly very serious. It was easy to see that Lucy's casual dismissal of the good old days bothered him. He had taken off his glasses, and he was rubbing them on his shirt with enough energy to remove dried paint.

Criscollo recognized a new target and attacked. "Not for us, Davey," she said. "Not for the fearless Sorrowers of sixty-eight. Hell, we girls used to kneel down on command so the nuns could check the length of our skirts. If you want to remember yourself as some sort of great iconoclast, fine. The way I remember it, they could have used us all for angels in the Christmas pageant."

"Have you forgotten Princeton?" Radici asked.

The cryptic question triggered the oddest moment of the long, odd evening. Plesniak tottered on the arm of the sofa. Criscollo and Ellis-Humphrey caught Radici in a cross fire of shocked amazement. Even Bill Pearson looked up from the floor for a moment.

Radici replaced his glasses and blinked at each of them in turn. "Sorry," he said. "Really. I'm sorry."

"For what?" asked the ghost by the fire. No one answered me.

SIX

BEFORE I COULD repeat my request for an explanation, Mary Kay stepped forward to fill the silence. "At least we got to college while the war was still on. There was a real sense that the world was changing then. Those were important days."

"Self-important," Criscollo said.

"Better than what came later," Mary Kay fired back. "it wasn't long after I finished graduate school that the biggest thing on college campuses was streaking."

"God help us," Libby said. "What was that ever about?"

"Beer," Criscollo said. "Rebels without a cause. The campus radical stripped of his Vietnam-era pretensions, naked to the world. What do you say, Mark? Could you have gotten behind that movement?"

"I would have followed you, Lucy. Eagerly."

Under the cover of the laughter that followed, Pearson got up and walked into the kitchen. I wiggled out of my suit jacket with the aid of Libby Radici, folded it into a square, and eased it under Ann's head, extricating my leg at the same time. Then I followed Pearson.

The kitchen was even smaller than the living room and dark, lit only by a single bulb in a dusty glass fixture over the sink. There was a table-full of unopened snack food in one corner and an auxiliary cooler of beer in another. The room was paneled in vertical strips of reddish pine. The same material had been used as facing for the cabinets and counter. A window over the sink looked out on the driveway.

Pearson was at the sink drawing a glass of water. He turned as I came in. "Headache," he said. Then he smiled and added. "I'm not used to late nights anymore."

His smile was still boyish, an impression helped along by the faint traces of old freckles on his broad face. In addition to football, Pearson had lettered in wrestling and the field portion of track and field. I'd gotten to know him on the track team, where he'd been as much cheerleader as participant.

"You're keeping in shape," I said.

"Coaching a little on the side," he said. I expected him to return the compliment, but he reached out instead and patted my stomach. "Getting a little soft,' he said. "Better watch that. A couple of laps around the old track wouldn't do you any harm. Are you running any these days?"

"Only to catch a streetcar."

"You probably settle for the next one a lot. Streetcars are like women. If you miss one . . ."

"You do without for years," I said.

Pearson gave me a closer look and chuckled. "I guess that is a truer punch line."

"Speaking of punch lines," I said, "what was this Princeton business Davey mentioned? I don't seem to recall it."

Pearson listened to the conversation in the other room until there was another burst of laughter. Then he said, "Not really supposed to talk about it, but that seems kind of silly now. It was senior year. A bunch of us went up to the university to mix with the college kids one night. There was a big protest rally going on. Things got kind of intense. A couple of impromptu bonfires, cops with dogs, people chanting and yelling. Tear gas even. It all scared the shit out of us. Well, we were just kids back then, even if we didn't think so ourselves.

"Anyway, like I said, I shouldn't even be talking about it. We sort of swore each other to secrecy on the subject."

"Why?"

Pearson had to think about that one. "We were afraid it would get back to our folks. Or worse, to the drill sergeant nuns at Our Lady of Sorrows. But it might have had more to do with our being embarrassed. We were the Sorrowers, right? We were better than everybody else." He considered the last swallow of water in the bottom of his glass. "That night we found out we weren't. That may be the big secret we've been protecting all these years."

He laughed to himself. "Isn't much of a secret these days, though. Is it?"

I should have followed up on that opening, but it was late in the day for me and subtleties. "I think you're all doing great," I said.

Pearson gave me another look and finished his water. "Maybe you're right. This head of mine is making me kind of whiny."

We heard the sound of a car out on the main road, and Bill looked up toward the window. He was still staring into the black night after the car had gone by without slowing. I remembered then that he had spent a lot of our high school years lusting after Maureen McCary. I wondered if we might both be waiting for the same woman.

"I wish Maureen would show," I said. "I didn't get much of a chance to talk with her at the hall."

"Neither did I," Bill said. He set his empty glass down in the sink. "She'll never spot the house in this jungle. I think I'll head out."

After Pearson had gone, I stood by the sink for a time, awake, but not truly conscious of my surroundings. Influenced perhaps by Ellis-Humphrey's paean to her college days, I thought of my own, of Mary and her future husband Harry, and of the old dream I'd dreamed that I would solve the mysteries that haunted me. The mysteries, still unsolved, were all I had left from those days.

Pearson's headlights came on in the driveway, drawing me back to the present. As if in response to his signal, the phone in the kitchen began to ring with a dated, mechanical resonance. I traced the sound to a dark corner of the room and located a wall phone.

"Hello," I said into the receiver.

"Owen? Is that you?"

I'd told myself that McCary would find me when she wanted me, but there was something eerie about her tracking me to a dark room in a dark corner of Hopewell Township.

"I couldn't come, Owen. I couldn't bring myself to drive up there alone."

"What happened to Roland?" I asked, picturing her blow-dried escort from the reunion.

"He had to go back to New York." Without the golden hair and spangles to distract me, I was able to concentrate on her voice. She sounded very young and very scared.

"I still want to talk things over with you. You're staying at the Howard Johnson on Route 1, right?"

"Yes," I said.

"So am I. I'm in room 121. Can you come by tomorrow morning at ten? Is that too early?"

It sounded only minutes away, but there was nothing I could do but tell her I'd be there, bright-eyed and full of helpful advice.

"Thank you, Owen. I knew I could count on you." I was still standing by the phone when the kitchen's ceiling fixture buzzed into life. Ann walked up before I'd stopped blinking. She was wearing my jacket across her shoulders. On her, it looked good.

"Time to saddle up," she said. "The evening's deteriorated into a debate on who's gained the most weight, a subject not dear to my heart."

"I thought you were asleep," I said.

"I was until you deserted me to come in here and stare at the paneling. I woke up freezing." She eased herself out of my suit coat, one shoulder at a time, and tossed it to me. "See that it doesn't happen again," she said.

"Right," I said a beat late.

We retrieved Ann's raincoat and her shoes and said our good-byes to our hosts, who seemed surprised by our decision. During that ceremony, I slipped one of Radici's cold beers into my jacket pocket, intending to make one huge boilermaker of the evening's whiskey.

Ann wisely insisted on driving us back. Her car was a Mustang II, an underpowered pretender to the original's throne. Not, I thought, that a man who drives a Volkswagen should look down his nose at other people's horsepower. I settled into the butterscotch-plaid bucket seat and opened my beer. Ann didn't seem to want conversation, so I watched the dark scenery.

She brought us safely down from the Hopewell hills to the Pennington Circle. Instead of sticking to Route 31 until it met the interstate, Ann turned off onto a winding old stagecoach tract, the Pennington-Lawrenceville Road. There she made the most of what power her little car had. I consulted the speed-ometer after an especially exciting turn. It told me we were do-ing seventy.

"I killed a cat along here once," I said. "At night. Came around a curve too fast."

"Afraid of meeting a ghost?"

"Afraid of becoming one. Could we go slower?"

"I go slow all the time."

We made it to the light at Route 206 in one piece. The light was red. While we waited for it to change, Ann said, "You're at the Howard Johnson, aren't you?"

"Everybody knows that," I said. Ann didn't ask me what I meant, and I didn't ask her how she knew. It didn't occur to me to ask. "If you make this right, I can pick up my car."

When the light turned green, Ann drove straight through the intersection. "You can pick it up tomorrow," she said.

She let me ponder the logistics of that for most of what was left of the drive. Then, as we were nearing the motel parking lot, she said, "You were certainly smiling a lot this evening."

"A world-weary, sophisticated smile, I hope."

"No, a goofy one. The one I remember from Our Lady of Sorrows."

I was happy to recognize a similarity between her descrip-tion and the yearbook portrait on the name tag hidden in my pocket. Maybe I wasn't so far removed from my better, earlier self after all. "I was smiling because the old crowd is doing so well," I said. "It's what I came here to see."

Ann asked her favorite question, "Why?"

I'd never worked that out. I took a stab at it now, my usual defensiveness broken down by alcohol and fatigue. "Just big-hearted of me, I guess. I'm not doing so well myself. I'm pretty much a lost cause, in fact. Never mind the details. But I feel vindicated when I see that someone I grew up with is making it. I mean, it seems to validate where I came from and how I was brought up. If I didn't grab the brass ring myself, maybe that was just bad luck."

My explanation sounded neatly tied together to me. I thought for a moment that it had also satisfied Ann. She followed my directions and pulled into a space near my room. Then she put the car in park and switched off the engine. I thought of high school dates ending in dark cars parked in quiet spots. Ann was thinking of something else.

"Suppose your happiness has nothing to do with your past and your upbringing being validated and everything to do with your failure being validated."

"Come again?"

"If a kid from your block makes it and you don't, then you can't blame your environment or education or the fluoride in your water. The fault is inside you."

"So I came all the way down here from Boston to confirm that I'm a loser and deserve my crummy life? And finding that out tickles me? That makes me a pretty sad case."

"What does all this private-eye business make you? Giving all your old friends a chance to laugh at you, as though the Sorrowers ever needed anybody's invitation for that. What does that make you?"

She was trying to get a rise out of me, but she couldn't. For one thing, I was too flattered by her concern for me, as I'd been all evening by her on and off attentions. "It just makes me goofy," I said. "Like my smile. Like I was ten years ago. I thought I'd changed, but maybe I haven't. Or maybe just the thought of being around you people again made me act the way I used to. Did you feel that way tonight?"

"Yes," Ann said. "And I saw it in a lot of people's eyes. The high school kid looking out again through the mask. In men's eyes mostly. Former boys, I should say. The old look you all used to give me. I wonder if there's any of you who hasn't imagined making love to me."

From Maureen McCary that line would have sounded impossibly egotistical and smug. Ann said it sadly, as though she had actually been used in some way by the imaginings of all those lost boys and marked by it for life.

I would have protested my own innocence if I'd been a better liar. Instead, I consoled her in a worse way than lying. I leaned across and kissed her, intending no more, I told myself, than to thank her for looking after me.

Ann interpreted the kiss differently and, perhaps, correctly. "I don't want to drive home tonight."

"Don't then," I said.

SEVEN

I AWOKE EARLY the next morning with the odd idea that I had
died sometime during the night. Then I opened my eyes and
realized that I was in far worse shape than that. Ann lay next
to me, curled up on her side, her bare back to me. It was a sight
and situation to marvel at, if I hadn't been too dizzy for marveling. I quickly determined that I was too dizzy for anything,
even lying quietly with my eyes closed. I staggered into the
bathroom and sat on the floor with my head back against the
cool porcelain of the tub.

The pain in my head reminded me of the apple-wine hang-
overs I'd suffered through in the earliest days of my drinking,
a high school hangover in other words, so appropriate to the
weekend that it almost seemed inevitable. As was my habit
when I woke up with an aching head, I started the day by trying to remember all the embarrassing things I'd done the night
before, the stupid remarks I'd made and the falls I'd taken. It
wasn't hard to remember the highlights of the reunion evening. I'd let Maureen McCary involve me in a mystery I wanted
no part of. And I'd made love to Ann Quinn, fulfilling her sad
expectation of everyman's desires.

I practiced keeping my eyes open. Luckily there was something interesting to practice on. I was facing the bathroom door,
across which hung a towel rack. On this plastic bar was Ann's
outfit from the previous evening, hung in reverse order. A pair
of sheer hose was on top, through which was visible her pant-
ies and bra. Under everything else was her amber dress. Each
piece was carefully folded and hung, quite a contrast, I knew,
to the way my own clothes had been tossed about the bedroom
in anticipation of Ann's entrance.

That entrance, as I now remembered it, had been perfectly
consistent with the deliberate order of the clothing on the rack.
Her walk had been slow and ceremonial. She'd been silhouet-

ted by the bathroom light, and I hadn't been able to read her eyes through most of her progress across the room. I'd been afraid I'd see the disappointed, tired look of the drive to the motel, but when she'd stopped a foot from me her eyes had been bright and her full lips had been drawn back in a wide, white grin.

"It's 1967 tonight," Ann had whispered as she'd pressed against me, softly.

"Nineteen sixty-eight, you mean," I'd managed to reply.

ONCE MY EYES WERE fully open, I decided that I needed some fresh air. I went back into the bedroom and dressed as quietly as I could in the wreckage of my reunion attire. I wasn't all that quiet, given my general unsteadiness, but it didn't matter. Ann never stirred.

The morning was cool and damp. That felt good to me at first. I stopped at the motel office long enough to collect a complimentary cup of coffee. The same man who had checked me in the day before was working behind the counter.

"How was your reunion?" he asked.

"Too wonderful for words," I said.

I saw the manager's smile reflected in the glass door on my way out, and then my own pale, bedraggled reflection. I would have smiled too, if I'd felt up to it.

I decided to take a walk around the motel grounds. It wasn't exactly a parklike setting. There were no trees, and only a narrow fringe of grass decorated the asphalt parking lot. A low concrete wall separated the lot from Route 1. The traffic on that road was constant and loud, eighteen-wheelers rumbling in procession over the old pavement. I could almost feel it breaking up through my shoes. Or it may have been that the pavement was fine and I was breaking up.

I had almost two hours to kill before my appointment with Maureen McCary. I used up a few minutes wondering why the idea of helping her frightened me so much. That was the problem certainly. For all my stupid posturing as a private eye and my longing after a younger self who had seen the world as one huge mystery story, I was genuinely afraid of stepping off into that void again. Afraid of solving a mystery because I knew from bitter experience that I would lose a lot and gain nothing in the process. I consoled myself with the thought that, in terms at least of illusions about my future, I had little left to lose.

As I finished the last of my coffee, I found I was standing before room 121, McCary's room. It was almost eight thirty. I considered using the time remaining to me to pack my bag and run out on her. There were two obstacles to this plan. One was Ann Quinn, still sleeping back in my room. I didn't want to desert her. The other objection was less noble but more daunting. My Karmann-Ghia was still parked back at the Lawrenceville firehouse. Unless, of course, it had been towed away or stolen.

My thinking then swung dizzily to the opposite extreme. I would make a virtue of not being able to run away. I would confront McCary now, before she was ready for me. I'd seize the initiative and use it to free myself. Maybe she'd even answer the door in hair curlers and a shapeless robe. A break like that would certainly steel my resolve.

I walked up to her door and knocked on it, not hard, but hard enough to move it slightly. I looked down and confirmed that the door hadn't been closed tightly enough to latch. I knocked again, more softly, as a way of marking time. I was suddenly sure there would be no answer.

I looked around the parking lot. No one else was stirring, and I couldn't be seen from the office. My only witnesses were rows of silent cars, still wet from the night before. I felt their eyes on me as I turned and pushed the door open.

I stuck my head into the opening, ready to call out Maureen's name. There was no one to call it to. The main room was dark and very empty. The door to the bathroom was open and the light was off. The bedroom had what television shows call "signs of a struggle." The sheets and blankets had been pulled from the bed and lay in a pile on the floor. Pieces of paper were scattered about. The Japanese-lantern shade of the reading lamp occupied the center of the mattress. One of the bureau drawers lay beside it. The other drawers were still in the bureau, standing open in varying degrees.

I stepped into the room and closed the door behind me without letting it latch. I thought of opening the drapes, but decided instead to flip the wall switch. That was a mistake. Light from the naked bulb hanging by the bed hit me like a blow between the eyes. I looked down in self-defense, and saw something snakelike protruding from under the bed. My head swam dangerously as I bent down to retrieve a pair of panty hose, twisted into a rope and knotted in the middle like a garrote. I dropped it quickly.

The hose inspired me to check the bureau drawers for other clothing. There was nothing in any of them, and nothing hanging on the room's little rack. The webbed suitcase stand beneath the rack was just as empty.

I wasn't thinking clearly, but I'd seen enough to convince me that the police were definitely called for. I was halfway across the room to the phone before I remembered the promise Maureen had extracted from me: no matter what happened, I wouldn't involve the police. Had she been expecting this?

"Expecting what?" I asked aloud. "What is all this?"

I noticed then that I was standing on one of the sheets of paper that littered the floor. I bent to retrieve them, groaning with emphasis as I picked up each sheet. Then I sat down on the bed to sort them out.

They were pages from the reunion program listing the graduates and giving their current jobs and addresses. Some of the names had been circled in red. I recognized the circled names; they were all members of the old gang, the Sorrowers. My own name was unmarked, as were Maureen's and Ann Quinn's.

I let the pages slip back onto the floor as a particularly sharp wave of nausea rolled through me. When my eyes focused again, I saw that one sheet remained in my hand. It contained an ad for a private detective agency. That's when I knew for certain I was going to be sick.

I ran into the bathroom and bent over the toilet. In the gray morning light, I could see pieces of paper floating in the bowl. At the last second, I moved to the sink and deposited my coffee there instead. Then I vomited dry air for a few minutes, for exercise. When I'd gotten bored with that, I knelt down with my head on the top of the vanity.

Anyone looking in the window at that moment would have thought I was praying. They would have been close to the truth. I wanted to open my eyes in another state, or at least in another motel room, with Ann sleeping quietly beside me. I tried it and found the last person I wanted to see staring back at me from the bathroom mirror. Owen Keane, private detective.

I got to my feet and destroyed more evidence by rinsing out the sink. Then I turned on the bathroom light, which almost made me sick again. The papers I'd seen floating in the toilet turned out to be pieces of a photograph. I retrieved them bit by bit and assembled them on the top of the tank like a wet puzzle. What I ended up with was a black and white of a blonde, naked and spread out artistically on a background of rumpled sheets. It was a photo of McCary, of course, the woman who had told me she was being blackmailed.

That cut it. I was calling the police now for certain, and maybe an ambulance for myself while I was at it. I would have made the call from the safety of my own room, but I didn't want Ann to hear me grovel. It was too long a journey in any case. I had to make the short walk to Maureen's phone in easy stages. First from the bathroom sink to the doorway, a short rest and then across the room to the corner of the bed. Finally, a slow flanking movement up the side of the bed to the phone.

I dialed the motel office and listened to four rings. Then two people spoke at once. One was my old friend the manager, who said, "Front desk." a second, more arresting voice came from the door behind me. It said, "Put down that phone."

EIGHT

THE SPEAKER WAS Ann Quinn. She was standing in the doorway of the room, barefoot and wearing her raincoat, her bare feet suggesting that the coat was probably all she wore. She hadn't shouted her instruction about the phone, thank God, or the shock of it would have laid me out flat. Her tone had been one of gentle disappointment, one a mother might use with a child who should have known better. It's an approach that's never failed to work with me. I placed the receiver back in its cradle.

Ann's sleep-arranged hair hung partly in her eyes. I felt an impulse to brush it back for her, but that would have meant deserting my post by the phone. "You don't understand what's happening here," I said. "I didn't have a chance to tell you last night. I don't have time now. I shouldn't tell you anyway. I don't want you involved. Go back to my room and get dressed. Then go home. I'll call you later if I can."

"Owen," Ann said. She shook her head, further tousling her hair. "It's a joke. A stupid practical joke."

I must have been too preoccupied with appearing in control of the situation to actually listen to her words. I reached for the phone again. "I'm wasting time."

"Owen, you're making a fool of yourself. The Sorrowers knew that ad of yours was a put-on the day the committee got it. They knew all along you weren't a detective. They worked all this up as a joke. When you owned up about the ad last night, I thought everything would be okay. Then you fell for this anyway."

"A joke," I said.

"Yes. Now come on. There's still time to get out of here before Maureen comes back." She turned in the doorway and then froze, waiting for me to move.

I stood up a little too quickly. The room revolved a half turn and then held fast. I walked past Ann and the open doorway and made it to the bathroom in one try. "What's this, then?" I asked her.

Ann brushed past me into the little room. She spotted the picture I'd reconstructed on the toilet tank and bent briefly to examine it.

"Maureen said she was being blackmailed, and I found that," I said.

Instead of turning to me, Ann delivered her response to her reflection in the long mirror over the sink. "You'd better update your reading. This is 1978. What would-be actress today doesn't have a trunk full of pictures like this? I'm surprised Maureen wasn't handing them out, autographed, at dinner last night."

She paused a full minute to let her words sink in. During that time, I watched Ann examining herself in the mirror. Her expression seemed slightly surprised to me, if in my befuddled state I was interpreting the subtle sadness in her eyes correctly. It was as though this new mirror had given her a new view of herself. Or a glimpse back at an old one.

Ann shook herself gently and drew her hands from the pockets of her coat. Then she began to collect the still-wet fragments of the photograph. "Where did you find this thing?"

"In there," I said, pointing to the toilet.

"How appropriate." She dropped the pieces back into the bowl and tripped the toilet's handle.

My immobility in the face of her wanton destruction of evidence told me that a great moment of epiphany had come and gone while I'd been staring at her reflection in the mirror. I now believed her.

I found that I had braced myself in the bathroom doorway like a man who expected the room to turn upside down at any moment. Actually, I was hoping it would right itself. "How did they know about the ad?"

"Lucy Criscollo was on the committee. She's a public defender now. When your ad came in she tried to trace your agency and couldn't. She had her office check with Boston. The police up there probably think you're some kind of con artist now. Lucy let the others know."

"And the Sorrowers worked all this out?"

"Not all of them. It was Maureen's idea mostly. She had several little projects going last night. Stunts, she calls them. She talked David Radici into throwing a party he couldn't afford. Then she told most of the Sorrowers not to go."

"Why?"

Ann stamped her foot in her frustration with my questions. "I don't know. She can always spot a person's deficiency. It's a gift she has. She likes to find the sore point and press it. Don't ask me why. She knows David doesn't have a lot of money, so she hit him there."

"What don't I have a lot of? Brains?"

I was looking for sympathy in the wrong place. "Self-respect," Ann said. She stepped toward me. "Now get moving. She's not due back here till ten, but she might be early."

"Where is she now?"

"At her mother's place. Across the river in Bucks County."

Ann took another step toward the door and me. This time, I got out of her way. I was still too stunned to be feeling much as I followed her careful, barefoot steps along the concrete path. The morning did seem crisper and brighter to me, though. So my first reaction to Ann's bombshell might have been a secret, guilty relief that the terrors of room 121 had been so easily explained away. It was a response that more than confirmed McCary's guess about my secret deficiency.

When we got back to my room, Ann retrieved her clothes from the bathroom and pointed to the shower. "Try running some cold water over your head. You'll feel better. Don't be in there too long, though."

A shower did help. So did a change out of my rumpled Nick Charles suit and into something more appropriate for a liquor store clerk: nondescript golf shirt and jeans and canvas deck shoes.

Ann had been gone when I'd come out of the shower. As I was tying my shoes she reappeared, carrying two more cups of the motel's coffee. She handed one to me. "You can drink this on the way to your car," she said. "I'll drive you over. Unless you want to check out first."

"I want to talk first."

"There isn't time." Ann undercut her protest by sitting down next to me on the bed. In spite of all I'd been through that morning, I felt an impulse to reach out and touch her. As a substitute, I sipped the coffee she'd given me. It was as sweet as syrup.

Ann smiled at my surprised expression. "I'm trying to elevate your blood sugar. It's basic therapy for a hangover."

"Don't tell me you grew up to be a doctor."

"No, a nurse." I must have looked surprised again, because she said, "I know. I don't like to tell my old friends what I do now because they never seem to believe me. Why is that?"

"I don't know," I said. I couldn't say what I was really thinking, that the job sounded too ordinary for her. "Maybe I expected you to be the actress, not McCary."

She shivered slightly at that thought. "I like what I do. I'm good at it."

"You took good care of me last night." I was attempting, awkwardly, to introduce an unexplained and delicate point. Namely, why had she ended up in my bed?

Ann ignored the opening. "When did Maureen get to you? When you were dancing?"

"Yes," I said.

"I meant to tell you about the whole stupid business this morning. You got away before I could. I would have told you last night, but you seemed so happy. Telling you would have spoiled it."

That didn't sound like the old disinterested Ann Quinn. "Why would you care one way or the other?"

"Not because I'm in love with you, Owen. Don't get that idea." She sipped her coffee, watching me over the brim of her cup, the depth of her eyes making me dizzy all over again. "I do like you though. I did in the old days, too. You were such an odd person then."

"Goofy," I suggested.

She shook her head. "Half the guys at Our Lady were that way. I meant that you were a special person. You stood out from the crowd. It's a dangerous thing to do, Owen. Especially when the Sorrowers are the crowd."

She stood up. "I'll get the car started."

I opened my suitcase to get my windbreaker. While sorting through the bag, I came across my little room bottle of J & B. The moment was the low point of my weekend, and maybe my year. I was seriously considering some hair of the dog as a supplement to Ann's blood sugar therapy. Or as a concession to McCary's judgment of me. Ann saved me from that surrender by sounding the horn of her Mustang. I stuck the bottle back in the bottom of the bag.

The first thing I did after climbing into her little car was roll down the window so I'd have a place to be sick if the spirit moved me again. Then I asked my keeper, "What was I supposed to have done next?"

"What do you mean? First tell me if we're stopping by the office."

"No. I'll check out later. I mean, how was McCary's stunt supposed to play out? What did she expect me to do?"

Ann pulled carefully into the traffic on Stone's Crossing Road. "I have no idea. I'd be surprised if Maureen does herself. She never used to think these things through. It isn't even important to her to be there to watch her victims react. Like last night, with Davey. It's enough for her to know she set the wheels in motion.

"She may not even come back here today. I'll bet she paid for the room in advance, using a made-up name or somebody else's. An unsuspecting Sorrower's maybe. She could have planted the seeds of another stunt that way. She and that gigolo she brought to the reunion probably stopped by here last night just long enough to set the stage. And maybe use the bed."

"Roland went back to New York after the reunion."

"Who told you that?" Ann looked at me like a tired teacher dragging a slow learner through the multiplication tables.

"Right," I said. "Scratch that."

"You can bet she set it up so she could deny ever talking to you, in case you actually called the police."

The realization that I very nearly had inspired me to lean my head a little more toward the slipstream. "Thanks for stopping me. I've really been a jerk."

"If that were true, you'd be halfway to Boston by now. You were going to do the right thing by Maureen, even if it got you committed. She may not have expected that, because she'd never stick her neck out for you or anybody else."

I thought it over and decided that Ann was right. Even if I could tie Maureen in with room 121, she would have some logical explanation for everything I'd found there. I ran through a mental list of the props they'd left me, looking for a clue to the mystery of what the Sorrowers had intended me to do next.

"There was something else in the room. Bits of a reunion program with names circled. All Sorrowers."

"Those you mean?" Ann indicated the back seat with a nod of her head. The sheets were there in a neat stack, along with the prop panty hose, sans twists and knots and carefully folded. "I went back to straighten up while you were in the shower."

I retrieved the program pages and read the circled names aloud. "Lucy Criscollo, Mary Kay Ellis-Humphrey, Bill Pearson, David Radici."

"They were all in on the joke," Ann said. "Maybe they hoped you'd drive around from house to house, grilling them. Maybe they have a whole plot cooked up."

"Maybe they do," I said. I folded the pages and stuck them into the pocket of my windbreaker. Ann observed the operation, but didn't comment.

We were passing Lawrence High, our old arch-rival school, which put us only a mile or so from the firehouse. I spent the last few blocks of the drive punishing myself with the memory of the party at the Radicis and the thought that all my old friends had been aware of my impending doom. Then I recalled something I'd wanted to ask Ann the night before.

"I heard at David's that the Sorrowers once attended a war protest on the Princeton campus. A riot actually. Were you involved in that?"

It was Ann's turn to sound disoriented. "What? No, I've never heard about anything like that. Who told you?"

"Radici introduced the subject while you were asleep. Criscollo was dismissing the old Sorrowers as a bunch of innocent kids. Radici shut her up with the word 'Princeton.' Turned out to be like setting off a grenade. Pearson told me later about the riot, and that the Sorrowers had sworn each other to secrecy on the subject."

Ann switched on her signal for the left into the firehouse lot. "I don't know anything about that," she said. "It's not connected to McCary's blackmail stunt, if that's what you're thinking."

We sat for a while after the oncoming traffic had passed. "It's okay to turn now," I said.

The Ghia was right where I'd left it, its protruding headlights giving me a doleful, Peter Lorre look. Ann pulled in next to it, with something very like a sigh of relief. "There you go," she said to the windshield.

I waited until she turned to face me. Then I said, "Thanks for the ride. And for taking care of me last night." I was struck again by how much she'd changed since Our Lady of Sorrows. "The old Ann Quinn would have kept her distance. She would have looked down on it all from above."

Ann nodded. "That was my deficiency," she said. "I was afraid of getting involved. Are you going back to Boston right away?"

I spent a foolish moment wondering whether she was really asking if we would see each other again. She snuffed out that daydream by adding, "It's a nice morning for the drive."

It was sunny anyway, as I'd noted earlier when Ann had led me out of McCary's trap. But I didn't feel like leaving. "I don't think I could make it. I may do some visiting instead."

Ann was still at least one step ahead of me. "Don't fool with the Sorrowers, Owen. Let that go. Count yourself lucky to have gotten off as cheaply as you have."

"Just now it doesn't feel like I got a bargain rate," I said. "Anyway, I've already paid for the ride. I might as well enjoy it."

NINE

AFTER ANN LEFT ME, I sat in the Ghia for a while, rubbing my lips gently to keep the memory of her parting kiss alive and wondering what I would do next. That's not quite true. I'd known very early on, as far back as the moment I'd left McCary's room, that I would go after the Sorrowers. I just wasn't sure how. I also wasn't too clear on why, beyond a vague idea that I wanted to get back at them in some way. I was too hurt and hung over for soul searching at that moment, or much of anything else.

It was quarter to ten. I decided that the firehouse would charge me rent if I sat there much longer. Besides, I had an appointment to keep with a client.

I drove out to Route 1 and found a coffee shop where I bought some doughnuts and refilled Ann's prescription of syrupy caffeine. I thought about stopping for cigarettes, but the steady ache in my head told me that this would be one great morning to quit again.

There was a discount men's clothier across from the Howard Johnson. I parked in the store's lot in a spot that gave me a discreet view of room 121. Then I sipped coffee and got powdered sugar on myself and waited.

A little before ten, a silver BMW with New York plates pulled into the motel's lot. The car's windows were so darkly tinted that I couldn't see inside. It pulled into a space on the outside row of the lot, backed into the space, actually, so it faced the room McCary had rented. No one got out. It was my client, I decided. Right on time for the curtain.

Now it was a waiting contest. Maureen was waiting for me to show up and stumble into her crazy fantasy world. I was waiting for my next brilliant idea to come to me. It promised to be a long morning for both of us.

I ended up being the more patient watcher, perhaps because I'd thought to bring along my breakfast. At ten thirty, the passenger side door of the BMW opened and a tall, thin figure got out. It was Maureen, in slacks and a light jacket and the rudiments of a disguise. Her golden hair was pulled up and partially hidden under a beret. She displayed dark glasses when she looked nervously around the lot.

McCary crossed to the door of room 121, walking in a caricature of stealth, almost on tiptoe with her hands slightly out from her sides. She listened at the door for a moment, then tried the knob. Ann must have pulled the door closed on her last visit. It appeared from Maureen's reaction that the room was now locked. She retreated to the BMW.

Ten minutes passed, during which I seriously regretted my decision not to buy cigarettes. Then the driver's side door opened and Roland, the absentee boyfriend, got out. He also wore dark glasses, but he'd forgotten his beret. He crossed stage right to the door of the room and inserted a key. Ann had been wrong about them checking out the night before. Roland opened the door slowly. Then his head disappeared inside, followed a moment later by the rest of him.

That must have been the signal that the coast was clear. McCary emerged from the car again and repeated her tightrope walk to the room's open door. It would have been the perfect moment for me to show up, all innocence, for my appointment, if I'd felt up to moving that fast. I only had a moment to consider the idea before the confused couple came out into the light. Then they were back in their car and on their way out of the lot.

I started the Ghia and followed them into the traffic on Stone's Crossing Road. My Boston driving habits held me in good stead then, as I had to face down an oncoming Cadillac and cut off a delivery van to join the traffic heading west. I was suddenly feeling much better. Maureen's corny beret and stagey mannerisms had almost made me smile. They'd certainly made the nasty joke she'd concocted for me seem more like a game she and I were playing together. Thanks to Ann, the game would now be played by my rules.

The silver car with the black windows turned onto the ramp for 1-95. My little red car with the dirty windows followed it. Roland headed west, toward Bucks County and McCary's mother's place. I could see no advantage to following them there, so I consulted the pages of the reunion program that Ann had thoughtfully provided. For three of the four circled names, Criscollo, Ellis, and Pearson, only out-of-town addresses were given. That left David Radici, my host of the previous evening. I pulled off the interstate at its intersection with Pennington Road and headed north.

Even if I'd been enough of a detective to figure out where the other Sorrowers were staying, I would probably have approached Radici first. I knew that Radici had also been suckered by McCary, and that gave me a bargaining chip. I intended to trade it for more information on the famous Princeton incident. Radici had already broken the Sorrower vow of silence on that subject, and the second fall is always easier.

Following up that Princeton lead was partly just good private-eye procedure. It was a given in my favorite paperbacks, the elegantly written stories of Ross MacDonald, that any ancient scandal, casually mentioned in the opening chapters, would turn out to be the key to the contemporary problem. I also had a less whimsical reason for following the Princeton trail, one based on something Ann had told me. Maureen McCary didn't really care how her jokes turned out, so the fact that her Owen Keane stunt had fizzled wouldn't be a great blow to her. It was enough for her to know her victims' weaknesses, their deficiencies. That was the key to evening the score in our little game. I wanted to know more about the Sorrowers' secret, hoping that it would give me a new angle on McCary. An unflattering one.

I surprised myself by driving right to the Radici mansion, with no map or sober memories to guide me. It was on Woosamonsa Road, which might have been Native American for "winding with bad pavement." In daylight, the house looked smaller than I remembered it and more tightly closed-around by trees. It was a ranch with gray board-and-batten siding and a mossy roof. A nice house, by my standards. At least for a couple who were supposed to be hard up.

One half of the couple was sitting on the front porch when I pulled into the gravel drive. It was Libby, in an old sweat suit that was loose enough to be one of David's. She was seated in a rocking chair, holding a yellow bundle. As I walked up, I saw that it was a baby. About eighteen months old to my inexperienced eye.

"You just missed Davey," Libby said in place of hello. Her dark hair was drawn back tightly in a pony tail. The arrangement seemed to have also narrowed her eyes, but that might just have been the way she chose to look at me. "He drove down to the Quality Market to get Daniel some lunch."

"Where was Daniel hiding last night?" I asked.

"At my mom's. Gave us a rare night on the town. And a chance to throw the party of the century. Care for a beer? We've got cases left."

My grimace made her laugh, which brought the baby to life in her arms. Libby raised him to her shoulder and began to rock. "Sorry to bring up a sore point," she said. She was referring to my hangover, but the mention of a sore point reminded her of her failed party. "It's a shame Daniel doesn't like onion dip and beer. He could stuff himself."

"Thanks for having us over," I said as a way of reminding her that I was one of the faithful few who had actually shown up. The strategy seemed to work.

"Sorry I'm a bitch this morning, Owen. Thanks for coming by last night. I wish you could have stayed longer, but then nobody did. Poor Mary Kay had to drive all the way back to New Brunswick last night. Come on up and sit down, if you have time for a visit."

I climbed the porch steps and sat on a bench next to her chair. In daylight, the view looking back down the drive was impressive, wooded hills and pastures seen through the shifting green filter of the Radici's own trees. "You have a beautiful place," I said.

"Thanks. We can only just afford it, and the taxes keep going up and up, but we love it here. It's our little retreat. Did you enjoy the reunion?"

The abrupt shift in topic caught me off guard enough to make me frank. "I did last night. This morning I'm not so sure."

Frankness came naturally to Libby. "I heard they worked up some joke on you last night. It wasn't too bad, I hope."

"Nothing I couldn't handle."

Libby rocked a little faster. "I'd like to ring a few Sorrower necks myself this morning. Davey was so excited about having the old gang over. Now he feels so let down, the poor jerk. It isn't really the money we blew. That's worrying me more than Davey. The old days are so important to him. He can't let go of them the way the rest of you have. When last night ended on such a flat note, it really brought him down."

I realized as I listened to Libby that Ann had been wrong about Radici's secret weakness. It hadn't been too little money. It had been too much nostalgia. I wondered if McCary had gotten it right.

While I was wondering, Libby was moving on. "Davey got so bummed out with poor Lucy last night. She was only saying what anyone might feel about their school days: that they weren't as great as we remember them. Davey can't feel that way for some some reason." Her rocking slowed to a stop. "I hope to God it isn't because he sees that time as the high point of his life."

I was almost used to Libby's plain speaking by then, but that remark yanked me back from my thoughts of McCary and the Sorrowers. Daniel was fussing again. Libby sat him on her knee and bounced him gently, his oversized head bobbing slightly out of time with her rhythm. One of the baby's socks had almost worked free of his foot. I reached over and pulled it up.

"I don't see how David could feel that way," I said.

"Thanks, Owen." She bent and kissed Daniel on the forehead.

As tender as the moment was, it didn't distract me from my reason for trekking to Hopewell. Libby's mention of the Criscollo/Radici debate gave me the perfect opening. "David said something to Lucy last night that I didn't understand."

"'Princeton,' you mean" Libby asked. "Wasn't that wild? I mean the way you could suddenly hear the crickets in the backyard after Davey said that."

"What did he mean by it?"

"I don't know. I asked Davey about it last night after everyone had gone, but he didn't want to talk about it. He didn't want to talk about anything."

"Do you remember hearing about an antiwar demonstration at Princeton that the Sorrowers got mixed up in?"

"No. Is that what it was all about? I'm pretty sure I would have heard about that. Davey's always talking about the peace movement. He's real proud that he was committed to that. But he really didn't get involved until college. Maybe that's what he misses, the war. I hear it's hard for soldiers sometimes after the fighting stops. Maybe it's the same for protesters."

"Maybe," I said. "You mentioned before that Mary Kay drove home to New Brunswick last night. What about Lucy? She lives in Delaware."

"She's staying at her folks' place down in the Burg." The reference was to Chambersburg, the old Italian section of Trenton. "How about Ann?" Libby asked. "Did she make it to her own bed last night?"

I concentrated on not reacting, but that only made Libby laugh. "When a man keeps that straight a face, I know there's something hot going on. Fess up, Owen."

I was spared that trial by the burly ring of the old kitchen phone.

"Damn," Libby said. "Davey probably ran out of gas again. Here. You're elected baby-sitter."

She plopped Daniel down in my lap. His expression was one of wide-eyed surprise, an able imitation of my own. The screen door of the house was slamming shut behind Libby before I could object. I shifted Daniel to my knee and tried a few tentative bounces. He smiled and gurgled a little bit. I bounced him higher, hoping to get a laugh out of him. Instead I got what was left of his breakfast in my lap.

Daniel had the good grace to look penitent. "There's a screwy kind of justice in the universe, kid," I told him. "Look out for it."

I was undoing the damage with a cloth diaper Libby had left on the rocker, when she slipped back onto the porch. "It's Maureen McCary," Libby whispered. "Do you believe it? Before I could call her a bitch for standing us up last night, she asked me if you'd been by here. I'm supposed to be off asking Davey right now. What's going on?"

"One of Maureen's jokes went a little haywire. I'm the wire."

Libby was more fluent in cliché than I. "You've turned the tables on her? Good for you! What do you want me to tell her?"

I'd already worked out my next move, and I couldn't think of a reason for not sharing it with McCary. "Tell her I've been here and gone, and I'm on my way to talk with Lucy Criscollo. And say that I was asking about something that happened in Princeton years ago."

TEN

IT'S BEEN my experience that a really good hangover is capable of a sustained second effort, like a seasoned marathoner who breaks through a wall of fatigue and finds a second wind. Just when you think you've beaten it, usually around lunchtime, the monster rises up again, and you spend the afternoon on the sofa watching a muted television through half-closed eyes. That is, you do if you're lucky enough to have a television and a sofa and a free afternoon. I had none of the above, so I settled for slumping down in the Ghia's seat and squinting a lot as I drove.

I'd gotten the Criscollos' address from the amateur detective's best friend, the phone book. At least I hoped it was their address since a number of Criscollos graced the Trenton book. The family I'd selected lived at 4331 Hudson Street, which was definitely in the Burg and seemed to ring a bell for me. One more bell added to the half dozen or so clanging away between my ears.

This would be the first trip I'd made into Trenton proper on this visit. Like a couple of million other people, I gave Trenton as my hometown because I'd grown up writing it as part of my address. But I'd never really lived in the city. I'd grown up in one of the suburbs served by the Trenton post office. These bedroom communities and I had come of age at more or less the same time, in the boom years after the Second World War. They were ungrateful children of the old capital, growing fat and prosperous while neglected Trenton withered away waiting for a call that never came.

I took Pennington Road down to Olden Avenue, and then followed that strip of discounters and car dealers into the old Polish north ward. There I rejoined Route 1, several miles south of my Howard Johnson base, and headed downtown through a landscape of oil depots and scrap yards. I exited Route 1 for an exciting half turn around the Trenton traffic circle that landed me on Greenwood Avenue. Then I drove east on Greenwood toward Trenton High along the tattered northern edge of Chambersburg.

If I was guessing right, by now McCary had telephoned Criscollo to warn her of my approach. There were two moves they could make, and the one they chose would tell me how much my Princeton lead was really worth. If the Sorrowers' accidental involvement in that ancient campus riot was as innocent as Bill Pearson had claimed, I could expect Criscollo to stick with McCary's original blackmail gag, either laughing off the Princeton angle or encouraging me to follow it up as a further waste of my time. On the other hand, if that Princeton story was a potential embarrassment to McCary and the Sorrowers, as I dearly hoped, Criscollo, under instructions from her chief, would make a clean breast of the blackmail stunt as a way of getting me to drop the whole thing.

I turned right at the high school and drove south a few blocks to pick up Hudson. The once-impressive homes on Greenwood gave way to never-impressive row homes of late nineteenth- and early twentieth-century vintage. Those along Hudson Street were narrow three-stories standing shoulder to shoulder with only cross streets and the occasional alley to break the line. They were mostly brick, some painted but not recently, some disguised with siding, their steep front steps ending in porchless doors. At intersections, the monotony was broken by a little business establishment or two, a bar or restaurant or beauty parlor. That was the view to my right as I drove along Hudson looking for number 4331. To my left sprawled Colonel Roebling's old factory that had once spun cable for the Brooklyn Bridge. It now sat boarded up and empty.

The Criscollos' house was white, or had been in the not too distant past. I squeezed the Ghia into the only space I could see for blocks. Cars were parked so tightly along Hudson that it appeared the locals pushed them in sideways. One car stood out from the rest, a dark blue Mercury Cougar, new and undented and parked in front of the once-white house. I checked the back of the car and found one of the classy, green plates issued by the stare of Delaware. I was surely on a roll.

Lucy Criscollo answered the door of 4331. Of course she would, I told myself, as she'd been warned of my approach by McCary. Maureen's call may have gotten Criscollo out of bed. She was wearing a robe and fuzzy slippers. I deduced from its excess material and loud floral print that the robe at least had been borrowed from someone much older. Lucy looked about the way I felt, which surprised me. Her dark hair had been combed through, but her eyes were smudged around with gray, as though she had slept in her eye makeup.

It was another comic moment, like my surveillance of cat burglar McCary at the motel. No visitor greeted by an apparition like this hung over woman in flowered flannel would dream of being asked inside the house. I realized there was an option open to Criscollo that I hadn't considered on my drive to the Burg, one more obvious and likely than the complicated scenarios I'd worked out. She could simply tell me and McCary to grow up and go play somewhere else. It suddenly seemed like a good idea.

"Sorry to bother you so early, Lucy," I said. "I'll come back some other time."

"No, Owen. It's no problem," Criscollo said. "Come in."

I stepped up into the house, wondering what hold McCary had on my host that would make her string along with the gag. Practical jokes had never really been Criscollo's forte. I remembered instead her acerbic wit. She'd used it to define the membership of the Sorrowers by ridiculing anyone and everyone outside the group. Her sharp tongue had made Lucy the one Sorrower aspirants like myself would be sure to play up to.

Criscollo wasn't dressed for receiving guests in the parlor. She led me past it and down a narrow hallway toward the smells and sounds of a kitchen. There I met the likely owner of the flowered robe, Mrs. Criscollo. She was tall and dark like her daughter but heavier and, this morning at least, happier. If she thought it odd that Lucy was entertaining with one foot in the grave, she never let on. She showed me to a chair with chrome legs and a plastic seat at a table with chrome legs and a plastic cover and gave me a much appreciated cup of inky black coffee. Lucy sat down opposite me. Mrs. Criscollo warmed her daughter's coffee and then returned to the stove. She turned down the heat under several pots, covering them at the same time. Lucy watched her mother's back, ignoring me until the old woman had bustled out of the room.

I got in the first lie. "Lucy, I'm worried about Maureen."

Criscollo held up a long, thin hand, interrupting me. "Owen, I've got a confession to make. It's about that ad you put in the program. I found out about that months ago, you see, and checked into it. I should have recognized it as an innocent joke, but, to be honest, I didn't. I thought, and this is going to sound bad, that you were trying to put one over on us. Now here's the worst part. I mentioned what I'd discovered to some of the Sorrowers. The upshot is that we set you up, or, I mean, Maureen did. She was never being blackmailed, is what I'm trying to say. Nor is she in any kind of trouble. None whatsoever. That was all a joke."

Criscollo ran out of garbled syntax at that point and picked up her coffee cup. She examined my expression as she drank. I'm sure it satisfied her. The way for me to play the scene was sincere surprise at what she'd told me. And that's what I felt, at least about the subtext of Criscollo's message. McCary preferred dropping her joke to having that long ago night at the Princeton campus researched. What had really gone on there?

Criscollo wasn't likely to tell me, but it didn't hurt to ask. First though I had to go through the formality of reluctantly admitting that I'd been duped. "A joke?" I asked trying to recapture the way I felt when I'd stumbled through this same scene with Ann earlier in the day. I used a finger to trace the pattern of leafy vines embossed on the plastic tablecloth before me as I worked through my summation. "I'm relieved that Maureen's okay. I really didn't know what I would do next. I guess I asked for it when I ran that ad. I don't know why I did it."

I considered sharing Ann's opinion that the ad and the whole reunion trip were ways of wallowing in my own failure, but that was taking method acting too far. "I wasn't trying to put anything over on anyone," I said. "It was pretty stupid, I guess."

Criscollo was relieved by my good sportsmanship and generous as a result. "I can see that now, Owen, really. I should have recognized it before. I think I know you better than the others do. You and I could open up to each other in the old days."

This claim brought my eyes up from the tabletop. Criscollo seemed sincere enough. "I remember your telling me about something that happened to you down at the shore," she said. "The summer before our senior year, I think. If I'm remembering right, you were at some kind of religious retreat. At Seaside Heights?"

"Seaside Park," I said.

"Right. Anyway, you met some kid who claimed to have been visited by God." I couldn't recall telling Criscollo about Jimmy, but I must have. I marveled at my choice of confidants while Criscollo talked on. "The whole thing seemed to really bother you. Why was that?"

"Because he'd made it all up. I'm not sure why he did." I was still wondering why I'd shared the story with Criscollo. I projected my likely motives onto Jimmy. "Maybe he was trying to impress us. Maybe he just wanted to belong."

"The thing I remember is that the experience seemed to change the way you looked at Our Lady. Why did it do that?"

I drank some bitter coffee and thought back. "Because the people running the retreat assumed that Jimmy had lied. They never considered the other possibility. One of them even set Jimmy up. Humiliated him in front of the rest of us. It made me wonder for the first time if anyone really believed. If it was really possible to."

Thinking of the black void that Jimmy's tale had opened in my old, secure view of the world made me aware, belatedly, of a more contemporary trap looming in my path. Criscollo's questions had brought us very close to a secret more embarrassing to me than anything I could hope to get on the Sorrowers: my failure in the seminary. I'd entered St. Aelred's as a deliberate challenge to the unbelief I'd first encountered at that retreat. I'd failed there because of my stubborn need to solve mysteries, to know the answers.

I might have panicked and bolted, if Mrs. Criscollo hadn't picked that moment to reappear. She shuffled back into the room, crossing to the stove. There she checked each pot in turn, sniffing and stirring and giving me a chance to think. The Sorrowers couldn't know of my failure at St. Aelred's, I told myself. If they had, they would have already used it against me. Maureen's stunt would have involved visions and vocations instead of private eyes and blackmail. Criscollo was only trying to distract me with her reminiscences. And I was letting her.

When Mrs. Criscollo left us again, I tried to regain the initiative. "Last night David Radici mentioned an incident from the old days. Something that happened in Princeton. What was that all about?"

Lucy tilted her head back and looked down her long nose at me. "That was nothing, Owen. Really."

"I've heard you all took an oath of secrecy. What were you afraid of?"

"An oath? Who told you that?" Instead of waiting for an answer, Criscollo leaned backward in her chair to peer down the hallway after her mother. Then she stood up and crossed the room to the cabinets under the sink. She returned carrying a bullet-shaped bottle of brown glass. My professional's eye identified it immediately as a coffee-flavored liqueur popular with the patrons of Nab's. "Join me?" she asked.

I put my hand over my cup. Lucy poured a generous dollop into her own coffee and then put the bottle back where she'd found it. "We weren't afraid, Owen. Just embarrassed," she said as she returned to her chair. "I'm not the only one involved, or I'd tell you the whole story."

"Come on," I said. "You and I could always open up to one another. Remember?"

Criscollo smiled ruefully and then drank deeply of her doctored coffee. "Okay. You'll probably laugh, though. It was just this crazy party we had in Princeton. There was no adult supervision, a little beer, and an even number of horny little Catholic-school boys and girls. There was also a consensus that virginity would be a handicap in college. None of us left the party handicapped.

"You remember those days. A lot of talk about liberation and free love and not much useful information being handed out. At least not at Our Lady of Sorrows."

She drank again. "Anyway it was pretty wild and pretty embarrassing the next day. We kept it quiet naturally. Not an oath of secrecy. Just a general agreement that we didn't want to be kicked out of school a week before we graduated. I'd pretty much forgotten all about it until David dredged it up last night."

If the liqueur bottle had still been on the table, I would have taken a drink from it. I stood up. "Sorry for being so nosy," I said. "And thanks for setting me straight about Maureen."

Lucy rattled on as we walked to the front door, reminding me more and more of her old self. "Poor David's really locked in that time. Living up there in the hills with Miss Granola of 1972 would do it to anybody. Life must be really dull for him these days."

"He misses the war," I said, repeating Libby Radici's insight. "He was really active in the peace movement. How about you? Were you a marcher?"

"Me? God, no. Why do you ask?"

"No reason," I said.

ELEVEN

SOMEBODY WAS LYING. The mysterious Princeton incident had evolved from a violent antiwar demonstration to a high school sex orgy. How had that happened? I thought it over on the walk to my car and came up with the name of a comedy team: Keane and Radici. I'd told Libby to scare Maureen McCary with a reference to Princeton, but I hadn't specifically instructed her to pass on Bill Pearson's tale of a Vietnam protest gone sour. Luckily for me, Libby hadn't volunteered the information. She couldn't have, or Criscollo would never have handed me a completely new explanation of the old scandal. When Lucy and Bill compared notes and realized their mistake, the story would probably mutate again, perhaps into a love-in on the steps of the marine recruiting office.

I sat in my car for a time, thinking of ways I could test the two stories. I trusted Pearson's version more than Criscollo's, as it had been more spontaneous. On the negative side, neither Ann nor Libby had ever heard of that wild night on campus. It was the easier story of the two to verify, though, so I decided to do that next.

I extracted the Ghia from its space and retraced my route along Hudson Street. Just west of the Roebling factory was a small park, perhaps a gift from the colonel to the city. The trees were tall enough to date from that time, and the playground equipment, battleship-gray swings and seesaws and a slide, looked old enough. As I was examining the park, I caught sight of a car in my rearview mirror. It was a silver BMW with tinted glass.

I looked straight ahead again and drove on with self-conscious carelessness. I was still winning my silly game with McCary. She was still on the defensive, reacting to my moves. She'd come in person to Hudson Street to see what I'd do next. The excitement I felt at having the upper hand for a change made me forget that scary moment in the Criscollo kitchen when I'd imagined the Sorrowers learning of my seminary days. That possibility still existed, and it should have been enough to make me scurry back to Boston, as Ann had suggested. It should have been, but I'd never had the sense to quit while I was ahead.

I headed back to Route 1, driving slowly and not running any yellow lights so Maureen—or Roland—would have no trouble staying with me. Once on the highway, I headed north until Route 1 emptied into yet another of the area's traffic circles, the Brunswick Circle. I thought of doing a few unnecessary circuits in the circle's bumper-car traffic, as a way of tweaking Maureen's nose, but I still wasn't feeling up to any merry-go-round rides. I got off as planned on 206 north and followed the signs for Princeton.

Once north of Lawrenceville, I began to notice changes in the scenery, one or two big industrial parks and a corporate headquarters where I remembered nurseries and sod farms. When I'd been a freshman at Boston College, I'd sometimes told people that I was from "the Princeton area" rather than Trenton. It sounded a whole lot classier, like ordering club soda instead of seltzer. Corporate America seemed to be discovering the same dodge. It was sad to think of the old university being slowly surrounded by concentric rings of capitalism, but that was the price it paid for being fashionable. The Age of Preppy was dawning, and Princeton was Mecca.

The BMW was still behind me, masked by two cars and a suburban transit bus. I'd accomplished my purpose by letting them follow me this far. They knew I was heading for Princeton and that I hadn't given up. There was no point in letting them watch me blunder around once I got there.

A few miles outside of town, I made a fast right onto a narrow road that was actually called Lovers Lane. The road hadn't been an inspired choice, as it was too narrow and residential to allow for a quick getaway. I was still in sight of Route 206 when the BMW turned in behind me. We drove along in plain view of one another until the lane ended at the Princeton Pike. I turned north on the pike, squeezing into a gap in the traffic not much larger than my late parking space on Hudson street. The BMW was still waiting to turn when I lost sight of it around a bend in the road.

The pike entered Princeton through its back door, the old part of town near the train station. This neighborhood was a tangle of little horse-and-buggy streets, just the right width for the Ghia. I drove into the rabbit warren, turning at every corner, first right and then left, until I'd almost lost myself instead of my pursuers. I finally popped out near the McCarter Theater. I made my way from there to Nassau Street and the center of town.

Traffic in Princeton seemed heavy for a Saturday afternoon, another indication that it had been a long time between visits for me. I passed up parking spaces on Nassau Street as too exposed and ducked down behind Palmer Square, where I paid way too much for the privilege of leaving the Ghia in a quiet lot. Then I walked back up the hill and crossed Nassau at the light near the wrought iron main gates of the university, scanning the traffic for the German sedan as I went. There were enough of them in town to give my neck a workout.

My destination was the Firestone Library. I've always had a weakness for college libraries, and the Firestone was no exception. I'd researched a high school theme paper there one rainy afternoon, which was as close as I had ever come to studying at Princeton. The low-slung stone building was unimpressive by the school's Gothic standards, despite its broad plaza. The interior was also utilitarian, with the exception of the wood-paneled reading rooms. The library's attraction for me wasn't its architecture or even the huge collection. It was the atmosphere. Within the Firestone, Princeton had struck me for the first time as more than a snobbish attitude and a staid dress code. It had seemed to me to be an incredibly beautiful opportunity.

The old feelings of envy came back as I entered the library, passing students more clean-cut and attractive than seemed necessary. The way they were dressed, in baggy earth tones and hiking shoes, and the knapsacks they carried, made them look like explorers, which was entirely appropriate. These lucky few depressed me more than their predecessors had ten years before, perhaps because I'd failed to return as a successful exception to their rule. I shook the mood off.

After several inquiries, I located the branch of the periodical section where back issues of the *Princetonian,* the university newspaper, were kept. The man behind the counter was wearing a shirt of blue oxford cloth with a button-down collar, unfrayed. He had wire-rimmed glasses of the same type as David Radici and a bad complexion. Too much time spent buried in the sub-basement, I decided. It may also have affected his attitude. He was certainly not pleased when I asked for the issues of the paper from September 1967 to May 1968.

"It's a daily paper," he said. "You're talking about a lot of material. Could you be more specific?"

Actually, I couldn't be. Pearson hadn't given me a date for the riot, only a school year. "I'm looking for information on war protests held on campus during that period," I said.

The pasty libertarian considered my request seriously, which improved my opinion of him. Finally, he said, "There were probably a number of protests that year."

"The one I'm interested in would have been more of a riot than a protest." I tried to visualize the scene Pearson had sketched for me. "A protest that got out of hand. At night. With fires and riot police and tear gas."

The librarian shook his head. "You have the wrong school, I'm afraid. At the height of the war, the worst we had at Princeton were sit-ins. Try Columbia."

"You're sure? You were here then?"

"Working here. Believe me, the only things our students threw at people were words. There was a time, though, when a group of us drove into Philadelphia." He was gazing right through me and into the dead sixties. "Mrs. Nixon was addressing an American Legion convention. We threw eggs at her limousine."

As he pictured his moment of glory, his expression of pride was replaced by puzzlement. After the weekend I'd had, I could easily sympathize with him. Some memories just couldn't survive out of context. I thanked him and left.

The basement librarian's testimony was enough to tip my mental scales against Pearson and his vivid recollections. I sat down on the stone steps at the edge of the library plaza to regroup. I was left with Lucy Criscollo's story, which was a dubious asset, as it had to be a lie. At least in part. My own experience with lying had taught me that it was better to remodel the truth than build from scratch as Pearson had apparently done. Assuming Lucy was liar enough to know that, her version would contain a kernel of truth. Which was what? That the incident had taken place in Princeton? That wasn't enough. Even Pearson had gotten the location right. That whatever had happened had happened at a party? A party at a private residence in Princeton?

I was making progress, if at a slightly slower rate than the trademark ivy growing everywhere around me. What Sorrowers had lived in Princeton? None of the principals in McCary's little charade had. Not the actress herself or Pearson or Criscollo or Ellis or Radici. Not Ann Quinn.

I got up and walked toward a public phone I could see some distance away on Washington Road. As I walked, I tried to recall the names of Lady of Sorrows' students who had lived in Princeton. The fragmented reunion program might have helped me, but I'd left it in the Ghia. Without it, the search was slow work. I was starting to think that the brain cells containing that data had all died in the great scotch flood of the previous evening, when I came up with the name Richard Gerow. Like me, Gerow had never risen above the second echelon of the Sorrowers. He'd been junior varsity in general, if I was remembering him correctly, runner up to Criscollo for class brain, vice president of almost everything and president of nothing.

I hadn't seen Gerow at the reunion, but I'd heard his name there. I wasted a minute trying to remember which Sorrower had mentioned him, before I realized that it hadn't been a Sorrower. I pictured the two women whose personal reunion had briefly blocked my entrance to the hall. One had made a nonsensical joke about Gerow. That he'd been turned away at the door. The other, Nancy somebody, hadn't thought that very funny.

If only I'd been rude enough to collar the pair and ask for an explanation. It was too late to do that now. Try as I might, I couldn't recall Nancy's last name or any part of the other woman's. That left asking Gerow himself.

I arrived at the phone, which resided in an aluminum box open on one side and supported by a pole the height of a parking meter. The box also contained a white pages, more or less intact. Gerows were not as common in Princeton as Criscollo had been in Trenton. There was only one family listed. I never even considered phoning them. That would have meant asking concise, direct questions, and I didn't have any of those.

I made my way back to my car, stopping at a liquor store on Nassau to ask directions to the Gerows' street, Woodland Drive. The store, though bigger and better dusted, inevitably reminded me of Nab's. I missed the place, which scared me, or rather the way I missed it did. The old store suddenly seemed very much like Our Lady of Sorrows, a piece of my past lost to me forever.

The liquor store clerk's directions took me north on Highway 27. A couple of miles out of town, Carnegie Lake appeared through the trees to my right. Woodland Drive would be a left, but the landmark I'd been told to look for was a boathouse on the lake. I spotted that easily enough, and something else. In a gravel lot in front of the boathouse sat the silver BMW.

I almost missed my turn in my preoccupation with the car and what its presence meant. I had somehow guessed my way to the one move McCary and company most feared I'd make.

The thought that I was a step away from beating the Sorrowers made me more nervous than triumphant. I drove up Woodland, an ordinary street of large tract houses, as though I were negotiating a mine field. The BMW didn't follow. I'd double-checked the reunion program before starting out for Woodland Drive. The house I pulled up to now was the only address given for Richard Gerow. It was a brick colonial, as innocent and ordinary as any on the block, but that only made me additionally cautious as I ascended the flagstone walk.

The front door was answered by a woman with iron-gray hair and matching eyes. She was dressed rather formally for a Saturday afternoon in a dark dress and a pearl necklace, like the mother from a fifties sitcom. Ricky Gerow's mother, I decided. She didn't open the door very wide, even after I'd identified myself as an old classmate of her son's.

"I live in Boston now," I said. "I came in for our reunion last night. I missed Rick, if he was there. So I thought I'd stop by and say hello. If he's home, that is."

"He doesn't live here," Mrs. Gerow said. She was as tall as Mrs. Criscollo and had the posture of a drill sergeant. Standing in the doorway, she had no trouble looking down at me.

"I wonder if there's some way I could get in touch with him," I said.

"My son doesn't live here," Mrs. Gerow repeated. "Now if you'll excuse me."

I didn't have a choice. I was halfway back to my car when I heard the front door open again. A man came out. Mr. Gerow, if I was still guessing right. I thought again of a television family from the black-and-white era. Gerow wore slacks and a golf shirt and a cardigan sweater. Robert Young on his day off.

Gerow wasn't as tall as his wife, but he was friendlier. "Sorry," he said as he hurried after me. "Sorry about that. My wife didn't mean to be rude to you, I'm sure. You're a friend of Richard's from Our Lady of Sorrows?"

"Yes," I said. I introduced myself. "I just wanted to find out how Rick's doing."

"Not very well, I'm afraid." Gerow's face was small featured and ruddy, except for patches of dry skin on his cheekbones and the bridge of his nose that resembled a light frost. His sandy hair was similarly touched with gray. "Richard's had some trouble over the years. He dropped out of the University of Pennsylvania. Did you know he'd gone there?"

I shook my head.

"Well, it was really only for one full semester. After that, well, there were bad times. Mother gets upset when she's reminded. We don't hear much from Richard now, even though he's living down in Trenton. West Trenton, actually."

"Do you think he'd mind me stopping by?"

"No. I'm sure he'd be happy to see a friend from the old days." He gave me an address on a street I didn't recognize. "He might be there or he might be at work. Do you know the Build-Lite factory?"

"On Lower Ferry Road?"

"That's right. You might check there if you have time." I thanked Mr. Gerow and started for the Ghia. He followed me down the walk. When we reached the car, he said, "If you should see Richard, tell him his father says hello."

TWELVE

THERE WERE NO silver sedans in the boathouse lot. Nor did any slide into line behind me after I'd joined the southbound traffic on Route 27. I didn't expect to see McCary or her fancy car again. Our little game of hide-and-seek had been called. The worst had happened as far as the Sorrowers were concerned. For all they knew, I already held their secret. That's why the game playing was over for them.

I didn't know the secret yet, but I was close. I was sure of that. Both the Pearson and Criscollo stories had lacked one important element: a reason why either would still be threatening to the group after the passage of ten years. All I'd uncovered prior to my visit to the Gerows was ancient history. Now I'd stumbled into the land of the living. Something bad had befallen one of our classmates, an aspiring Sorrower. I didn't know what had happened to Gerow, but I'd glimpsed some of the collateral damage in his father's eyes. That's why the game playing was over for me.

In place of some vaguely defined revenge against McCary and the Sorrowers, I now had a new motive. Or rather, a very old one. It was the desire to solve mysteries, the need to know the answers, especially those that couldn't or shouldn't be known. I was crossing a line I'd crossed before, and never with happy results. The time had come, in other words, to point the Ghia north toward Boston. So I headed south.

It took me almost an hour to drive from Princeton to West Trenton. The last part of the trip was on I-95, which I left at the exit for Mercer County Airport. Then I was asking directions again, this time at a barbershop at the intersection of Bear Tavern Road and Upper Ferry. Gerow's residence was on Grand Avenue. It turned out to be a large white structure with the shingle siding and gabled roof of a house and the fire escape and security door of an apartment building. There were six different doorbells on the front porch. I pushed the one marked "Gerow" and got no answer.

It was after four o'clock, a good time for calling it quits. I decided to try Gerow's place of employment instead. I took Parkway Avenue east past the Naval Turbine Test Station to Lower Ferry. The Build-Lite factory was on this old colonial road, hidden behind a block of state office buildings. I could smell the factory well before I saw it. I had a vision of a newspaper lying out in the rain on an unprotected front step. That was the smell, but on too small a scale. To produce what I was driving into now would have taken a wet copy of the Sunday *Times* on every front porch in the city.

The approach to the factory was along a narrow drive that paralleled railroad tracks and ended at a guard shack. A middle-aged woman in an olive uniform sat inside. When I pulled up, my car's lawn mower impersonation was almost drowned out by the play-by-play of a Phillies game.

The guard leaned out her window without bothering to turn down her radio. I said, "I'd like to see Richard Gerow."

She responded by cupping a hand behind her ear. I switched off the Ghia and repeated my request.

Mike Schmidt took a pitch low and outside while the guard thought about it. "Paint shop," she finally said. "Take a right and follow the road around to the back lot. It's a gray building near the stacks."

I was so pleased at being admitted without a challenge that I didn't pause to ask her if she meant smoke stacks or something else. I took the right turn and drove past a row of loading docks and a long, blank block wall. Behind the factory, I found a parking lot, half empty on this Saturday afternoon. Seen lengthwise, the plant appeared to be a half dozen buildings of different sizes and ages, all squeezed into one jumbled shape. A skeleton of ducts and pipes covered the outside of the buildings, making the plumbing look like an afterthought. Close to the factory, a row of parked semitrailers held bundles of scrap paper, each bundle the size of my car. Bits of loose paper blew about the yard.

I soon understood the guard's reference to "the stacks." Along the perimeter of the factory grounds were wooden skids holding sheets of gray-colored board. The loaded skids stood in stacks of varying heights, creating a dark, irregular wall, like the ramparts of a ruined fortress.

I parked in the lot and walked toward what looked like a king-sized garage. The man I sought was working in front of the building. At least it appeared from a distance to be Gerow. The closer I got, the less sure I was. The height and build were right—short and slight—and the almost delicate features were the ones I'd remembered while talking with his father. But the detail work was off, the pony tail and reddish beard surprising, the earring just plain wrong.

Gerow was filling a pail from the spigot of a fifty-five-gallon drum that rested on a wooden cradle outside the shop. He looked up as I approached, but his half-closed eyes showed no recognition. "Help you?" he asked.

"Hello, Rick," I said. "Remember me? Owen Keane. From Our Lady of Sorrows." That announcement didn't rate a blink. "We missed you at the class reunion last night."

"Missed my invitation, too, I guess." He grinned with the left side of his face. "Sent it to my folks, I bet. My mom probably trashed it." He transferred the pail to his left hand and extended his right. His slender forearm bore a blue and red tattoo of a dragon.

"Reunion, huh? Sorry I missed that. Owen Keane. Algebra II. Sister Athanasia."

"Right," I said.

"'My salad days, when I was green in judgment,'" Gerow said.

"What?"

"Shakespeare. I was reading him this morning on break. So what have you been doing with yourself, pal?"

There was no reason to put on airs for Gerow. "I work in a liquor store."

"Drug dealer, huh? Well, everybody's got to live. I'm not exactly doing social work myself." He pointed a thumb in the direction of the plant.

"What is this place?"

"Paperboard factory. Can't you smell it? I'm so used to it now I don't anymore. They grind up scrap paper, throw in some starch, and spit out construction-grade cardboard." He set down his pail and turned toward the paint shop's open door, gesturing for me to follow. The single, poorly lit room was divided from just inside the door to the back wall by a row of old metal lockers. A desk occupied one of the far corners. The other held a tall metal box like a shower stall with no door, its interior a crazy design of a dozen different colors.

"Spray-painting cabinet," Gerow said, following my gaze. He led me to a wall of shelves. They held books and cans of paint, the cans acting as bookends for the volumes wedged between them.

"What we mostly get is old newsprint," Gerow said. "But we get books, too. Awful, right? Grinding up books to make some crappy cardboard. I save all the ones I find. The guys who run the pulper let me come up and poke around the scrap on my break. I read them, too. As many as I can. I figure maybe the answer's in one of them."

"The answer to what?"

"You name it, pal."

He pointed to a row of fat maroon books. "A complete O. Henry. Well, almost complete. I'm missing volumes six and seven. One through four came in a bundle of scrap five years ago. Then last year, I found five, eight, and nine. What do you suppose the odds are of that?"

"I don't know," I said.

"Me either. But it's enough to make you think. If six and seven show up, I'll figure it's a sign. I'll be looking those books over pretty closely, you can bet on that."

Before I could ask him how he intended to decipher the books' message, the dark room was darkened further by the arrival of a figure in the doorway. The man was only Gerow's height, but he was as wide as the opening in which he stood. Seen in silhouette, his upper body seemed disproportionately large, his hands dangling down almost to his knees.

"Yo, Ricky," the man said. "Your main man around?"

"On a Saturday?" Gerow asked. "Are you kidding?"

"Mind if I look?"

"Nope."

The man entered the ship, looking behind the lockers, under the desk, and inside the spray-painting cabinet. He was well tanned for the month of May, nearly bald, and he had a very thin aquiline nose, far too fragile looking for his face. As he walked past us to the door, he said, "Tell him I'll be back."

"That's Vince," Gerow said. "He runs the numbers game here at the plant. Cal, my shop foreman, likes to play on credit. Cal and Vince have been playing hide-and-seek since we got our checks yesterday. Someday old Calvin's number is going to come up. Then Vince can hide from him."

He turned back to his library. "I'm starting to pile up some duplicates. You see anything you need, a Bible or a complete Shakespeare maybe, just take it."

"Thanks," I said. "I've still got boxes of books from college."

"Right," Gerow said. "That figures."

He led me back out into the sunlight. Then he picked up a paintbrush, thick with school-bus yellow, that had been lying on the gravel. He stooped over the pail he'd been filling when I arrived and began to stir its clear liquid with the brush. The result was instant yellow soup.

I thought my attempt to introduce the subject of college had failed. Then, without looking up from his work, Gerow asked, "Where'd you do your four years, pal?"

"Boston," I said.

"University?"

"College."

Gerow continued to swirl the brush in the yellow soup, but he looked up at me now, squinting into the afternoon sun. "I'm a university man myself. University of Pennsylvania."

"I heard that," I said.

"It's funny, but I remember Our Lady of Sorrows a lot better than Penn. Course I was at Our Lady longer. I just had a semester and change at Penn."

"What made you drop out?"

"Bad dreams, pal. That's the way I remember it, at least. Those days seem like one long bad dream sometimes."

He stood up and began flicking the brush at the ground, each quick movement of his wrist sending an arc of yellow solvent downward toward the gravel. "Not that my memory's any too reliable," he said. "Some guys lost legs and arms in 'Nam. I lost memories."

"You were in Vietnam?"

"Hell, yes. That's where I did my post-graduate work, you might say. In chemistry." He pantomimed the act of injecting the contents of a needle into his tattooed forearm.

"How about you, pal?" He gave me another narrow-eyed examination. "You stayed out of the whole sorry mess, I bet."

"Yes," I said.

"Well, you were lucky." He paused to examine the brush. There was a collar of yellow where the black bristles met the silver band. Gerow looked around for a long minute, finally bending to retrieve something from under the drum of solvent. It was a wire brush with a curved wooden handle. He began to force it through the last of the yellow paint.

"I fucked up big time in 'Nam," he said. "Tied knots for myself I've been untying ever since. That's mostly what I work at these days, untying knots. It doesn't help that my memory's so bad. Seems sometimes like I used to know how to work things out, but the part of my brain where I kept the secret got fried." He glanced briefly toward the shop, perhaps thinking of the books he'd collected in search of the answer.

"Your memory seems okay to me," I said. "You remembered me and Sister Athanasia."

"Damned if I didn't," Gerow said, much impressed with his feat. "Crazy, isn't it?" He put the bucket back under the spigot of the drum and squatted next to it. Then he turned on a trickle of solvent and held the brush under it. "I've lost whole years, but I can still remember that nun. I can remember every line in her face, and there were hundreds. Thousands. I've seen that face quite a few times over the years. In my mind, I mean. What would Sister Athanasia think of me now, her algebra angel? That's what I ask myself."

He said it as though he'd long since worked out the answer. I gave him a new one to chew on. "Were drugs the reason you dropped out of Penn?"

Gerow carefully turned off the spigot and then stared at it. "You sound just like Minerva," he said.

"Who is she?"

"Sort of my guidance counselor. I tell her and I tell her that I didn't do drugs till 'Nam. Tell her and tell her and tell her. But she always finds her way back to that same question. Doesn't believe me, I guess."

He turned his head toward me without standing and looked up at my face. There was an imploring look in his bleached out eyes.

"I believe you," I said.

Gerow compared my answer to my expression for a time. Then he stood up, stiffly. "End of the day for me, bro," he said. "Thanks for stopping by." He carried the bucket of yellow solvent to the back of the shop and emptied it onto some rainbow-colored gravel.

I'd used my standard interrogation technique with Gerow, saving my most important questions until it was too late to ask them. I tried to tack them onto the ragged end of our conversation. "Do you remember the Sorrowers?"

"The Sorrowers." Gerow smiled and repeated the name like he hadn't thought of it in years. "The Sorrowers. The old gang."

"Right. Did you ever throw a party for them at your folks' house?"

Gerow froze in the act of shaking out the bucket. "How could you know about that?"

"Then there was a party?"

"Only in my dream. My bad dream."

"The dream you had in college?"

"And in the jungle. I'd wake up from it happy to be in 'Nam. I had that dream for years. But there was no party, pal. Just a dream about one. A bad, bad dream."

"Tell me about it."

"Now you really sound like Minerva. She's always on the trail of that dream. You think the secrets are in a dream? That sounds crazy to me."

I thought it beat the hell out of waiting for an odd volume of O. Henry to tumble from a bale of scrap paper, but I was in no position to knock another man's system. "Are the Sorrowers in your dream?"

"You're not, pal." That seemed to settle my right to ask questions as far as Gerow was concerned. "You must not have been invited, like me and the reunion. You're just lucky, I guess. You missed 'Nam and you missed the dream. You're one lucky guy."

I was startled by the sound of a locomotive-class whistle close behind me. Gerow chuckled at my reaction. "Five o'clock whistle. Quitting time. I've got to go punch out. See you later."

As Gerow sauntered past me, I said, "I know a Minerva on Prospect Street. Minerva Esposito. Is that your friend?"

Gerow grinned hugely at my artlessness. "Minerva Fine," he said. "Spruce Street. Tell her Ricky said hello. And stay lucky, bro."

THIRTEEN

I WAS BACK ON Lower Ferry Road before I remembered the greeting I was supposed to pass on from Mr. Gerow to his son. I could do that later. I had a feeling that my business with Gerow was far from over. For the moment, though, I'd had enough of his company. Gerow wasn't big enough to be intimidating, but I'd felt threatened by him throughout our conversation. Perhaps it had been his casual allusions to Vietnam, a name that evoked countless demons for a man of my generation. Or perhaps it had been Gerow's disjointed memory. I'd been comfortable enough with my old friends at the reunion, even though they'd almost qualified as strangers. We'd all still had enough in common to remind us of our shared roots. Gerow's connection to those roots had been severed harshly, making him as comfortable to be with as a visitor from another planet.

I intended now to locate Minerva Fine and learn her version of Gerow's history. I headed that way, more or less. By accident or design, my route took me past a McDonald's on Olden Avenue. My hangover had finally gone belly up, leaving me extremely hungry. So I stopped long enough to buy a sack full of Styrofoam-encased dinner. Before leaving the restaurant, I looked up Minerva Fine's exact address in a phone book chained to a wall near the men's room. If the book hadn't been chained, I might have carried it off with me as a souvenir of my day. I felt as though I'd spent most of it thumbing through those inky white pages, looking between the lines for a hidden secret à la Richard Gerow.

I took my food back to the Ghia and set out again, but not for Spruce Street. It occurred to me as I drove that the unconscious goal of my circuitous route had not been the McDonald's after all. It couldn't have been, because I was still inclined to wander. Everything around me was familiar now. I passed a funeral home I'd visited as a boy, remembering how I'd "borrowed" packages of smelling salts with the home's name printed on them, intending to include them in the detective kit I was always assembling. I'd planned to use them to revive fainting witnesses, never dreaming that I'd grow up to be the kind of detective who often needed smelling salts himself. I next spotted my old parish church and its grammar school where I'd read Hardy Boys epics like *The Yellow Feather Mystery* and *While The Clock Ticked* during class by slipping them inside the anonymous paper covers of my textbooks. If only I'd read Tom Swift instead.

It was no mystery now where I was headed. The Ghia knew the way, making a right a block past the church and following a winding, tree-lined street whose houses grew smaller the farther we got from the main drag. I pulled up in front of an undistinguished Cape Cod whose gray shutters needed Richard Gerow's professional attention. I was disappointed to see that an old beech tree that had stood on one corner of the front yard was now only a two-tiered stump. I wondered how its relation in the backyard, in whom I'd once had a tree house, had fared, but I didn't get out of my car to see.

Instead, I sat and ate my hamburgers and remembered the people who had lived in the house, my scattered family. If the exercise was my antidote for the unsettling time I'd spent with Gerow, the rootless man, it backfired. I left my old street feeling very rootless myself.

THE PHONE BOOK LISTING for a Fine on Spruce Street had included the first name Walter, from which I'd deduced that Minerva was married. This was supported by the appearance of the lady herself, who answered the front door of her apartment holding a girl of two or so. Mrs. Fine was black and in her late twenties. She wore her hair extremely short, which emphasized the prominence of her cheekbones and the size of her eyes. The girl in her arms also had large eyes, which I only briefly glimpsed. After a quick look at me, she buried her face in her mother's shoulder.

"Sorry," Fine said. "She was expecting Celia, her favorite baby-sitter." A man appeared in the room behind Mrs. Fine. He tied a tie and listened while the woman with the child asked me my business.

"My name is Owen Keane," I said. "I'm a school friend of Richard Gerow's. I think you know him."

"He's a client of mine," Fine said, her large eyes searching my face. "How did you find me?"

"Ricky told me where you lived." I used Gerow's high school nickname to bolster my claim to be an old friend.

"He's never been here," Fine said. "I only see him at the office." She wasn't doubting my word, only marveling aloud at an unexpected facet of Gerow, a reaction familiar to me. "What can I do for you?"

"I'd like to find out what happened to Ricky. I want to know more about his bad dream."

"Honey," the man said. When Fine turned to look at him, he pointed to his watch.

"Right," Fine said to his retreating back. Then she turned to me. "Look, I normally wouldn't discuss a client with a stranger, but I'm as curious about Richard's dream as you are. If there's anything you could tell me about his high school days, I'd really like to hear it. I'd be willing to share what I know in exchange for any information that might help him.

"But the thing is, we're fifteen minutes away from being late for a wedding reception. So if you could come by my office on Monday..."

"I'll be in Boston on Monday," I said. "I'll be gone tomorrow. If you can spare me five minutes right now, I'll take them."

She really was curious about Gerow. "Come on in then," she said. "You can stay until Celia shows up."

The Fines' apartment building was one of three modern-looking brick cubes set well back from Spruce Street and fronted by a service road that paralleled Spruce, creating a grassy esplanade. The living room into which Fine now led me lived up to this classy exterior. The carpet was sculptured shag, and one wall was paneled in smoky mirrors cut to form a series of arches.

Another child was in the living room, a boy of five or six who was lying in front of a console television, watching a "Lone Ranger" rerun from my own childhood. Mrs. Fine turned down the set as she passed it on her way to the couch. I sat in an armchair of matching sky blue damask. The little girl squirmed free of her mother's arms and went to join her brother on the floor.

"So what do you want to know?" Fine asked me.

"You said Ricky was a client of yours. He called you his guidance counselor. What are you really?"

"I'm a county social worker. I specialize in rehabilitated drug users. Substance abusers, they want us to say now. People who have successfully gotten through a recovery program but still need help keeping their day-to-day lives in order."

"Gerow's a graduate of a drug rehabilitation program?"

"Ricky, you mean?" Fine asked, leaning heavily on the nickname I'd unconsciously dropped.

"Yes."

"He's been through a number of programs. Methadone maintenance included. He's weaned himself from even that, thank God."

I glanced at the children huddled together on the shag carpet. Minerva said, "Don't worry about them. They're in a different world." I thought she was referring to the influence of the television set until she added, "For now at least."

"How long have you been seeing him?"

"Years. Longer than most ex-addicts we get from rehab. They usually backslide or get on with their lives. Most successfully pick up and move on, believe it or not. Richard won't do either. He's been straight for years, the whole time I've known him, in fact. But he just can't let go of whatever it is that's holding him back."

"Vietnam?"

Fine glanced toward the doorway behind me. "Don't let my husband hear you say that. He was in a rifle company over there. He hates the cliché that every Vietnam vet is a time bomb waiting to go off. Or else a burned-out drug addict."

"Isn't that a good description of Gerow?"

"Yes. The question is, did 'Nam do that to him or did the war just bring out a problem that was already there?"

"He told me you've asked him about using drugs before the war."

"It's the only time I ever really provoke him. He swears he hadn't so much as smoked a joint before he went overseas."

"Do you believe him?"

Minerva turned to examine the television. Clayton Moore and Jay Silverheels were in the process of slipping away before a grateful schoolmarm could thank them. "I believe that he believes it. He's perfectly frank about his drug use in the army and after the army, so I don't know why he would lie."

She looked back from the set to me. "Did Ricky use drugs when you knew him?"

It was payback time. Time for me to tell her the secret that would help her cure Gerow. The problem was, I didn't know the secret. I was closing in on it, though. "Tell me about his dream."

Instead of registering annoyance with my stalling, Fine nodded as though I'd provided some valuable confirmation. "You're right. That dream is the key. It's what first made me think that Ricky had at least experimented with drugs before the war."

"Why?"

"Because I don't think it's a dream at all. It has all the characteristics of a flashback. An involuntary replay of an intense, drug-induced experience. A bad trip, they used to call it."

That term suggested only one drug to me. "You're thinking of LSD?"

"I think it's the most likely candidate. Did Ricky describe the dream to you?"

"I know it had to do with a party in his parents' home."

She picked up on my evasive wording. "Did Ricky tell you that?"

"Not exactly."

"Then how do you know?"

There was no avoiding a serious contribution to the conversation now. "I think it was a real party. I heard a mention of it last night at my high school reunion. Ricky Gerow's high school reunion. I went to ask him about it today, but he said there hadn't been a party. Only a bad dream about one."

"A nightmare," Fine said. She looked down at her children and lowered her voice, leaning toward me at the same time. "In the dream, he's in his own home, but it has the quality of a fun house, a maze of distorted perspectives that has him trapped. He's surrounded by friends, but he knows their smiling faces are just masks hiding some kind of monstrous deformities. His own body is deformed, his hands are large, useless balloons, his legs and arms, long and limp. And he thinks he's going to die. He knows it. It's the root of the panic he feels when he can't find his way out of the maze."

"That's the dream that hounded him out of college?" I asked, whispering now myself.

"Yes. It reoccurred throughout his freshman year, probably brought on by the stresses of that first year in the real world. He didn't tell his parents; his relationship with his mother has never been good. And he didn't try to get professional help, which was a worse mistake. He stuck it out by himself and failed instead."

"And then the army got him."

She nodded. "And the nightmares continued because, of course, the stress was now much worse. Eventually, he responded to it and to the nightmares with heroin, which was like using gasoline to put out a fire."

We sat and thought about it while the moment of the wedding reception came and passed. On the television, the theme music of the next program, the "Jetsons," marked the top of the hour. I caught sight of my own shadowy reflection in the wall of mirrors and was startled by the pockets of darkness where my eyes should have been.

I roused myself with the thought that I was already working on borrowed time. "Is this kind of reaction to LSD common?"

"No. It's uncommon. Even on the initial trip, which is the most dangerous, most users don't experience a bad reaction. But if the environment is threatening or the user feels isolated or insecure, these feelings can be exaggerated by the drug. And," she added, speaking slowly for emphasis, "if there are pre-existing psychological problems or emotional difficulties, the chance of a bad trip is much greater. Unresolved conflicts can be brought to the surface, catching the user by surprise. In some cases, this emotional upheaval can outlive the residual effects of the drug, making it hard to say where the chemicals leave off and the psychological problems start."

The doorbell rang. Walter Fine emerged from a back room, wearing a suit jacket now and a scowl for me. Both children ran to greet the person I most feared, Celia the baby-sitter. Minerva walked me to the front door.

"I'll get the car," her husband said as he hurried out.

"Meet me out front," she called after him.

She kissed her children and followed me out into the hall-way. I was asking my next question before the apartment door closed behind us. "Could Gerow have experimented with LSD and forgotten about it?"

"No, not forgotten. But he might have blanked it out," she said. "Suppressed the memory. It has to be that if the party was real." She shook her head. "It's all so conjectural. Are you sure there really was a party?"

"Yes," I said.

"Do you have any proof?"

"No. Nobody will give me a straight story." The Fines' apartment was on the first floor. We stepped through Plexiglas security doors into the soft, purple light of a mild evening. "Will you press Gerow about it?"

"Not on your life," Fine said. "Not unless you can tell me exactly what happened that night. And maybe not even then. Ricky's achieved a kind of peace. It may not be perfect, but at least he's not having nightmares anymore. Or injecting himself with poison. I'm not going to risk bringing his monsters to life again, unless I can be sure of killing them off."

"Gerow's not satisfied," I said. "He wants to know more."

"Who doesn't?" she asked a little harshly. Then she reached out and touched my forearm lightly. "We all have problems to figure out. My job isn't working that miracle for my clients. It's helping them get through their days and nights while they're doing their own figuring."

A car came around from behind the building and onto the service road. Fine walked to meet it.

Instead of "thank you" or "good-bye," I threw another question after her. "Did Gerow mention any of the names of the friends in his dream?"

She turned back to me as the car pulled up at the curb. "He did, but I can't remember them. They're in my notes, back at my office." She opened the car door and began to climb inside. Then she said, "I do remember one name. A nickname. Angel Annie."

FOURTEEN

ANN QUINN didn't smile when she opened her front door and found me there, perhaps because like Lucy Criscollo earlier in the day, she wasn't dressed for company. Her straight, golden brown hair looked as perfect as it had at the reunion, but she wore no makeup. I was struck again by the fine lines imposed on the face I remembered so well. Her outfit was an oversize T-shirt over tattered bell-bottoms. The boy standing behind her in the doorway was dressed the same way. He was perhaps six or seven, a tow-headed kid with a bandage across the bridge of his nose.

I'd been running across children all day, but I was still surprised to find one here. I covered my surprise with tactlessness. "Whose kid?" I asked.

"Mine," Ann said. "Jack, honey, go and play with your train."

Jack hesitated long enough to give me a warning look. Then he marched off, leaving Quinn and me and an awkward silence.

Even in an old T-shirt and jeans, Ann was striking enough to rout my mental forces. It took me perhaps a minute to marshal enough of them to word a simple question. "Can I come in?"

Quinn's house was an ancient brick cottage, neatly kept. She led me to the kitchen, another reminder of my visit to Lucy Criscollo, this one doubling as a warning to me to be on my guard. As the kitchen was in the back of the house, the trip was also a tour of the first floor. The living room had hardwood, a high ceiling, and a fireplace of wheat-colored tile. A sun porch off the living room was set up as a den. Jack sat there assembling pieces of plastic track. The dining room had a glass-topped table supported by rattan legs. It shared an old oriental rug of reds and blues with half a dozen mismatched chairs. The kitchen was small and old-fashioned, with white cabinets, imitation-marble linoleum, and a rounded refrigerator whose long chrome handle looked like the hood ornament of a forties coupe. The room was lit by a layer-cake-shaped ceiling fixture.

Ann crossed the room to an enameled range and took a steaming kettle off the fire. Then she sat down on a bench in a tiny breakfast nook. I took the bench opposite her.

On my drive south on I-95 to Brookshire, the old Philadelphia suburb given as Quinn's address in my fragmented reunion program, I'd written some tough-guy dialogue for myself. Finding Ann at the heart of Gerow's mystery had been a worse blow by far than the one that had started my day, the revelation that I'd been played for a sap by Maureen McCary. I felt genuinely betrayed now, as though I'd been the victim of that long-ago party and not Gerow.

The wounded feelings I'd brought with me to Quinn's cottage were not eased by the discovery that she had a son. I remembered Ann assuring me as we'd left the reunion dance floor that there'd been no great love in her life, which made me feel doubly betrayed. I forgot the tough questions I'd prepared, or rather, I thought of new ones. "Where's Jack's father?"

"He's dead." Ann raised her eyes from the tabletop. The look she gave me pressed my back against the wall behind me. "Don't play the jealous lover with me, Owen. What happened last night doesn't entitle you. I thought I'd gotten that across."

"You also told me not to go digging into the Sorrowers' secrets. I thought you were trying to protect me."

"I was."

"And yourself, coincidentally. You were there that night."

"Where was I, Owen?"

"At Ricky Gerow's house in Princeton. You remember Ricky. Sweet little guy. Math club type. It was probably an impromptu graduation party. One his parents didn't know about. It had a very select guest list. Just Gerow and the cream of the Sorrowers. You experimented with drugs that night. LSD, probably. You all came through okay. The Sorrowers, I mean. Gerow didn't make it. He still hasn't."

I'd forgotten the tough questions I'd come to ask, shocked out of my prepared script by Ann's casual dismissal of my jealousy. Instead of maneuvering her into a confession, I'd spilled out the little I knew or had guessed. Ann could now deny the whole thing and have done with me. She didn't, though. She took up the role I'd abandoned, the unrelenting questioner.

"Did you talk with Ricky?"

"Yes," I said.

"Where did you find him?"

"In West Trenton. He works at Build-Lite on Lower Ferry."

"Doing what?" Her eyes had returned to the table.

"Painting things. And saving books."

Ann ignored that non sequitur. "How is he?"

I shrugged. "Better than he's been. He dropped out of college before the rest of us were juniors."

"I'd heard that," Ann said. "Did he tell you why he'd dropped out?"

"He was having bad dreams about your little party. They followed him to Vietnam."

I'd run through my supply of offended feelings. I no longer wanted to hurt Ann, but I stumbled on anyway. "He picked up a tattoo there. And a drug habit."

Ann hadn't heard that, judging by her expression of sharp pain. She asked, "He's gotten over that?" But I understood that she meant, "Please tell me that he has."

"He's gotten past it," I said. "He may never be over it. He's not the Richard Gerow we knew. Just a fragment of him. He isn't really sure how he landed where he is. He's suppressed the memory of your experiment with LSD. That party is really just a haunting dream for him."

Ann had run out of questions. She sat with her head bent forward, her long hair hanging just above its reflection in the table's varnish. Her hands were folded before her as though for prayer. When I reached across the table to touch them, she drew away.

That simple reflex seemed to bring her back to life. "So you've figured out the Sorrowers' secret?" she asked.

"Yes," I said, not sure where she was headed.

"That we happened to be there the night Ricky played with fire?"

"That you played, too, and got away with it."

"So we swore each other to secrecy because we were ashamed of being lucky?"

Worded like that, it did seem a little thin. "One of the Sorrowers must have supplied the drugs. That's probably what you're all covering up."

Ann almost smiled. "You'll never be much of a detective, Owen. You pile up deductions fast enough, but you don't follow through. You really don't want to know the ugly parts, so you don't ask. You'll never be any good at understanding people until you learn to think the worst of them. I'll start you on your way, if you like."

"Go ahead," I said.

"What happened at that party was worse than fooling around with drugs or even supplying them. Ricky Gerow didn't experiment with drugs that night. The Sorrowers did. Ricky was just the guinea pig. Do you want me to go on?"

I nodded.

"Ricky's parents were away, as you guessed, on some overnight trip. Maureen found out about it somehow, and she dragged a few of us over there for a surprise party. Ricky wasn't exactly thrilled to see us. He was scared we'd mess up the place. But in the end, he let us in.

"Sometime during the evening, somebody gave Ricky a drink spiked with LSD. It was another stupid practical joke."

"Whose joke was it?"

Ann shook her head and said nothing.

"Maureen McCary's?"

"What Maureen told me later was that Mark Plesniak actually brought the stuff. Just to show it off, I think. It was Maureen's idea to slip it to Ricky. She didn't know what would happen. None of us did."

"Who's us?"

"Bill, David, Mary Kay, and Lucy were all in on the stunt."

"And you?"

"Yes. It was horrible, Owen. Ricky got dizzy and disoriented almost right away. But he wouldn't be still, even though he could barely stand by himself. He ran around, bumping into things until Bill and David held onto him. Even then, he shook uncontrollably.

"Ricky didn't seem to know where he was. He was seeing lights that hurt his eyes in a darkened room. His heart was pounding. He was so frightened. Sweat poured out of him like blood from an artery. He scared us all.

"Everyone but Bill and David took off. I would have gone too—I wanted to—but Ricky kept calling my name. So I stayed to help look after him. But we couldn't quiet him down. He babbled on and on for hours."

I asked a question for Minerva Fine. "What did he talk about?"

"His parents. Our Lady of Sorrows. About not being liked. About being afraid."

"Of what?"

Ann shrugged. "Of the things we were all afraid of then. College. Life. The future. Only Ricky was terrified of it all. It might only have been the acid. I don't know."

She drew her arms up across her chest. "And he talked about me, Owen. How much he loved me. Wanted me. I didn't expect that. I mean, I knew he had a crush on me, but I didn't think it was any big deal. It was to him. I tried to hold him, to quiet him, but that was a mistake. He got wild. Pushing me down, tearing at my clothes. Bill had to pull him off me."

The memory actually made Ann's hands tremble. We sat and watched them for a time. Then she closed them into fists and went on.

"An hour or so after that, Ricky decided that he was going to die. Right then and there. He was so sure of it that he convinced the rest of us. I don't know whether all his little fears had combined to create one big fear or if the big one had been there, behind all the others all the time. By that point, he didn't seem to be able to move. He was just lying there, sobbing and moaning. I could hold him then. It was all right. I rocked him and talked to him. Eventually, he fell asleep."

Ann was rocking herself now, ever so slightly. "What did you do then?" I asked.

"I left. It was late. Early, I mean. Early the next morning. First we put him to bed. Then Davey and I left. Bill stayed with Ricky. I caught hell when I got home. I cried and cried when I got to my own bed. I was so happy to be away from him and safe.

"That's all I know firsthand. Bill told me later that Ricky slept until late the next morning. He woke up sick, but he didn't seem to remember anything that had happened. Not even that the whole gang had been there. Bill convinced him that he'd had too much to drink.

"We were all safe. We graduated right on schedule. We thought we'd gotten away with it. Ricky, too."

"And you swore to keep it a secret."

"Not right away. We kept quiet about it, of course. The following spring, we heard that Ricky had dropped out of Penn. We should have tried to help him then. We should have told his parents everything we'd done. Instead, we closed ranks. We took our dirty oath."

FIFTEEN

WE SAT FOR A WHILE studying the patternless swirls and knots in the wooden planks between us. That's what I was studying anyway. I couldn't even guess at Ann's thoughts.

After a time, she said, "I have to put Jack to bed."

I started to get up, but she held me in place with a hand on my arm. "Wait a bit, Owen. Please. I won't be long."

I sat down again, switching my attention from the tabletop to the wallpaper behind Ann's empty bench. It was surely as old as the other antiques in the kitchen, a cream paper slipping toward brown on which were printed repeating pictures with a Dutch motif. Windmills alternated with groups of tulips on every other strip. The competing version had kissing children in wooden shoes and fat, steaming teapots. The wallpaper's cheerful domesticity failed to comfort me. It seemed like an artifact from a lost civilization, indecipherable now and meaningless.

Ann's confession had answered the conundrum of Ricky Gerow, the man who experienced flashbacks from drugs he had never taken. Gerow hadn't forgotten his experiment or even blanked it out. He'd simply been excluded from the secret in the first place. Gerow had aspired to the inner circle of the Sorrowers, but he'd never made it. In a very real way, that failure had shaped his life.

I'd also learned why Gerow's "trip" had been so bad. Minerva Fine had told me that a threatening environment or pre-existing fears and problems would be enough to trigger a dangerous reaction. All those elements had been present for Gerow, one threat being the pressure of making good on his big chance to impress the Sorrowers. Even if Gerow had been a willing participant in the experiment, the outcome would probably have been bad. Because he hadn't understood what was happening to him, the result had been terrible.

I felt again as I had when I'd visited my old home earlier in the evening: detached and disoriented. The Sorrowers hadn't been the heroes I'd always thought them to be. It was a modest enough discovery, a normal enough one, albeit years overdue. It shook me nevertheless. My hometown now seemed like the house in Gerow's flashback, a familiar, unfamiliar place of constantly shifting perspectives in which I was trapped.

For the second time that day, I wanted to run away; I actually stood up from the table to sneak out. I was stopped, as I had been that morning in McCary's room, by the thought of Ann Quinn. I'd learned my answers at the expense of her peace. I couldn't leave without trying to restore a little of that, even though the effort seemed hopeless.

I walked into the sun room where Jack had been playing. He'd completed a little oval of track and set his train on it. There were other projects scattered about the room: a tower of bright, snap-together blocks, a pirate ship made from a shoe box, complete with masts and sails made of plastic straws and paper napkins.

A stereo stood in one corner of the room and next to it a rack of LPs in jackets held together with yellowed tape. I poked through them and came across *Parsley, Sage, Rosemary and Thyme,* the Simon and Garfunkel album that had been playing at David Radici's party in those last happy hours of my innocence regarding the Sorrowers. I set the record on Ann's turntable and played it, softly. A lullaby for Jack and me both.

Ann found me before the first dewy cut had ended. She sat down heavily on a worn sofa whose back was covered by a loosely woven afghan.

I remained standing. "Ann, I'm sorry," I said. "I had no right to come here and accuse you. What happened to Ricky..." I broke off then, unprepared for the sympathetic look in her eyes.

"Owen," she said, shaking her head. She patted the sofa beside her, another echo of Radici's party. When I sat down, she took my hand. "You can't stand to leave me with my guilty conscience, no matter how much I deserve it. You're way too soft to be a detective. You should have stayed in the seminary."

Like a skillful conjurer, Ann had saved her most dramatic revelation for last, but I was almost too numbed by its predecessors to take it in. "You know about that?" I asked.

"Yes. A cousin of mine works in the archdiocesan offices in Trenton. She was a year behind us at Our Lady of Sorrows. She told me you'd quietly approached the archdiocese about the priesthood. And that you'd been sent to a seminary in the Midwest. And that you'd quit. I've always been curious about that. I couldn't see you in the priesthood, Owen. I couldn't see you even trying for it."

"Who else knows?"

"Which Sorrowers, you mean? I don't think any of them do. That's one of the reasons I came to the reunion. I wanted to be sure that whatever else they did, they didn't hit you there."

She really had been looking out for me. From the start. I felt again an unhappy kinship with Richard Gerow. I'd been rocked in Ann's comforting arms just as he had been. But I had misinterpreted the gesture.

The insight was a straight left to my jaw, and I dodged it instinctively. "That might explain why you were there last night, but what about the other Sorrowers? Why did they risk it? Suppose Gerow had wandered in?"

"Lucy was on the reunion committee, remember? They knew Ricky didn't have a reservation."

"Even so, why would they want to be reminded of Gerow and what they'd done to him?"

"They didn't come back to remember. They came back to forget."

Her riddle brought to mind my own reason for attending the reunion, the boozy idea that I could get in touch with an innocent, happy time. "They were looking for their earlier selves?"

"For the good old days, Owen. At least half our class was looking for those times last night, people who hadn't done anything as terrible as we had, people who were just falling a little short. Think of how much more the Sorrowers wanted the old days back.''

"What do you mean?"

"We didn't just poison Ricky Gerow that night. In a way, we poisoned ourselves. We've all been damaged."

"Right," I said. "McCary was shocked so badly her hair turned blond."

Ann let my hand drop onto the sofa. "I'm not saying we all reacted the same way. We didn't. Maureen turned her back on everything she'd been taught at Our Lady. That was her way of avoiding the guilt. It's been 'me first' for her ever since. Mark Plesniak might have taken that same way out. If so, he's the only other one.

"Poor Bill Pearson hasn't been able to untangle himself from the old values. He's still beating himself up with them. You couldn't really tell that at first. That night at Ricky's he held us all together. But there were hairline cracks in him even then. There must have been. A little more of him has broken away every time I see him."

"What about Radici? He still thinks the Sorrowers are God's chosen people."

"That's just another variation, Owen. Don't you see that? Davey's stunted, like a child whose legs are broken so badly they stop growing. He sees what we did as some wild act of rebellion. You didn't have to tell me this morning that it was Davey who'd brought up Princeton. I could have guessed it. He's the only one who could possibly be proud of it. But it's all symbolic to him, like burning a flag. It has to be. Davey wouldn't hurt a fly."

I turned to watch the play of lights on the stereo receiver while Ann worked her way through the supporting cast. "Lucy and Mary Kay are both atoning by trying to make the world a better place, one through law and the other, journalism. I think that's what they're doing anyway. It's a little beyond me."

I turned back to her. "Is it? Isn't a life of service your own solution?"

"Emptying bed pans isn't striving for social justice, Owen."

"At least you're accomplishing something."

"The point is that we were all drawn there last night by some kind of heartsick nostalgia. Even you."

I didn't like the company Ann was placing me in. "I did go into the seminary and I did leave it, but I left on my own two feet. They didn't tear the buttons off my uniform or break my sword."

"I'm glad they didn't," Ann said. "But I wasn't thinking of the seminary. I was thinking of something that happened to you earlier. The summer before our senior year. You came back from some shore retreat a wounded person. Someone filled with doubts."

My earlier feeling that I was recreating my visit with Lucy Criscollo returned with a vengeance. Who hadn't I told about that damned retreat? Telling Lucy had been enough, I decided. Every bit as good as taking out an ad in the school paper.

"That's why I said that I couldn't see you trying for the priesthood, Owen. Why did you?"

"Just stubborn, I guess," I said. And terminally curious.

Ann took up my hand again. "Sorry I beat you up last night about celebrating your failure. I should have realized that you were only there to escape like the rest of us. Back to the time when we all believed we had guardian angels watching over us.

"You're really one of the Sorrowers now, Owen. We lost our faith, too. Faith in ourselves, our values, our times. We've been searching for a solution ever since. Just like Owen Keane."

My head felt too heavy to hold upright. I couldn't stop it from sagging toward my chest. "Owen Keane, private eye," I said.

"The last person who really believed the Sorrowers were worth caring about. Sorry to have taken that from you, too."

We sat through the rest of the album's first side in silence. Philosopher to the end, I was considering Jack's oval of plastic track, a closed loop that always carried the train back to its starting point.

When the music ended, Ann asked, "Are you going to tell Ricky what you've learned?"

I thought of Minerva Fine's refusal to reawaken Gerow's monsters if she couldn't be sure of killing them off. It made running out on Gerow seem almost noble. "No," I said. "I won't tell him."

"What will you do?"

"I don't know."

That morning in my motel room, with the embarrassment of McCary's joke a fresh blow and my hangover at its apogee, I'd still been moved by an impulse to reach out for Ann. Her physical presence was that intoxicating. Even now, if she'd given me the slightest encouragement, I might have forsaken whatever remained of my pride and clung to her. Instead, she patted my hand as though I were a schoolmate of Jack's who had lost his way.

I stood up. "Take care of yourself," I said.

Ann walked me to the front door. When I was safely out on her porch, she said, "Let me hear from you sometime. Let me know what you're doing."

It was that rare moment when a lifetime's careful study of detective patter actually pays off. "The next reunion suit you?" I asked, forcing a grin.

"That won't be till eighty-eight."

"I'll try to have done something by then."

SIXTEEN

THE HEAVY TRAFFIC on I-95 was still flowing south toward Philly. It was Saturday-night traffic, inbound and hopeful. I had the northbound lanes almost to myself. I drove back to the Howard Johnson, but not to stay. I packed my things, settled my bill, and headed north again, this time on Route 1.

I now knew what the Sorrowers had done to Richard Gerow and to themselves. I knew what they had come to the reunion seeking, what we all had come there seeking. I even understood Ann's whispered prayer to 1967, the benediction to our lovemaking. It had been a sad glance back to the time before her fall from grace and my own. Finally, I'd learned that my smug sympathy for Richard Gerow was misplaced, that he and I were sharing the same trench in the same hopeless fight.

I'd solved the mystery, in other words, and ended up a loser all the same. The emptiness that rode north with me on Route 1 was an "I told you so" from the dark universe beyond the Ghia's feeble headlights.

Somewhere ahead of me in the sprawling megalopolis, my old college friends Harry and Mary had a town house. I knew I'd find it, even though it was one tiny point of light among millions. I wasn't much of a detective, but I could play the white pages like Isaac Stern played the violin.

Harry and Mary had often asked me to visit. I suddenly wanted to, badly. I would let Mary fuss over me and pretend we'd never been more than good friends. If Harry tried to talk me into taking that job with his firm, I'd let him do it. I'd failed to save Ricky Gerow, but maybe I could save Owen Keane. It was worth a try. I'd break with my past. I'd pick up and move on.

BOOK TWO

ONE

ONCE UPON A TIME, Osborne Island had been called Mystic Island East, tying it to Mystic Island, a romantically named but very ordinary spot on the edge of Great Bay. That was before casino gambling in Atlantic City created a real estate boom in the surrounding Jersey shore towns. Mystic Island, which was neither mystic nor an island, became a working-class bedroom community, its modest summer homes drafted into a year-round service their builders had not anticipated. Mystic Island East underwent gentrification, emerging as Osborne, an area of larger homes and matching pretensions.

It also had a small beach. I drove there one Sunday with a friend for a walk and breath of bay air. It was an overcast, cold day in mid-November. The year was 1988, ten years and a few months after my last contact with the Sorrowers of Our Lady of Sorrows. I hadn't seen any of them since I left Ann Quinn's house, except for my old adversary Maureen McCary, who had visited me often through the black magic of television. In the early eighties, she'd been the spokesperson for a New York bank that advertized during Yankee games. The bank had eventually bellied up, a fate I'd attributed directly to McCary's own smiling insincerity.

The intervening decade had been an eventful one for me. I'd taken a job as researcher with my friend Harry Ohlman's New York law firm, but it had only lasted a few years. Going to work for Harry had been more than a career move; it had been an experiment in living life without mysteries. I'd tried to spend those years not asking questions, or rather asking only the simple little questions whose answers could be found in carefully indexed books.

My companion on the drive to Osborne Island was a friend from those years spent hiding in libraries. Her name was Marilyn Tucci, and the library in which I'd done most of my hiding, the New York Public, had been her personal domain. In those days, Marilyn had worked as a research assistant, and I'd depended on her to help me with my assignments as I'd sleep-walked through my days. We'd been sometime lovers, too, until my experiment with normalcy had ended abruptly.

We parked a few steps from the flat, gray water of the bay, next to a sign threatening litterers with a five hundred dollar fine. The prolittering faction was represented by half a dozen brown and white gulls who were working the flotsam at the water's edge. When Marilyn and I stepped from her car, a very practical Japanese station wagon, these birds gathered in a noisy, demanding delegation.

"Pigeons on steroids," Marilyn said. "I feel like I'm back in Bryant Park."

The reference to the park next to our old library was one of several bits of nostalgia Marilyn had tossed off since her arrival that morning. The sentimentality was as unexpected as her visit. Marilyn was normally a practical, unsentimental person, although that's understating the case. She actively disliked anything romantic, spiritual, or mystical. She believed in herself implicitly, woman of her times that she was. Everyone and everything else were suspect facts subject to continual verification.

All of which made Marilyn and me as natural a pairing as tequila and scotch. Even so, we'd bumped along together adequately as long as I had successfully played the part of an uninspired office worker. But when a mystery reached into my library hiding place and yanked me out by the nose, our relationship had ended.

We walked south toward the grassy point of land that marked the mouth of the Mullica River. Along the beach before us ran parallel lines of blackened pilings, the tallest standing three or four feet above the sand.

"What was this?" Marilyn asked.

"An old boardwalk," I said. "It burned down. There was a pavilion up there." I pointed to the dunes to our right, which were covered by brown grass and shaggy, green-black cedars. "It burned, too."

"You tracked the arsonist down, I assume," Marilyn said. "Was it some greedy condo developer?"

I played along with her joke at my expense. "No, it was a stranded extraterrestrial. Turned out that when viewed from above the boardwalk and pavilion spelled out SOS in Martian. The arsonist was just trying to hitch a ride."

Marilyn kicked sand at a persistent gull. "One of your more routine cases," she said.

The thing you noticed first and remembered longest about Marilyn was her hair, which was auburn and coarse and strong willed. At the moment, it was escaping in all directions from beneath the broad brim of her white knit hat. The brisk wind blew it back from her face, at the same time making her small, flat nose and broad cheekbones glow. Her thin lips, in contrast, were almost colorless. From her neck to her knees, she was disguised by a down-filled coat of shining green.

"What are those things sticking out of the water?" she asked, pointing past me to the bay. Out of the glassy water poked thin, bare branches, like the topmost limbs of a drowned forest.

"Markers for clam beds, I think," I said.

"And what's that way out there?" She pointed to a blue blur of buildings on a distant headland.

"That's a deserted cannery," I said. To tease her, I added "I think it's haunted."

"You think everything's haunted," Marilyn said.

Some time after my experiment with ordinary living had failed, Marilyn had undertaken an experiment of her own. She'd married. It had struck me as an uncharacteristically romantic move, until I'd met her husband, as practical, realistic, and self-confident a person as Marilyn could have found. Or so he'd seemed. Around the same time, Marilyn had left the library, taking a job in the research department of a Manhattan-based publishing conglomerate. Her career there had gone well, but her marriage had not. It, the marriage I mean, had ended, badly, not many months before our beach walk.

"I'm haunted," Marilyn said. She made the admission in a soft voice and covered her embarrassment by bending over to pick up a stone.

"Is that why you came to see me?" I asked. "For an exorcism?"

Marilyn tossed the stone to the waiting bay. "For an explanation," she said. She negated that compliment immediately by adding, "It was you or the National Psychic Hot Line."

I supplied the topper. "And their line was busy."

Marilyn smiled. "Correct."

The blow that had ended our relationship years before had been my decision to take up again what Marilyn had begrudgingly called my "quest." My decision to turn away from a life without questioning and back to the search that had led me to the seminary and then driven me from it. My reappraisal of the old, crazy idea that I could find in the mysteries of this life clues to mysteries not of this life, signposts, like the bare branches poking out of Great Bay, that pointed to secrets beneath the surface. It was a quest for which Marilyn had had no time or sympathy.

And yet here she was. It was a triumph for my view of the world, or would have been if, after years of solving mysteries and even witnessing a miracle, I'd put together anything like an answer.

I decided to prepare her for the worst. "Suppose I don't have an explanation. What then?"

Marilyn slid one pillowy green arm under mine. "Then we'll just have to spend the afternoon in bed."

The beach ended in a series of pools filled with the deposits of the last high tide. We searched them, but found nothing worth rescuing. Across from the pools, near the last few feet of the Mullica, was a muddy tidal flat. On its edge stood two fishermen in hip boots. We watched several cycles of casting and reeling, but never saw them land a fish.

"Looks like they're wasting their time," I said.

"The justification for fishing isn't catching things, Keane. It's the trying that matters. You should know that if anyone does."

Marilyn's cosmology *had* been shaken up. I put my arm around her padded shoulders. "If you expect to spend the afternoon in my bed," I said, "you'd better start calling me Owen."

TWO

WE GOT BACK to my house in Mystic Island about two. Actually, it was my uncle's house. His summer getaway and my aunt's when she'd been living, a place they'd come to catch fluke and blue crab and escape the heat of Cherry Hill on weekends. In the winter, my uncle rented the house to college students. Or at least he had until he heard that his ne'er-do-well nephew needed a quiet place to hide out.

The one-story house was white and L-shaped, the inside of the L roofed over to form a carport that sheltered the front door. The tiny yard was entirely covered in low-maintenance white pebbles. The stones behind the house ran up to the edge of a lagoon, a man-made alleyway of water that led to the bay. Inside, the house had two bedrooms, one bath, a kitchen with dining area, and a living room, which doubled as the front entryway.

Marilyn parked her little station wagon at the curb in front of the house. As she shut off the engine, I reached over to examine a small spray can attached to her key chain.

"Breath freshener?" I asked.

"You've been away from the Big Apple for a long time. That's Mace. You know the saying: 'Don't leave home without it.'"

"Nice home," I said.

"Right. Like the natives around this burg don't all have gun racks in their pickup trucks." Marilyn the New Yorker thought Georgia started a few blocks south of Newark.

"This native doesn't," I said. "I'm allergic to guns."

"I would never have guessed," Marilyn said.

I retrieved the front door key from its hiding place in one of the porch lights and unlocked the door.

"You must be right about this burg being safe," Marilyn said. "You'd never get away with that trick in New York."

"There's only the one key," I explained. "So my uncle and I share it. I'm going to have a duplicate made someday."

"While you're at the hardware store, pick up a bigger mailbox." She pulled catalogs and envelopes from the box on the side of the house while I waited in the open doorway. "How long's it been since you emptied this thing?"

"A week last Tuesday," I said. "It's usually stuff for my uncle and somebody named Resident."

Once inside the house, Marilyn dropped the mail on the kitchen table along with her floppy hat. Her knee-length ski jacket went next, onto the back of a chair. Then she was unbuttoning my coat.

"I do that pretty well myself now," I said.

"If you're this modest about your jacket," Marilyn said, "I'll be all day getting you out of your underwear."

That schedule suited me, as it offered me time to figure out what was going on. Marilyn had always dictated the terms of our physical relationship, so her aggressiveness didn't surprise me. But her transformation from the pensive, vulnerable woman of our beach walk did.

"Let's talk about your being haunted," I said.

"I said horny. You must have misunderstood."

She spoke with a businesslike certainty that was an echo of the old days. She was telling me that any spiritual intimacies, like our physical ones, would proceed according to her schedule.

"I must have," I said. "Can I show you something in a bedroom?"

"Yes," she said. "Your skinny butt."

AFTERWARD I MADE US a late lunch while Marilyn prowled around the house. The menu was only salad and some canned soup, but as Marilyn considered cooking to be a lost art, I was confident it would pass. I was less comfortable with her restlessness.

"Shouldn't you be stretched out exhausted somewhere?" I asked.

"Would you like me to purr contentedly while I'm at it?" Marilyn asked back. "You must be dreaming."

She disappeared into the living room while I stirred lumps of tomato soup in a saucepan of milk. She called her next question out from around the corner: "Does Harry Ohlman know you have a portrait of his wife hanging on your wall?"

"He gave it to me," I called back. And drew it, I added to myself. The pencil sketch of Mary had been part of my payment for a case I'd handled for Harry and his daughter, Amanda. The rest of the payment had been the chance to witness the miracle I mentioned earlier, Harry regaining the love of his dead wife. I could have done without that bonus, as it had made my life seem even emptier. Two years had passed, and the feeling of hopeless separation was still with me.

Marilyn wandered back into view, stopping by the sliding glass doors that overlooked the lagoon. "Tell me about this job you've found," she said.

"I'm working at one of the casinos."

"Head of security?"

"Assistant bartender."

"Keane. I could get you on at McGraw-Hill tomorrow. You could do research again."

"I've never stopped doing research," I said.

"Right. I forgot. You probably interrogate all the drunks who come in, trying to find the one who saw God last. Or are you expecting Him to stop by Himself?"

"Or Herself," I said.

"That would serve you right." Marilyn was standing over the kitchen table, flipping through the mail she'd rescued earlier. "Here's something for you. In a plain manila envelope no less."

"Who from?"

"From whom. There's no return address."

I carried a salad over to Marilyn and took the envelope in exchange. My name and address were typed on the front. It had been posted in New York City three days earlier. "Typed by a left-handed tobacconist," I said.

"Shut up and open it."

I shook the envelope's contents down into one end and tore off the other. Inside was a blue booklet and nothing else. On the booklet's cover was a semiprofessional drawing of a sprawling building. Above the drawing was printed: "Our Lady of Sorrows High School." And below it: "Twentieth Reunion Class of 1968."

"Did you hear me, Keane?" Marilyn asked. "I said the soup's foaming up."

I dropped the booklet and ran to the stove just in time to see the soup rising above the top of the saucepan like an angry, red souffle. I held the pan aloft until the crisis passed. Then I ladled the soup out and returned to the table. Marilyn was already eating her salad. And reading my mail.

"Do your reunion people always send you a program along with your tickets? I've never heard of that."

"There are tickets?"

"Two. Stuck in the front of the program." She pulled one out. "For someplace called Angelo's in Hamilton. Friday, November twenty-fourth. That's a week from last Friday. Cocktails at six. Dinner at seven-thirty. Everybody should be good and sloshed by then."

"Speaking of which," I said in my best disinterested voice, "do you want a beer?"

Marilyn gave me her best skeptical look. "You didn't know this stuff was coming?"

I took that for a yes and crossed to the refrigerator. "I didn't know that stuff was coming. I got an invitation to the reunion a few months back, but I never answered it."

I held a bottle out to her, a frosty symbol of the truth I was asking her to accept. She hesitated a second before taking it. "They don't let you in these things for free." She consulted the ticket again. "These are thirty-seven fifty a pop."

A skin had formed on the soup in my bowl. I poked through it and played with the pink liquid underneath. Meanwhile, Marilyn Tucci, researcher, went to work. First she reexamined the envelope, hunting for subtle clues I might have overlooked, like a cover letter. Then she began to study the program itself, pouring over every page in search of answers.

While she searched, I double-checked my own story. I *had* thrown away the invitation for my twentieth reunion. After tearing it up. Its arrival had sparked the same unpleasant memories of the tenth reunion that were starting to replay as I watched the top of Marilyn's auburn mane. Pictures of photograph fragments floating in a toilet, of tattered books held upright by paint cans, of windmills on yellowed wallpaper.

Marilyn interrupted this montage with a question. "Did you notice that a page has been torn out of this? What do you suppose that means?"

"That the page contained a clue to the sender," I said. "It may have been a listing of the reunion committee. The sender has to be on the committee or have some contact on it to have gotten a copy of the program this early."

After rechecking the first pages of the program, Marilyn gave me a look of grudging respect. "No committee list," she said before resuming her reading.

In addition to memories, the reunion invitation's arrival had inspired an emotion: disbelief. I felt it again. Could ten years really have passed since my Pyrrhic victory over the Sorrowers? Those years had come and gone, and much had happened in them, but, all at once, none of it seemed to matter. I might have left Ann Quinn's house the evening before for all the difference my ten years of searching made. I had no desire to face the Sorrowers again.

"This is screwy," Marilyn said. She pushed the program away and turned her attention to me, noting first my soup bowl, which was full, and then my beer bottle, which was empty. "What's the story, Keane? There is one, isn't there?"

"An old one."

"How old?"

"Pre-Tucci."

"Let's have it."

I got up to collect the next round of drinks, meaning a fresh beer for me. "Let's make a deal," I said. "I'll tell you my story if you'll tell me yours. Why did you come all the way down here today?"

If I thought that stratagem was going to get me off, I was underestimating Marilyn. "Okay," she said.

It turned out to be an easier deal to make than make good on. Marilyn stared out toward the lagoon for a time while I poked at my salad.

"You know all about the business with Tony," she said without preamble. "As much as I do anyway. I thought I'd worked it out, but I haven't."

Tony was Marilyn's former husband, Tony Corelli, and the "it" she hadn't worked out was his death. For a man still in his thirties, I knew an unhappy number of widows and widowers. My uncle, for instance, at whose table we sat. Harry Ohlman, my friend and benefactor. Marilyn.

"That wasn't your fault," I said.

"Thanks, Monsignor. How many Hail Marys do I say? I didn't come down here for absolution. Especially not your knee-jerk variety. I know it wasn't my fault. I know it. I don't feel it."

"What do you feel?"

"Mixed up." She took her first sip of beer. "I wasn't there for Tony. That's what it comes down to. I ran out on him. He needed me, and I let him down. If he'd had cancer or been crippled, I would have stood by him. I know that. But it doesn't do me any good, because he didn't have cancer. He was just lost. And I couldn't stand the thought of being lost with him."

"That's not your fault either."

"Give it up, Owen. You can spend your whole life looking for first causes. They're just excuses. Sooner or later you'll have to take responsibility for yourself."

She rapped the phony marble of the tabletop, hard. "That's my problem. I rap my knuckles on everything I come across. On everybody. I want to know they're solid. Real. Tony was real. At first." She rapped the table again. "But toward the end I couldn't feel the solid anymore. My knuckles were passing through into nothing. Into a void. I was scared to death of being pulled inside."

I was familiar with Marilyn's knuckle test, at least in theory. I'd been another, earlier subject of it, and I had failed, too.

She straightened in her chair. "Your turn to talk," she said.

"Wait a minute. You haven't told me why you came down here."

Marilyn rolled her eyes. "You really need things spelled out, don't you?" She rapped the side of her shaggy head, lightly. "I'm getting less solid, Keane. And I'm scared."

She stood up and opened the sliding glass door, almost lifting it off its track in her haste. Then she marched out into the November afternoon. I collected our overcoats and followed her. I found her out on my uncle's floating dock, which was grounded at the moment. He and I had taken it out of the water when the weather turned cold. It sat on the edge of the sea wall and Marilyn sat on it, dangling her Reeboks above the lagoon. A lone mallard bobbed on the water in their reflection, waiting for a handout.

I wrapped Marilyn's coat around her as I sat down. Her eyes were wet, and her nose was red. "Your story had better be great," she said.

It made up in length what it lacked in greatness. I took her back to the first reunion invitation, the one that had found me in Boston in seventy-eight, and ran her through my whole adventure with the Sorrowers. From the phony ad I worked up to set things going all the way through to my late night drive to Harry and Mary's after Ann Quinn had yanked the last rug out from under me.

Marilyn's nose was still red when I finished, but now it was from the wind. "So what happened to Gerow?" she asked.

"I don't know. I never tried to check up on him." I felt a pang of guilt over that, worn smooth at the edges like the stones we'd found at the beach, and it reminded me of Marilyn's own confession. "It was like you and Tony. I was afraid of getting dragged down by him so I went away."

I was trying to win Marilyn's confidence with that association and maybe even cheer her with the reminder that she was far from the only sinner in the world. I looked into her eyes for a sign that I'd succeeded, and found a haunted look.

"It's more like Tony and me than you think," she said.

She got up and led me back into the house, holding her coat around her like a blanket. She stayed wrapped in it as she bent over the reunion program. "I thought I recognized that name. Richard Gerow is dead."

She slid the program across the table to me. Under the heading "In Memoriam" were eight names, the first of them a young woman who had died of leukemia before our graduation. Gerow's name was at the opposite end of the list.

I carried the program with me into the living room. The house had been furnished with my aunt and uncle's castoffs, pieces too dark and heavy for a shore house. I sat down in a wing chair that smelled faintly of my uncle's pipe.

Marilyn knelt at my feet, balancing herself with a hand on each of my knees. "I'd tell you it wasn't your fault," she said, "but you'd probably hit me."

"Kick you, you mean," I said. "When my knee jerked."

"You don't know that you could have helped him, Keane."

"I know that I didn't try." It was no good telling myself that I'd come across Gerow during my personal Dark Ages, the time before I'd resigned myself to my true calling. I knew I could have gone back for him. I knew I should have.

Marilyn wouldn't give up. "It wasn't your responsibility."

I almost smiled at the way she and I had traded roles, and at the awkward way we'd each tried to comfort the other. We would have done as well or better by going back to bed, our old tried-and-true method of comforting.

I pushed a lock of hair away from her forehead. It fell back into place immediately. "Somebody thinks it's my responsibility," I said. I held the program up. "That has to be what this means."

She snatched the booklet from my hand. "This is a joke. Another sick joke. So Richard Gerow happens to die. So what? He wasn't the only one. Look at all the people your class has lost, probably from drinking the water in Trenton. Some joker, one of these almighty Sorrowers, gets the idea of sending you an anonymous program. Probably the sicko who set you up the last time. What was her name again?"

"Maureen McCary."

"McCary, right. For the price of a chicken dinner with a side order of pencil points, she's hoping you'll come and play Sherlock Holmes again."

"Nick Charles," I corrected. "And they sent two tickets, so they must be hoping for two fools. Want to come along and play Nora?"

"You should live so long," Marilyn said. When she heard her own words, her eyes grew wide.

I recognized, too late, the trap I'd led her into. Here was another call for help from one of the unsubstantial people of the world, and she had instinctively turned it down. I took hold of her cold hand. "I'm sorry, Marilyn."

She pulled her hand away slowly as she stood up. "It's getting dark," she said. "I'd better be starting back."

THREE

MONDAY WAS A workday for me, spent behind a casino bar waiting for God to come in and order Herself a daiquiri. At least I was there physically. While I mixed old-fashioneds and whiskey sours for senior day-trippers from the four corners of the Delaware Valley, I thought about Richard Gerow. He was dead now, according to the mysterious reunion program. That was all I knew, or thought I knew. I kept alive the silly hope that the program was a fake, that Gerow's name had been added to the list of dead students in one copy only, mine. Aside from that act of creative desperation, I held my mind firmly in check. I forced myself not to speculate before I had more definite information. By no means did I entertain thoughts of foul play. Or of the Sorrowers. That out-of-character restraint was probably a mistake, as it left me with only Gerow himself to think about, a mixed-up little guy with a beard, an earring, and a very incomplete library.

I did manage to do two things Monday that were more constructive than wandering in memory. I scheduled vacation days for Tuesday and Wednesday. And I tracked down Minerva Fine. She had been the one reliable source of information on Gerow ten years earlier, apart from his father. I wanted to put off contacting Gerow's parents as long as possible and avoid the Sorrowers forever if I could. So I used the phone behind the bar to conduct a search for Mrs. Fine, who, when last seen, had been a Mercer County social worker.

It took me three calls and as many phony cover stories to find her. Minerva no longer dealt with drug users, at least not reformed ones. She was now working for the State of New Jersey, heading up a child abuse project. I called her number between martinis and got her secretary, who asked me for a name.

Without really thinking, I used a trick that had opened a door for me before, replying with the name of the person I was trying to research. "Tell her it's Ricky Gerow," I said.

Fine came on the line quickly and angrily. "Who are you?" she demanded. "And why are you using that name?"

I struggled for my next breath, the wind knocked out of me by the force of her indignation. Gerow *was* dead. Fine knew without asking that, whoever her caller was, it couldn't be Gerow.

"I didn't think you'd remember my name," I said. "It's Owen Keane."

"You were right," Fine said.

"I came by your apartment one evening ten years ago. To ask about Ricky Gerow. You were nice enough to speak with me."

There was a beat or two of silence. Then Fine said, "I remember you. What do you want?"

"I need to know how Gerow died."

This time there was no pause. "I don't think so, Mr. Keane. I confided in you ten years ago because I hoped it might help Ricky. There's no chance of helping him now."

"Then you don't have any questions about Gerow's death? Just tell me he died of natural causes with no loose ends, and I won't bother you again."

Fine picked up on the note of supplication in my voice. "I'm sorry. I can't tell you that. I have questions. Do you have something to tell me about Ricky's death?"

"I can tell you about his first one. The one he revisited in his nightmares. I know all about that party now." And have since Carter was president, I thought.

There was a rustling of paper. "I've got some open time tomorrow morning. At nine."

"I'll be there," I said.

I STARTED OUT FOR Trenton at seven the next morning, allowing two hours for what would probably be an hour and a half's drive. I still planned trips using the cruising speed of my old Karmann-Ghia, though I hadn't driven it in over a year. The Ghia currently resided in a barn on my brother's place near

Vineland, awaiting a massive restoration that I would probably never get around to. In its place, I now drove an eighty-six
Chevrolet, a boxy two-door with a romantic name, Cavalier. It
was red, like its predecessor, but glossier, as it lacked the pati-
na of memories and associations that covered the Ghia. The
Cavalier did have a heater, however, which went a long way toward reconciling me to my loss.

I took Highway 539 out of Tuckerton, which led into the
isolation of the Jersey Pine Barrens. It wasn't true, as Marilyn
had suggested, that I believed in haunted places. But I kept an
open mind about the Pine Barrens, perhaps because I'd come
close to haunting that primeval place myself once, years before. On that visit, I'd been told a ghost story by a man who
was now a ghost himself. The story had left such a lasting impression on me that I never drove through the old forest without scanning its tangled pines. For wandering deer certainly,
but also for the dead.

I wasn't expecting to see the ghost of Richard Gerow, not
outside of my own haunted dreams. But the closer I got to
Trenton, the more nervous I became. My mental discipline of
the day before collapsed without the busywork of the bar to
prop it up. I speculated freely now, with no more to build on
than the mailing I'd received and Minerva Fine's unspecified
questions about Gerow's death.

Fortunately, I also had a secret ingredient, my own guilt. My
favorite explanation for the mailing was still the one I'd pro-
posed to Marilyn. It was an indictment of me sent by someone
who thought I was responsible for Gerow's death. I'd lived for
ten years with the knowledge that I hadn't helped Gerow, but
I'd also believed that I hadn't hurt him, that my visit to his
paint shop had left him no more than bemused or puzzled. I
beat myself up now with the antithesis of this, the idea that my
brief reappearance in his life had somehow destroyed his hard
won peace.

I stopped for breakfast at a log cabin restaurant outside New
Egypt. A log burned in a tall stone fireplace and a Hank Wil-
liams, Jr., record played on the jukebox. I took a seat at a
roughly made cedar counter and ordered toast and coffee.

The waitress who served me had the dry-gulch voice and leathery face of a long-time smoker. "Haven't seen you in here for a while, Paul," she said. "How's business? Still in real estate?"

"Yes," I said, happy to be someone else for a while.

She stopped by my stretch of counter several times to refill my cup and complain about the price of houses. It was too late to correct her, so I just nodded and hoped the real Paul wouldn't show up to claim his seat. I wondered how he was doing, this doppelganger of mine. I wished him a wife and kids and a big house in one of the sandy developments springing up on the fringes of the Pines. What the hell, I gave him a dog, too.

As long as I stayed in the restaurant, the jukebox noise and the chatter of the other customers drowned out my bad conscience. Drowned it out, but didn't soothe it. The old worm started gnawing on me again as soon as I unlocked the Chevy's door.

There were two very tangible objections to my idea that the anonymous mailing was an accusation directed at me, namely the two reunion tickets. No one recriminating me for failing to help Gerow or for knocking the props out from under his uneasy peace would reward me with an evening of dinner and dancing. Marilyn's theory, that the mailing was yet another Sorrower joke, covered both the program and the tickets. In her version, Gerow's death was just a coincidence that worked to the Sorrowers' advantage.

But who among the Sorrowers could see any humor in Gerow's death, however innocent or natural it might have been? Not Bill Pearson, the man Ann had described as flaking away under the weight of his guilt. Not Ann herself or Mary Kay or Lucy, all of whom had been working off the same debt when I'd last seen them. Not even David Radici, for whom the poisoning of Gerow had had some crazy symbolic value. That left only Maureen McCary, Marilyn's number one suspect. But even she had been damaged by that long-ago sin, according to Ann.

Then there was the problem of motive. I was still a threat to the Sorrowers' collective peace of mind. I knew what they'd done to Gerow in 1968. I could still expose them, however belatedly. Why would any of them prod me into it with another stupid joke?

Motive was also the weak link in a third explanation of the mailing, the one I most feared: that the program and the tickets were the sender's way of taunting me with his or her involvement in Gerow's death. Why would anyone dare me to poke around in something so dangerous? And why draw me back to Trenton for the reunion? Why bother with me at all?

The more I thought about it, the more I felt like an item on somebody's list of unfinished business. As Ricky Gerow had been.

FOUR

THE DIRECTIONS I'd gotten from Minerva Fine took me to downtown Trenton and Hanover Street, not far from the Old Barracks, where Hessian soldiers had been sleeping it off when George Washington and the boys dropped in. Fine's building was also a historic landmark. For me, at least. It had been a department store back when I'd been young enough to visit Santa Claus. Since then, the windowless building with art deco pretensions had been taken over by Trenton's only boom industry, government.

Fine's office was on the third floor. The upper half of her office walls were glass, designed to give the occupant a view of the ten or so paper pushers squeezed into the surrounding bull pen. The glass was two-way, though, so I was able to study Fine while I stood in her reception area. She was seated behind a large metal desk, talking on the phone. She'd let her hair grow out since our previous meeting. She wore it straight and brushed it back from her face without a part. When the large, earnest eyes I remembered so well looked up and met mine, it was over the half-rims of reading glasses. I wondered how I'd changed to her. Was she noting the gray in my hair or my prematurely furrowed brow? Or just wondering what rock I'd crawled out from under?

I was reminded again of the passage of years when Fine waved me into her office. A folding frame on her desk contained pictures of her children. The girl she'd held in her arms ten years before was now a novice teenager. Fine's son had to be in high school.

"Ewing High," Fine said, guessing my thoughts.

"Congratulations."

She nodded, first in acknowledgment and then toward an empty chair. She wore a formal-looking, cream-colored blouse with a high collar. Wrapped around the outside of the collar was a band of the same material, tied in front in a loose cravat. A stock, General Washington would have called it.

When I'd seated myself, Fine said, "As I recall, I did most of the confiding the last time we met. In fact, I was fairly indiscreet. This time, why don't you talk."

"Would you tell me first how Gerow died?"

"He committed suicide. The actual cause of death was a drug overdose." She watched my reaction and then said, "You really didn't know that, did you?"

"No. I only found out two days ago that he was dead. Could it have been an accident?"

"That's always a possibility with a heroin overdose, because the user can never be sure of the purity of a given sample. But I don't think Ricky's death was any accident."

"Why not?"

"Because he died of such a massive overdose. No experienced user could accidentally inject himself with the amount of heroin they found in Ricky. No matter how unlucky or out of practice he was."

"When did it happen?"

"Last April."

"You can't still have been counseling him. How did you stay in touch?"

"It seems to me I asked you to talk, Mr. Keane. Not interrogate."

"Sorry. Habit of a lifetime. What would you like to hear?"

"Something like an explanation of why you called me."

My ten-year-old investigation of the Sorrowers was fresh in my mind, as I'd recounted it for Marilyn only two days earlier. I summarized my discoveries for Fine as though our last interview had been sometime the previous week and not the previous decade.

"You were right about Gerow's nightmare. It was a flashback. Gerow was talked into hosting a party for some high school friends in 1968. They gave him some LSD without letting him in on the joke. They never let him in on it. You know more than I do about his reaction to it and what his life was like afterward."

Fine took off her glasses and folded them carefully. "Poor Ricky. He was telling me the truth all along about not using drugs back then. He never knew what had happened to him. Or did he find out?"

"I'd like to know the answer to that myself. I know I didn't tell him."

Fine's "Why not?" was never actually spoken aloud. It took the form of a quizzical expression. When that passed, she asked a question I dreaded even more: "When did you learn all this?"

"The same night I came to your apartment. I found out more than I could handle that night. I took off and kept going."

I expected a stronger reaction to my confession than I received. "I see," she said. "How did you happen to hear that Ricky had died?"

"Last weekend, I received an anonymous mailing. The timing has to do with Our Lady of Sorrows High School class of sixty-eight reunion. It's a long story, but I was here in Trenton for our tenth reunion when I first heard about Gerow's troubles."

"I remember your telling me that," Fine said.

"This Friday we're having our twentieth reunion. Someone sent me a copy of the reunion program containing a mention of Gerow's death." I patted my pockets for the program, but, true to form, I'd left it in the Chevy. "The sender may have been someone who was at Gerow's party twenty years ago."

"Why would anyone do that?"

It was the question I'd been asking myself all the way to Trenton. Fortunately, it was rhetorical enough to ignore. "You said on the phone that you had questions about Ricky's death. Would you feel comfortable discussing those with me?"

"I'd feel more comfortable if I understood your part in all this," Fine said. "And don't tell me that Ricky was your friend. Ten years ago, you'd completely lost touch with him. When you found out about his troubles, you deliberately cut all ties with him again. For all you knew, he could have died the day after you last saw him in seventy-eight."

Fine's directness was quite a contrast to the mutual absolution session Marilyn and I had run for each other on Sunday.

Here was a woman for whom the bottom line was responsibility. I took it as my theme. "When I called you yesterday, I was afraid Gerow *had* died in seventy-eight. Or not long afterward. I thought I might have stirred something up back then."

"You still could have set the wheels in motion."

"They would have to have been pretty slow wheels, if Gerow didn't kill himself until last April."

Fine batted that objection away with a wave of her folded glasses. "If Ricky's suicide is tied somehow to his LSD experience, it was in the works for twice ten years. There's no statute of limitations on people's problems. Especially if they involve an addiction."

She opened a desk drawer and reached inside. I could have guessed all day about the contents of the drawer and not named the object she pulled from it. It was a pint bottle of Jack Daniels, unopened, its neck decorated with a yellow ribbon.

"I've had this in my desk for almost seventeen years now. Can you guess why?"

"You were an alcoholic."

"I *am* an alcoholic, Mr. Keane. I haven't had a drink in seventeen years. This little bottle is a symbol of that for me. Every day I don't open it is a day my life stays together."

I nodded toward the bottle. "Why have that so close?"

"To help me stay focused. There are a million bottles around me all the time. I can't fight them all off. So I concentrate on this one. It helps me forget the others."

"What does the yellow ribbon mean?"

"That was a gift from Ricky Gerow. I showed him this bottle when I was counseling him. Do you remember when everyone was putting out yellow ribbons?"

"For the hostages in Tehran."

"Right. He brought me this ribbon back then."

"To symbolize what? A captivity?"

"Yes. To the addiction. A hostage crisis that never ends, Mr. Keane. So don't tell me that the passage of years washes the slate clean. It doesn't always."

I suddenly felt very exposed in the fishbowl office. "You think I may be responsible then?"

"No. I think you did the right thing ten years ago, although probably for the wrong reasons. I think you were right not to tell Ricky the truth about that party.'

"Why?"

"You asked me earlier how I stayed in touch with Ricky. It was actually the other way around. I hadn't been his counselor for eight years at the time of his death. But I heard from him at least once each and every year. On April second."

"Your birthday?"

"Ricky Gerow's rebirth day. The anniversary of the day he originally gave up drugs. It's the most important day in the calendar for any former substance abuser. Liberation day, some programs call it. Ricky always sent me a card or a letter on April second, telling me how the previous year had gone for him. Every year for the past five or six, the letters got more and more positive. The note I received this year was short, but extremely upbeat. Ricky seemed to have put his demons behind him.

"If you'd come in here with your story the day after I read that last card, I would have shaken your hand for not telling Ricky. He seemed that well, that contented."

"But now he's dead."

"By his own hand. Only weeks after he wrote me that card. That's the biggest question I have concerning his death, the number one problem: reconciling his last words to me and that awful act."

"What did Gerow say in his last card?"

"Nothing specific." She looked up toward the ceiling. "He was never specific. Just that he was finally enjoying his life and that he was actually looking forward to the future."

"How had he changed his life for the better over the past five or six years?"

"He hadn't. Not outwardly. He still worked at that factory in West Trenton. He still lived alone in the same apartment. The changes he made were psychological. Or spiritual. As I said, he was never very specific."

"Did he leave a suicide note?"

"No. I asked about that when I spoke with Ricky's father. Mr. Gerow was also taken by surprise by Ricky's suicide. He never stopped thinking of Ricky as he'd been before Vietnam."

"What about Mrs. Gerow?"

"She died in the early eighties. Mr. Gerow is living in a retirement community near Rocky Hill."

"Ten years ago you hinted that Gerow and his mother had a bad relationship. What was that all about?"

Fine blinked dramatically. "I really was indiscreet with you, wasn't I? I think your expression is to blame, Mr. Keane. You give the false impression that almost everything is going over your head."

"It's not entirely false," I said.

"Ricky's problems with his mother were of a very common variety. That is to say, it isn't uncommon for a young man with a dominant mother and a passive father to resent his mother. And coming of age can be additionally challenging for a young man who lacks a strong role model. Any number of problems can result from this, the most common ones being insecurity and a fragile sense of identity on the part of the son."

"Were those Ricky Gerow's problems?"

"I think so. As I said, it isn't an uncommon situation or especially crippling. If your mutual friends hadn't intervened to alter the course of Ricky's life, he would probably have worked it all out by himself."

"But they did intervene," I said.

"What are you getting at?"

I took a turn looking up at the ceiling. It was the only restful view in the office, a flat expanse of white acoustical tile, yellowed in spots by somebody's cigarette smoke. "I'm looking for an explanation of why Gerow's life changed for the better. His mother died in the early eighties. He dropped out of counseling around the same time, and his annual reports to you got more and more upbeat."

"I don't think so, Mr. Keane. Ricky had come to terms with his mother long before her death. Back around the time he kicked his drug habit. They weren't exactly friendly terms, but that's often the way that scenario plays out. I think you have to look elsewhere for an explanation of the change in Ricky's life.''

I backed out of that dead end and began again. ''You said that Gerow's timing is your number one problem. Is there a number two?''

''Yes, his method. That he took his life with heroin, I mean. I've spoken with the counselors who inherited Ricky when I found a new job, let's see, eight years ago. Gerow finally graduated from counseling a few years after that, with the blessings of my successors. They were confident that he wouldn't backslide. So was I.''

''He may not have,'' I said. ''Even if he hadn't been using heroin again, it might have seemed to him the symbolically correct way to kill himself.''

Fine nodded impatiently. ''I know, I know. He could have been consciously or unconsciously completing the suicide he'd begun in Vietnam. It's an attractive theory, but I don't believe it. For someone like Ricky, who has successfully cleansed himself of drugs, the needle is a symbol of something worse than death. Putting a gun to his head would have been many times easier for him than injecting himself with a drug. To put it in archaic terms, it would have been the difference between simply dying and being damned.''

They were archaic terms that meant a lot to me. I sat and thought about them until Fine made a show of checking her watch. There were other things to ask her, detailed questions on the circumstances of Gerow's death and the routine of his last years. I thought of another source for that information, perhaps a better one.

''Would you trust me with Mr. Gerow's phone number and address?'' I asked.

''Telling Mr. Gerow what happened to his son in 1968 won't help anyone now,'' Fine said.

''I'm only interested in last April.''

''Do you think the person who sent you the reunion program is involved somehow in Ricky's death?''

''**I**'d rather not think that,'' I said. ''But I have to know.''

Fine smiled for the first time in our acquaintance. "That's another thing I've noticed about you. Someday I'd like to find out why that is." She took a book from a drawer of her desk and copied a few lines onto an index card. "In the meantime, I'd settle for sharing whatever you learn about Ricky's death."

"Deal," I said.

FIVE

I STARTED OUT for Rocky Hill with the thoughtless arrogance of the native and promptly got lost. My wanderings carried me north to Skillman. There a filling station attendant fielded me like a grounder that had gone through the shortstop's legs and flipped me east southeast.

My careless navigating might have been due in part to nerves. It was one thing to admit my desertion of Richard Gerow to his ex-guidance counselor and quite another to confess it to his father. That is, it would be if I actually got around to making a confession. Minerva didn't think that rehashing the Sorrower's crimes with Mr. Gerow was a good idea, and I had a history of using her sound judgment as an excuse for silence.

I was also apprehensive on my drive to Rocky Hill because I half expected to find Mr. Gerow in a nursing home. I'd done some investigating in nursing homes in the past, and the results weren't among my happier memories. I relaxed a bit after I'd closed in on Mr. Gerow's retirement community. The place was called Rockingham, and it looked more like a country club than an old folks' home. Behind a massive stone wall were nicely scattered apartment buildings, surrounded by shedding trees and the mothballed holes of a golf course. I paused twice for speed bumps at golf cart crossings on my way up the winding drive. Just short of the community's office, I was stopped again, this time by a gaggle of once-wild geese crossing the drive on their way from one pond to another. I wondered if they were northern geese wintering here or Jersey geese who had yet to head south.

A man vacuuming leaves from the office sidewalk directed me to Hearthstone, Mr. Gerow's street. His apartment was on the first floor of a stone and cedar building, and it had its own street door complete with a brass knocker. A bunch of Indian corn was wired to the knocker, so I used the bell.

I'd just about decided that no one was home when the door's dead bolt snapped back. Mr. Gerow had changed less in the past ten years than had Minerva Fine, or so it seemed to me. He still had the look of a boy left outside on a frosty night. He was even dressed the way I remembered, in a cardigan sweater over a golf shirt and plaid slacks. As we shook hands, I entertained the odd idea that he'd changed his residence to match his outfit.

"You're a friend of Richard's and you and I have met before," Mr. Gerow said, summing up my rambling introduction.

"I came by your house ten years ago and you gave me Ricky's address," I said.

He smiled and shook his head at the same time. I interpreted the combination to mean that my claim was plausible but didn't ring any bells. "Come on in," he said. "Excuse the mess."

There was no mess to excuse beyond a few pages of newspaper dropped at the foot of an easy chair. The front room was overfurnished in pieces too big for it, survivors from the Gerows' Princeton home. I took a seat on a French provincial sofa, thinking of my house in Mystic Island and its displaced furniture. I also thought of my uncle. Mr. Gerow was yet another entry in my growing list of widows and widowers.

I suspected that the wall hangings had not been in the Gerows' Princeton living room. There were six in the series, all detailed drawings of imaginary and very bizarre golf holes. In one, a foursome teed off from a mountain peak toward a tiny green on a neighboring alp. The next print featured tiny golfers struggling across a glacier. The last one on the wall I faced had a hole laid out along the base of an active volcano, with rivers of glowing lava for hazards.

"I get a real kick out of those," Mr. Gerow said, nodding toward the prints. "Do you play golf?"

I almost said, "Not yet," but I caught myself in time to shorten it to "No."

"It's a great game. Some people call it the game you can play your whole life." He paused for effect. "But I don't think a round should take more than four hours myself."

I tried to imitate Gerow's chuckling, wondering at the same time how I could change the subject to his dead son.

Gerow made the transition for me, his head sagging a little as he abruptly downshifted. "You heard about Richard, I guess."

"And Mrs. Gerow," I said impulsively. "I'm sorry."

"Thanks." Gerow looked around the crowded, empty room while I mentally kicked myself for dividing his attention by mentioning his wife. He wasn't distracted for long.

"They were both blows, but losing Richard was the harder of the two. That's hard saying, but it's true. I think it's because Alice's death seemed part of the normal order of things. It was well explained. The doctors explained it. The priests explained it. No one has been able to explain Richard's death for me."

He held up a frosty white hand to stop himself. "That's not right exactly. The police gave me an explanation. I just couldn't accept it."

"What was their explanation?"

Gerow might have told me it was none of my business, but he didn't. Lonely people cut nosy people a lot of slack.

"They said it was a drug overdose. He was found in his apartment, lying on his bed. Very peacefully," he added as though to comfort me. "There was a needle on the bed beside him. On his nightstand was the paper packet the heroin had come in, a candle, and a spoon. They use a spoon, you know, and the heat of a candle to dissolve the drug in water. His were the only fingerprints on the spoon and the needle."

Mr. Gerow paused for a breath and then soldiered on. "Richard's landlady found him. His foreman at Build-Lite, Cal Hart, called her when Richard didn't show up for work. Called her the first day Richard didn't appear," Gerow said proudly. "That's how regular Richard had always been. It was a Monday afternoon when she found him. The police said he'd probably died the previous Friday night."

"But you don't believe the police."

"Oh I believe them on that kind of thing all right. Time of death, cause of death. They can work that stuff out with their eyes closed. Type of death, now that's another matter. I'll never believe Richard took his own life. All the needles and fingerprints in the world won't convince me."

"Why not?"

"Because he was a survivor. A fighter. That boy had been through more hard times than I've known in almost twice as long a life. A lot of them he caused himself, I know, but he never gave up, not at the lowest, darkest moment. Why would he suddenly quit when things were going well for him?"

His question reminded me of a loose end from Minerva Fine's testimony. "How were things going well? He was still at Build-Lite. He was living the way he'd always lived."

Gerow's emphatic nod was almost a bow from the waist. "Outwardly, things hadn't changed, except that he was having his hair cut shorter and he'd given up his beard and that earring thing he'd worn since the army. But outward things aren't important. Alice always hated where he worked, a boy who could have been anything, but in the end a job doesn't matter either. Being happy matters. That's what you really have to wish for your children. Happiness. Richard wasn't happy for a long time. He was restless. Discontented.

"You'll think this is trite or stupid, but Richard—before he changed, I mean—reminded me of a ghost from some old Halloween story. One who'd lost his head and had to walk the earth searching for it. I don't know what lost piece of himself Richard was searching for, but he finally found it."

"When did this change take place?"

Gerow tapped his chin. "Not overnight. I'd say I started to notice it just before his mother passed away. He'd call on the phone to talk with us when he never had before. He'd even drive up to see us. Not often, but sometimes. And when he did, he'd be smiling. And he'd talk about the Mets or my golf game, the kind of silly things contented people talk about when they visit."

That observation reminded him that he was playing host again. "Hey, can I get you a cup of coffee? I was just going to have one myself when the doorbell rang."

He was out of his chair before I could turn down his offer. I followed him into the kitchen, unwilling to give up the momentum our conversation had developed. As we walked single file down a narrow hallway, I addressed his narrow back. "The last time I talked with Ricky, he told me about the troubles he'd had in Vietnam."

Gerow didn't reply until we reached the tiny kitchen. It was as neat as the rest of the house, but brighter, its oak woodwork and white tile floodlit by November sunlight streaming through sliding glass doors. After directing me toward a two-person dinette, Gerow filled two mugs with tap water and set them inside a microwave. Then he turned to face me.

"Drugs, you mean?" His tone was so casual, he might have been asking me if I took cream in my coffee.

"Yes," I said. "Is there any chance that this happiness Ricky found..."

Gerow completed my question with the very euphemism I'd been hesitant to use: "Came out of a needle? You can speak as plainly to me as you want to, son. I had my consciousness raised on the subject of drugs twenty years ago. Raised and calloused over.

"The answer to your question is no. There was only one recent track mark, needle mark, on Richard's arms. The one that killed him. All his other scars were old."

"There are other ways to use heroin besides injecting it."

"I know that, but Richard wasn't doing any of them. I can give you more reasons for that belief than I have fingers and toes. He couldn't have held down a job, for starters. Not and used drugs for any length of time."

The microwave chirped three times and then shut itself down. Gerow removed the steaming mugs. He sprinkled just enough instant coffee into each to darken the water and then carried them to the table.

"And there's the problem of money," he said as he sat down. "Richard didn't make a lot, and any he had left over he spent on his car."

"His car?"

"Yes. Would you like to see it? It's out back. Bring your coffee."

We went out through the sliding glass doors and down a leaf-strewn drive that ended in a row of carports. The third stall contained a car under a canvas cover that had been tailored to its sleek outline. Mr. Gerow made little progress removing the cover until I set my coffee down and helped him. We folded it back onto the trunk of the car, a pristine Pontiac Firebird from the mid-seventies. It was gold with mag wheels and it made me think of the "Rockford Files." I could easily imagine James Garner, or rather Jim Rockford, driving it in one of the high-speed chases that wrapped up all his investigations.

"I don't drive it myself," Gerow said. "I've been meaning to sell it, but I haven't gotten around to it yet."

And wouldn't for some time, I thought. I sipped my dish-water coffee for its warmth alone while the old man pointed out all the custom features Gerow had added to the car. It was odd to think that Richard Gerow had had so ordinary a hobby, a man who'd grappled with the basic questions of his existence, as odd as finding out that Descartes had been a croquet champ on the side. Maybe Ricky had figured out in the end that a nice car was the secret of life. A lot of people before him had. Maybe the budding happiness his father and Minerva Fine had noticed was just Ricky's gradual surrender to the material, af-ter the fashion of his nemesis, Maureen McCary.

The chill air got to Gerow after five minutes or so. We re-treated into the kitchen, where I turned down his offer of more coffee.

"Sorry for running on so about Richard," my host said. "He's on my mind a lot." Made nearsighted by his obsession, he seemed not to have recognized my own fascination with the subject.

I decided to ask the question that had been sharing the apartment with us ever since Gerow had denied the possibility of his son's suicide. "You think the police got the type of death wrong, meaning you don't think it was a suicide."

"Couldn't have been," Gerow said.

"If Ricky wasn't using drugs, it couldn't have been an accident either. What does that leave?"

"Murder," Gerow said promptly. "Sorry. I thought you understood that."

I asked my next question because it seemed like the correct, innocent question to ask. "Who would murder Ricky?"

"That's the problem the police had with the idea. It would have to have been premeditated murder if Richard didn't have the heroin and needle lying around, and, of course, he didn't. And he didn't have anything worth stealing, except maybe his car. So it had to be an enemy, and Richard didn't have any enemies. The people he worked with at Build-Lite and the folks at his apartment building all liked him. He didn't seem to know anybody else."

"How about someone from his past?"

"I've thought about that. A lot of the time on television programs old army buddies show up to cause trouble for people. I've wondered if the murderer wasn't somebody Richard knew in the army. Somebody like that might have known that Richard once used heroin, which would have made it a logical way to kill him."

Mr. Gerow seemed oblivious to the fact that he was currently talking with a person from Ricky's past. If this were one of his television programs, I would have been screwing a silencer onto my pistol while he fussed over the sink, rinsing out our coffee cups. Luckily for him, we weren't on television. When he finished with the cups and turned to face me, my hands were empty and my expression was a study in innocence.

"I'd like to show you some things," he said. "If you have time."

"I have time." I said.

I followed him back into the furniture museum front room. In one corner there was a secretary inlaid with several different kinds of wood and held together visually, if not literally, by a heavy coat of varnish. From the top drawer of the desk, Gerow extracted a hinged-top, cardboard cigar box. I had a vision of the marbles and jacks and baseball cards I'd once kept in a similar box. But when Gerow opened his, I saw that it contained only paper.

"What do you think of these?" he asked. "I found them in Richard's desk."

He handed me a packet of preprinted deposit tickets for a personal checking account. The bank was Hunterdon National of Flemington, New Jersey, and the account holder's name was William Porter. Below the name, in smaller type, was a Flemington address.

"Do you know this Porter?"

"No. And I can't remember Richard ever mentioning him."

"Have you gotten in touch with him?"

"I tried. Not right away. For a little while after Richard died, I couldn't really bring myself to think about it. It was July or August before I made up my mind to write to him. My letters came back marked "addressee unknown."

"Is there anything else?"

"Yes. I found these in the glove compartment of the Firebird."

He stepped over to a coffee table and upended the cigar box. Four paper bands dropped quietly onto the table. They were used money straps—their seals unbroken—preprinted with an amount in bold red ink: five hundred dollars.

I sat down on the sofa to examine the bands. Each was hand stamped with a date and the name of a bank, First Penn. The dates were roughly one month apart. The first fell in December 1987, and the other three in January, February, and March of the current year. Each strap had been initialed by a different person, the tellers who counted and strapped the money, I decided.

"Who did Ricky bank with?"

"New Jersey National. He had a checking account."

"Any five-hundred-dollar deposits?"

"No. Just his paychecks every week. The account balanced to the penny," Gerow added.

"Have you looked into these?" I asked, holding one of the straps out to him.

He declined to touch it. "I didn't know what to do with them." It was clear that Gerow found the little bracelets of paper disturbing.

So did I. "Would you mind if I checked them out?"

"You?" Gerow asked.

"Yes. I do a little investigation work on the side." When I wasn't sticking tiny plastic rapiers through olives. "I'd like to find out what happened to Ricky."

"Why?"

"Because I didn't do anything to help him ten years ago."

One more *why* out of Gerow and I would have been there till dinnertime, telling him the tangled history of the Sorrowers. He saved us both from that ordeal by reaching out and touching the back of my hand with his cold, dry fingertips.

"I appreciate your saying that, Owen. A lot of people wanted to help Richard. None of us could figure out how."

"We still might," I said.

SIX

I LEFT ROCKY HILL with Mr. Gerow's cigar box on the passenger seat of the Chevy. By taking it, I'd tacitly promised to follow up the leads it continued, but I didn't set out to do that. I thought of the box as an item of emergency equipment, a break-glass-in-case-of-fire step that I hoped I wouldn't have to take.

I told myself that I was being systematic, which was my favorite rationalization for putting off dirty work. Minerva Fine and Mr. Gerow were both convinced that Ricky hadn't fallen back into drug use, but I was not. I was equally skeptical of their shared opinion that he hadn't committed suicide. I'd accepted much less reliable testimony often in past cases, leap-of-faith detective that I was. This time, though, I wouldn't even go near the cliff. I wanted proof.

My drive south was like a highlight film of my investigation of the Sorrowers. Highway 27 carried me between the Gerows' old neighborhood and Carnegie Lake, at whose edge Maureen McCary's BMW had once lain in wait for me. Princeton itself seemed unchanged, although more traffic-ridden. Not so its suburbs. The budding commercial development I'd noted around the university ten years earlier had run riot since. I cut over to Route 1 on Washington Road and found a solid wall of malls, hotels, and corporate offices along each side of the old highway.

I was recreating the very drive I'd made a decade earlier, when I'd traveled from the Gerows' home to their son's less-posh West Trenton apartment. This time, I didn't have to stop for directions. I drove straight to Gerow's address on Grand Avenue, as though the many visits I'd made in memory had been real ones.

The small apartment building still didn't live up to the name of its street, but it was holding its own. Two girls who should have been in school were roller-skating on the cracked front walk of the building. Bundled up in sweaters and knitted leggings, they were going through the motions of an elaborate figure-skating routine. The would-be Olympians watched me mount the front porch and ring the bell for the office. Then they studied my waiting technique. When I was reaching to ring the bell again, one of the girls said, "Mrs. Nix is over there."

She pointed to the west and obligingly held out her fuzzy blue arm until I could walk around behind her and sight along it.

"At the laundromat?"

"She runs it," the girl said.

"Thank you."

"Nooooo problem," she replied as she bumped away on one skate, her arms outstreched.

A more sensitive detective might have guessed at the relationship between the apartment building and the laundromat. Both had a dogged sort of respectability. It turned out to be a characteristic of the lady who ran both, Mrs. Nix. I spotted her at a desk at the far end of the laundromat's single, overheated room. She was overdressed for the place, in a red suit and white blouse. Mrs. Nix didn't hear my approach, understandably. Frank Sinatra was belting out a number through ceiling speakers in competition with the rumbling of half a dozen dryers. Somewhere in the back-to-back rows of washers, a machine was undergoing the tortures of the spin cycle.

Mrs. Nix was making entries in a ledger. She looked up when I spoke her name. She had shrewd eyes half hidden by red-veined lids and a mouth so pursed it appeared to be lipless. "Yes?" she said. "What is it?"

I abandoned any hope I'd had for small talk. "I'm looking into Richard Gerow's death for his father. I wonder if you have a moment to speak with me."

Her face softened briefly. "Ricky, Ricky," she said, shaking her head. "I still can't believe he did that."

She spoke with an English accent, as unexpected a find in a Trenton laundromat as a guardsman in a breastplate and plumed helmet.

"His father doesn't believe it either. That Ricky killed himself, I mean."

"He wouldn't, would he? It would be an awfully hard thing for a parent to accept. I hope you're not encouraging any false hopes as a way of taking Mr. Gerow's money. He seemed like a nice man, but not a practical one."

"I'm doing this as a favor to Mr. Gerow. I was a friend of Ricky's."

"As was I," Mrs. Nix said. "Not that I understood him or even approved of him entirely. I just liked him. He liked me," she added. Then she paused, giving me a chance to express my disbelief. I passed.

"He was a good tenant," she continued. "Not too loud. Quiet in fact, compared with most young men today. His appearance was off-putting, certainly. Years ago, I mean, before he cut his hair. I remember some of my older guests being quite nervous when he first moved in. Once they got to know him, they liked him and even came to depend upon him. He was always doing little favors for people. And odd jobs for me."

"What odd jobs?"

"Painting mostly. He was a meticulous painter. You wouldn't have guessed it by looking at him."

"How did you pay him?"

"By barter. That is to say, by discounting his rent."

"No jobs paid for in cash?"

"Certainly not."

"You found his body, I understand."

"Yes, when the gentleman from Ricky's workplace called. But I can't help you there very much. I never actually went into his apartment. Not that morning. I unlocked the door and stuck my head in. There was an odor."

She drew her lips in even farther. "I could see in through the open bedroom door to Ricky's bed. I called to him—I don't know why. I knew it would do no good. I should have been scared out of my wits had he answered."

One of Mrs. Nix's customers interrupted us at that point. The vending machine that dispensed tiny boxes of detergent had failed to live up to its end of the bargain. Mrs. Nix stood up without a word to me and marched over to the offender, which hung on the wall near the laundromat's back door. She literally marched, her short arms working as hard as her legs as she advanced against the enemy.

"Once more unto the bleach, dear friends," I said aloud, my irreverence made risk-free by the noise of the machines and the harmonies of the Andrews Sisters.

Mrs. Nix delivered a straight right to the machine's solar plexus, which may have been simply for her personal satisfaction, as no soap appeared. Then she pulled a formidable ring of keys from her pocket, unlocked the front of the machine, and cleared the jam.

She was dusting off her hands, one against the other, when she rejoined me in front of the desk. "Was there anything else?" she asked.

"Ricky's front door. You say it was locked?"

"Just the lock in the knob. I used my master key to open it. There's also a dead-bolt lock, worked by the same key, but Ricky hadn't set it."

"How about a security chain?"

"There was one—is one I should say—on all my apartments. Ricky hadn't used that either. I don't know that he ever used it. He wasn't what you would call security conscious. His flat was broken into once, but that didn't change Ricky's thinking. Perhaps because nothing was taken."

"When was this?"

"Only two weeks or so before his death. The window next to the fire escape was forced."

"Any sign of a forced entry on the weekend he died?"

"No, there was nothing like that. All the windows were locked from the inside, including the one on the fire escape. I'd had that one repaired, of course. The police paid special attention to it."

"How long had Ricky roomed with you?"

"Thirteen years. I was struck by that coincidence when he died. Silly, isn't it?"

"Did you notice any changes over time?"

"Everyone changes over time, Mr . . . ?"

"Keane."

"Mr. Keane. Ricky certainly mellowed. We all mellow."

If Mrs. Nix had mellowed, she'd been one tough nut to start with. "Was there anything out of the ordinary about the way he behaved toward the end?"

"I didn't talk with him that last week."

"I mean over the last few months."

She chewed her invisible lips and thought about it. "He was spending more and more time away from us. On weekends, that is. That tendency began about a year before he died."

"Tell me about it."

"There's nothing to tell, is there? He was just spending his weekends away. I thought he was visiting his father. I'm almost certain that Ricky led me to believe he was. But when I later spoke with Mr. Gerow, I got the distinct impression that his son's visit's were almost always quite short. Most weekends, Ricky would be gone from Friday night to Sunday evening."

"But not that last weekend."

"No. I knew he hadn't gone away then, because that fancy car of his was parked all weekend in the stall Ricky rented from me."

A female singer I didn't recognize was crooning to me over the loudspeakers, promising to see me in all the old familiar places. The song reminded me of the next step in my agenda, one I wasn't particularly anxious to take. I dug around for other questions to put to Mrs. Nix.

"Did you ever see Ricky high? Intoxicated, I mean."

"I know what you mean." She squared her shoulders and raised her chin. "And the answer is no. Not once. The police didn't find so much as a beer in his apartment."

"They found an empty needle," I said.

"I know," Mrs. Nix said. She was momentarily less sure of herself, less in command of her little corner of the empire.

I thought I understood why Ricky had liked her. She made me think of the nuns at Our Lady of Sorrows: gruff, no-nonsense women with soft hearts. I wondered if Mrs. Nix had reminded Ricky of Sister Athanasia, the embodiment of the high standards from which he'd fallen away.

I thanked her for her time and left.

SEVEN

CAL HART, paint shop foreman, was so intent on his work that he didn't notice my arrival outside his door. He was standing at a workbench, bent over it actually, his weight resting on his elbows. Propped up before him was a plank painted white and lettered in gold. Hart held a brush in his right hand and his right wrist in his left hand.

I decided he needed a break and knocked on the paint shop door. Hart came over, smiling unselfconsciously although there were several gaps in his discolored teeth. I guessed his age to be just short of fifty and his last shave to have been the day before yesterday. His hair was crew cut and his ears were in the Clark Gable class. He was muscular and walked with the practiced grace of an ex-athlete, but he had a hard, protruding belly like a woman in her fifth month.

"Mr. Hart?" I asked when he opened the door. It would have been a good lesson to me in the dangers of jumping to conclusions if he had said no and shut the door in my face. Instead, his smile widened to reveal more bad teeth, telling me I'd guessed right.

"Come on in out of the weather," he said. "Give me an excuse to rest my eyes."

None of the changes I'd noticed on my drive into the Build-Lite grounds had been for the better. The guard shack hadn't been staffed, and I'd driven unchallenged to the paint shop past a row of idle loading docks. Little tumbleweeds of scrap paper still blew around behind the plant, just as I remembered, but their wanderings had been the only activity I could see. The stacks, the skids of surplus paper board that circled the factory, had looked higher and deeper, as though the old plant's principal work now was fashioning its own tomb. The process seemed to me to be nearly complete.

I introduced myself to Hart and told him that I'd come to talk about Ricky Gerow at his father's request.

"The day doesn't go by when I don't think about Ricky," Hart said. "I was thinking about him when you knocked." He pointed with his brush to the sign he'd been working on. I could see now that the golden letters spelled a name: S. Fletcher. I could also see that the lettering was as irregular as Hart's smile.

"Fletcher's the president of this joint. He wants a sign for his parking space. This is the fourth one I've made so far. He threw the first three out his office window. I can see this one taking the same route. My hand's not steady enough for this stuff."

"Was Ricky's?"

"Hell, yes. He could paint the trim on a window and never touch the glass. He was great at signs and stuff like that. If any of the guys bought a new truck and wanted his name painted on it, he'd bring it to Ricky. The little guy'd do it for nothing."

"Doesn't sound like his drug habit bothered his nerves," I said.

Hart looked genuinely scandalized. "That was all a long time ago. Back in 'Nam. Ricky didn't do that shit anymore."

"How long did you know him?"

"Twelve, thirteen years. He hired on here working the dryers, about the hardest job in the place. The dryers are these monster machines that heat the raw boards and press the last of the water out of them. They come out of the machine heavy and hot, eight foot by twelve, and the operators stack them on a trolley. It ain't like working in an oven; it is working in an oven."

I broke in at that point, afraid Hart would drag me back through the cardboard process to the original tree in the original forest. "But he ended up here in the paint shop."

"Right. When I got authorization to hire a full-time assistant, Ricky applied for the job."

"It was just the two of you?"

"Except in the summer. Before the big slowdown around here, they'd hire a bunch of college kids every summer, and we'd get five or six. Ricky would be assistant foreman then. He'd really run those college boys' butts off. He loved that."

The reference to college reminded me of Ricky's library. I turned to the paint shelves behind me and saw that the rescued books were still there. Some of them anyway. The O. Henry volumes on which Ricky had staked so much were missing.

"Ricky collected that shit," Hart said. "Don't ask me why. I've been meaning to throw it all out."

Just like Mr. Gerow had been meaning to sell the Firebird.

Hart seemed completely at ease with me. It was the moment to ask the question I'd come to ask. "Where would Ricky have bought drugs around here?"

Hart tossed his paint brush at the workbench. "Didn't I just tell you that Ricky wouldn't touch that shit anymore?"

"Ricky died of that shit," I said. "He had to get it somewhere. Was there someone in the plant who could have sold it to him?"

Hart drew back from me without actually moving away: dropping his hands to his sides, making his small eyes smaller, and compressing his lips in a fair imitation of Mrs. Nix. Then he said, "I don't know nothing about that."

"Who would?"

"Damned if I know."

"Do you still play the numbers? Or have you switched over to the Jersey lottery?"

Hart relaxed slightly, mistaking my new tack for a new subject. "There's no taxes on the numbers game," he said. Besides, they, ah . . ."

"Let you play on credit?"

Hart's grin returned. "Right."

"Is Vince still running the game around here?"

"How did you know that?" Hart asked, his voice hushed in awe as though I'd worked a minor miracle.

"Ricky told me once." The miracle was my remembering it.

"Yeah, he still is."

"Where can I find him?"

This time, Hart actually took a step backward. "What for? Ricky never played the numbers. He said it was for suckers."

I spelled my brilliant plan out for him. "Vince is doing something illegal. He's likely to know who else is doing illegal things around here. Like who might be selling heroin."

"Man, Vince would break your arm for looking at him sideways. Don't mess with him."

"Are you going you going to tell me where to find him, or do I have to ask Mr. Fletcher?"

Hart mentally washed his hands of me. "Drive back around to the southeast corner of the plant. There's a railroad spur that goes right into the building. Vince bosses the loading crew. Ask for him there. But don't tell him I sent you."

I had my hand on the knob of the paint shop door when I thought of another question. "Did Ricky ever say where he spent his weekends?"

Hart shook his head. "I know where he's spending them now, though. You'll be spending yours in the same place if you mess with Vince."

I KNEW I'D FIND VINCE, because the prospect scared me, which meant that the Keane luck, always perverse, would work to bring us together. It had been easy to play tough in front of Cal Hart, a man who, according to Ricky, had routinely hidden from Vince. Bearding that lion in his den was altogether another proposition.

I thought about walking around to the railroad spur, as a way of putting off the confrontation, but in the end I followed Hart's advice and took my car. I knew I wouldn't feel like a long walk back after Vince got through breaking my arm. I drove back out by the deserted guard shack and took what was the left fork for people entering the Build-Lite grounds. I found the spur at the far corner of the building. It dead-ended at a thirty-foot garage door of corrugated steel. There was a person door next to the railroad train door. I parked as close to it as I could and went in.

It was like stepping into a cathedral. Visually, that is. I was struck by the vast expanse of air unbroken by pillars and beams and yet trapped beneath a roof, an enclosed space whose scale invoked thoughts of boundless space. The tracks ran into the plant for at least the length of a football field. A single brick-red boxcar sat at the far end of the line, filling the acreage before me no more effectively than a bicycle fills a garage.

What did fill the place was noise. Two noises, actually: men yelling and something that sounded like a half dozen bass drums being beaten randomly and simultaneously. A concrete loading platform ran down the left side of the tracks. I walked down it toward the boxcar, my long stride a bit of affected nonchalance. The bass drum sound was resonating from the car itself. Pairs of men were carrying four-by-eight sheets of Build-Lite board into the car's open door and shouting bits of conversation to one another over the booming.

I didn't have to ask for Vince. He came out of the boxcar while I was still some way off and spotted me immediately. He walked toward me, and we came together about ten feet from the yelling crew. I was heartened by Vince's appearance. He'd been gray-haired ten years before, but prematurely so. Now he seemed definitely old and wasted, his skin baggy and sallow. The large hands at the ends of his long arms were mottled with brown spots.

"Got business here?" he asked me.

"Business with you," I said. "I want to put a bet down."

"I know you?"

"I know you." So far, I wasn't scoring any points for clever dialogue, but I hadn't gotten an arm broken, either. The company of the work crew made me bolder. "I want to ask you some questions."

Like the rest of his head, Vince's prominent brow was almost hairless. He looked up at me from beneath it with eyes as dead as any shark's. I began to appreciate Hart's continuing respect for the old man.

I was still in the early phases of this reevaluation when Vince turned his head to address his crew. "Quitting time," he said in a normal speaking voice.

The two men who had been picking up a board from the skid dropped it back into place and repeated the announcement for the benefit of the men in the car. The booming within fell silent immediately. It was an order that seemed to need no elaboration. While Vince and I stood facing one another like a pair of nearsighted gunfighters, the two men at the skid were joined by four from inside the car. Three of these carried hammers, which accounted for the booming noise I'd already begun to miss. The six trooped off toward a passage at the far end of the tracks without a good-bye glance at me.

"Let's talk private," Vince said. He turned and started for the car door before his meaning sunk in. It was too late by then to do anything but follow him or get out of West Trenton, fast. I followed him.

It was early evening inside the car, the faint light made gray by the paperboard in which the interior had been paneled. The job was almost complete. Only one shadowy end of the car still showed its metal walls and rough wooden lathing. A keg of nails stood at the center of the car's plank flooring. A forgotten hammer lay across one side of the keg's open top. As he passed the keg on his way to the unpaneled end of the car, Vince picked up the hammer and a single nail.

"This is for protection," he said, indicating the paperboard with a wave of the hammer. He didn't face me when he spoke. He didn't have to. His flat voice bounced around the inside of the car and found me near the open doorway, where I'd taken root.

"Otherwise," Vince continued, "when we pack the car the boards we pack on the outside will get beaten up. From rubbing."

He arrived at a sheet of board that hadn't been completely secured. He set the nail he carried in place in the soft board with a tap of his hammer, then drove it through into the wooden lathing with one quick blow. The resulting boom echoed in the car as he walked back toward me. "What do you want?" he demanded.

I found my voice as he drew abreast of the keg of nails. "The name of the local heroin supplier."

Vince froze in his tracks. "Heroin? I don't know nothing about heroin."

"Right," I said. "You're just an honest businessman."

He raised the hammer to the height of his belt. "Go down to Trenton if you want drugs. You'll find all you want down there."

"I'm not buying. I just want to talk with the dealer."

"Right," Vince said, parroting my earlier sarcasm. "You're just an honest citizen. What do you really want?" I made a mistake then. Or rather, another one. I decided that I wouldn't mention Ricky Gerow. I didn't want to accidently make trouble for the hapless Cal Hart. "Just tell me who he is. I'll tell him my business."

"Or else what? What's the threat? You gonna turn me over to the cops?"

"Maybe I am a cop."

"Balls. You look like a fucking accountant."

"You're right, Vince. I am an accountant. Tell me what I want to know, or I'll pass your name on to my fraternity brothers at the IRS."

Vince already looked gray around the edges in the half-light of the car, but as I watched he went grayer. "I could make some calls," he said.

"I'd appreciate it."

He turned and tossed the hammer toward the keg of nails before starting for the door where I stood. Where I had been standing, I mean. I was well out onto the loading platform before he cleared the car.

"Wait here," he said.

He went off toward the exit his crew had taken, walking with his head bowed. I paced the loading dock, my relief giving way to excitement at having seized the initiative for once. The Gerow case suddenly seemed less an investigation than a creative act. Instead of following clues, I was making them follow me toward the conclusion I wanted to reach.

I was still riding my irrational high when Vince limped back in. "Know the Extension Bar?" he asked.

"On Dwyer Avenue?"

"Right. Be there at six. There'll be a gentleman there to talk with you."

"How will I know him?"

Vince smiled the way I remembered Ricky Gerow smiling, using only one side of his face. "He'll know you."

THE EXTENSION BAR wasn't easy to find. I'd been there once before, during a long-ago break from Boston College, but I almost drove past it now. The low, stuccoed building was set back from the stores on either side of it, and there was no roadside sign. The bar's name referred to the fact that its stretch of Dwyer Avenue had once been an extension of an older road, a post-World War II gamble on the potential of undeveloped suburbia. The hoped-for development had long since taken place. It had swept over the area like a storm tide and then receded, leaving the shells of empty stores and parking lots covered in weed.

The Extension must have been doing better than its neighbors; there were no weeds growing in its gravel lot. A sign over the front door proudly proclaimed it to be "the longest bar in New Jersey." It was also a front-runner for the title of darkest. The room's narrowness accentuated its length, reminding me, ominously, of Vince's boxcar. The actual bar ran down the left side of the room. Small tables stood along the right wall. The whole place was paneled in wood darkened by decades of stale air. The euphoria I'd danced with back on the loading platform had walked out on me, and I'd taken up again with my old standby, doubt. I had the unhappy feeling that I'd simply traded one trap for another.

The Extension's happy hour crowd consisted of a half dozen men widely scattered along the bar. There was one exception. A shadowy figure with a beard sat at a table at the very back of the room. As far as I could tell in the semidarkness, I had this gentlemen's rapt attention.

The bartender's blond hair had been teased into nervous exhaustion. It would have been a relief to have stopped and shot the breeze with her about our mutual profession. Instead, I nodded to her as I ambled past. The patrons at the bar seemed very young to me. The Extension had always gone after the college crowd, although it wasn't exactly adjacent to a campus. The upper half of the dark walls were decorated with pennants, items of sports equipment, and other knickknacks from Trenton State and Rider College, the two local schools. The drinkers who followed my progress behind them via the bar's smoky mirror looked like underclassmen, not drug dealers. Not that the two groups were mutually exclusive, as I knew from my own experience. I couldn't imagine a campus drug peddler servicing the Build-Lite account, however, which left me with the bearded man in the corner.

He was still studying me, comparing me to the description of the rough CPA he'd been told to expect. In age, he was somewhere between me and the boys at the bar. His hair and beard seemed unnaturally black and curly, and I wondered if they were real or part of a disguise. A nearly neon sign advertising Budweiser gave his skin and the whites of his eyes a red cast.

The bar had a back door marked "emergency exit only." I was trying to decide whether my rising panic qualified when I arrived at the bearded man's table.

"Have a seat," the man said. When I'd sat down across from him, he asked, "You the guy interested in heroin?"

"Yes," I said.

"You have money?"

I'd thought of that on my drive from the Build-Lite factory. I couldn't squeeze information from this stranger by threatening him with exposure, as I'd done with Vince. I'd very likely have to pay for what I got, and I didn't have much cash with me. I decided I could only bluff it out.

"Some," I said.

"Let's see it."

So much for bluffing. I reached for my wallet, casting a guilty glance toward the bar as I did so. When I looked back to the bearded man, I saw that he'd pulled out a wallet of his own. He opened it to display a badge, a silver one with Budweiser red highlights.

"You're under arrest," he said.

EIGHT

In keeping with tradition, I was allowed to make one phone call. I didn't have to ponder the question of whom to call for very long. Harry Ohlman, my Boston College roommate and one-time employer, had bailed me out of trouble so often that it almost constituted his second career. Actually, looking after me was probably no better than Harry's third or fourth career. His talents were that numerous and his singleness of purpose that spasmodic. At the time of my latest SOS, Harry was semiretired from his family's law firm and struggling to become a professional artist. His curt manner on the phone suggested that I'd called between two extremely important brush strokes. I told Harry what I had been up to and where it had landed me. He told me that, given the lateness of the hour, I should resign myself to at least one night in jail.

That was easy enough advice to give. I was put in a large holding cell that was surely known locally as "the tank." Eight other guests had already checked in. Tuesdays were always slow, according to the old policeman who deposited me. The cell had bunk beds for forty guests, although calling them beds was stretching the term considerably. Each bunk was actually a flat sheet of metal without bedding, surrounded on all sides by a three-inch metal lip. The bottom of the resulting tray was drilled through in spots with holes the size of a quarter. The holes were intended to prevent a drunk from drowning in his own vomit, I decided. It was a feature that made the lower bunks somewhat unattractive.

I found an upper berth in a quiet corner of the cell. The bed next to mine was occupied by an older man who was dressed, as I was by then, in a rumpled suit. He introduced himself simply as Cranny, speaking with the overprecision of a parson accused of raiding the sherry. Actually he was a professor of

English Literature from Rutgers University who had been hauled in for driving while intoxicated.

When Cranny found out that I'd been an English major in the dim past, he bent my ear with descriptions of prison conditions from the works of Charles Dickens. I found Cranny's prattle comforting, as it made my surroundings seem unreal, a dream from which I would surely awaken.

The cell was kept in perpetual twilight, a cold, November twilight. I started out with my suit coat rolled up under my head, but I was soon using it as a blanket.

When he'd squeezed Dickens dry, Cranny jumped right into a theory he had on madness in literature. "Don Quixote and Captain Ahab were brothers," he said by way of a catchy opening.

"What do you mean by that?" I asked as quietly and evenly as I could. I scanned the cell at the same time, accidently making eye contact with a large gentleman several bunks away. I made contact with one of his eyes, that is, his left one. His right eye had swollen shut, and he dabbed periodically at a split lip with the back of his hand.

"They were brothers in madness," Cranny said. "Now follow me on this. Both Quixote and Ahab were madmen who had such powerful visions they were able to infect the people around them with their madness. With me so far?"

"Right next to you," I said.

"Good," Cranny said. His bright eyes looked out at me through matted bangs of black hair mixed with gray, reminding me of a Scottish terrier I'd once known. "In both cases the madness was caused by a shock, the stunning realization that we are alone in a godless universe."

The steel underneath me grew a few degrees colder. I sat up and gave Cranny a closer look. I didn't know him, and he couldn't know me. He was just another stranger who had spotted the "kick me" sign tattooed on my back.

Cranny blinked under my examination. "Happen to have a cigarette?" he asked.

"No."

"Oh, well. Where was I?"

"Alone in the universe."

"Right. We all are. Mankind as a whole and each soul of us individually. The thing that made them different, Quixote and Ahab, I mean, was their reaction to their isolation, to the idea of godlessness. Their reactions, I should say. The knight-errant constructed a fantasy world that took the place of his lost faith, a place in which he could quest after an impossible belief."

"To dream the impossible dream," said a bundle of clothes lying on the bunk below Cranny.

Cranny ignored the remark. "The sea captain rejected the idea of a meaningless universe. He cast a white whale in the role of an omnipotent being and then wrestled with it for its secrets."

"To fight the unbeatable foe," the man in the lower berth added, singing now.

"Quiet," Cranny said. "What we have then are two projections of imagination on the world at large, one benign and the other violent. Quixote infected people with nobility. His madness made them better than they were. Ahab destroyed the people around him. His dream brought death and destruction."

"Why?" I asked. "What made one dream ennobling and the other destructive?"

"Unbearable sorrows," the kibitzer sang in reply.

That last interruption knocked Cranny's needle into a completely new groove. "I had an interesting idea the other day regarding *Huckleberry Finn*," he said. "Specifically, the Tom Sawyer episodes that open and close the novel."

I tried several times to drag Cranny back to the subject of the mad brothers. I badly wanted to know the difference between the bright and dark roads they'd taken in their searching, hoping it would tell me which path I was on myself. The answer seemed all too obvious, given that Gerow was dead and I was sitting in a cell. I wanted Cranny to show me a loophole, but I couldn't get through to him. My interruptions only produced additional requests for cigarettes.

No one in the cell seemed to mind Cranny's rambling lecture and my useless interjections, probably because it was conversation to sleep by. One by one, our companions all dropped off. I did too, finally, missing the end of Cranny's insight into the symbolism of body odor in the *Brothers Karamazov*.

I dreamt that night that I was arraigned before Minerva Fine with Harry Ohlman standing by my side. I was charged with deserting Richard Gerow and impersonating an accountant. When I looked over at my lawyer, I saw that it was now Mary Ohlman, Harry's dead wife, standing next to me. When Fine asked if she had anything to say in my defense, Mary replied, "His whale is winning, your honor."

NINE

My DREAM ARRAIGNMENT was the only one I had to face. Early on the morning after my arrest, a different old policeman came and removed me from the cell. He led me to a waiting area aglow with fluorescent light. There Harry Ohlman looked on while I signed for my tie and belt and the odds and ends that had been in my pockets.

Harry's mood had improved sometime during the night. He was actually smiling as I walked over to him. Harry was a big man who carried the extra pounds the years had brought him comfortably. He also seemed reconciled to the steady thinning of his dark hair. He wore what remained combed straight backward in a short, fatalistic style. He was almost dressed like a lawyer this morning, in a camel overcoat over a tweed jacket, a red and white striped dress shirt open at the collar, and tan slacks. A lawyer called back unexpectedly from vacation was what Harry actually looked like, although, in his case, the vacation had stretched on for years.

"Sorry for not coming last night," Harry said. "I didn't want to leave Amanda. She's just getting over her quarterly ear infection."

"Thanks for coming at all," I said. "How did you manage to get me out?"

"It was a combination of the Ohlman charm and the fact that you hadn't actually been charged with anything. That guy you hassled back at the factory must be well connected. This whole exercise seems to have been about nothing more than putting the fear of God in you."

"The joke's on them," I said. "I never go anywhere without that. Shouldn't we sue them or something?"

"There's a thought. They'd have to get you convicted and sent to prison to cover themselves."

"Let's get out of here."

We stepped out of the police station onto Perry Street, no garden spot even by Trenton standards. The morning was overcast and raw, but it felt like the first day of spring to me.

"You were being held on suspicion," Harry said, "which is police talk for 'because we damn well feel like it.' I only had to convince them you were a harmless innocent."

"That couldn't have been too tough."

"It wasn't. I had a little help from our old friend Pat O'Malia," Harry added, naming a policewoman we'd both run afoul of a couple years earlier. "I spoke with her last night. She put in a call on your behalf to a drinking buddy she has on the Trenton force. Fight connections with connections, as my dear old dad always says. I helped the cause by driving over bright and early this morning to relate some choice episodes from your past. I had those doughnut hounds on the edges of their seats."

"I'm surprised they didn't throw the key to my cell into the reservoir."

We arrived then at his car, a very, very red Porsche. Harry had yet to shed all the trappings of a successful lawyer.

"Oddly enough," he said, "it's actually getting easier to explain you to people as your career gets longer. To pass you off as a real person, I mean. Your biography is so fantastic now, it's actually credible. No liar would come within a mile of it."

"Irony," I said. "Nothing I like better first thing in the morning. Maybe someday I'll be so famous that you won't have to travel around explaining me to the police."

"That would be nice," Harry said.

Rescuing the Chevy from the police impound lot turned out to be more work than springing me, but we eventually got it done. We drove in tandem to an old-fashioned stainless steel diner out on Route 1. While Harry used the Ohlman charm to distract the help, I slipped into the tiny rest room with an overnight bag I'd stowed in the trunk of the Chevy. I washed and shaved and struggled into a change of clothes and came out nine-tenths ready for Harry's inevitable lecture.

I sat down opposite him and sipped the coffee he pushed across to me. "Was this hot back when they poured it?" I asked.

"Piping," Harry said after finishing off the last of his own. Before he could set his empty cup down, a waitress was on her way to refill it. She took our orders and then poured a last dollop into Harry's cup as a parting gesture of devotion.

"You must tip in advance," I said.

"I just look as though I intend to eventually," Harry replied.

"Touché. How's the painting going?"

"It's hard." He held his big hands out before him and extended his fingers as though checking them for wear. "But I'm still enjoying it. And Amanda's still rooting for me. At the moment, though, she's more fascinated by her Uncle Owen's latest exploit. She told me to be sure to get the whole story."

"That's more than I have myself, but you're entitled to all I know." I started by reminding Harry of the evening in seventy-eight when I'd appeared on the front door of the Ohlman town house, as unexpected and helpless as a baby in a basket. To my surprise, Harry not only remembered the evening but also the story of Ricky Gerow. That is to say he remembered the first part of the story, the part that ended with me scurrying for cover.

I filled him in on the sequel while we waited for our breakfasts. I knew from having worked for him that Harry liked concise reports. I opened with a brief description of the anonymous mailing I'd received, producing the program itself for his inspection. Then I synthesized the testimony of Minerva Fine and Mr. Gerow, adding the minor contributions of Mrs. Nix and Carl Hart as footnotes. That brought us up to the part of the story I'd already told him over the phone, my dramatic encounter with Vince, the well-connected numbers runner.

Harry was still shaking his head when the pancakes arrived. "I've seen you ricochet off into the great unknown before," he said, "but this has to set the record. What were you thinking of, going after that Vince character? Have you started reading Mickey Spillane? You're lucky you didn't wake up in a hospital this morning. In fact, you're lucky you woke up."

I was beginning to wonder. "It's called being methodical," I said. "Gerow died of a drug overdose. The police think it was suicide. If I could have found the guy who sold Ricky the heroin, it would have supported the idea that he took his own life. It would have answered a lot of people's doubts."

Harry interrupted me with a wave of the knife he'd been using to spread his syrup. "Excuse me, but I don't think this was about being methodical. Roulette balls are more methodical than you are. This was about grasping at straws. You want the official explanation of Gerow's death to be correct, even after everyone who knew him has told you it couldn't be."

The efficient waitress interrupted at that point with another coffee refill. Harry's smile clicked off as soon as her back was turned.

"I can't understand it, Owen. You didn't used to be such a fan of suicide." He was trying to be glib, but his voice caught on the last word. He hurried on to cover his embarrassment. "Back when you were doing research for me in New York, you would have twisted yourself into knots making a murder out of suicide." This time he forced himself to say the word without hesitation. "Now you won't even consider the possibility of murder. Why is that?"

"I've mellowed," I said. If my evasion was an echo of Mrs. Nix, Harry's reply was straight out of the gospel according to Minerva Fine.

"Seems like you've also gotten dishonest. You know damn well that proving Gerow killed himself won't close this case. These Sorrowers of yours are still responsible for what they did to Gerow, even if it took him twenty years to die from the wounds."

"Then I'm still responsible, too. For not helping him."

"Exactly. There's no way out for you if it was a suicide, just more useless guilt to add to the not inconsiderable load you're already carrying around. You're better off if it was murder."

"How do you figure that?"

Harry washed down a hasty mouthful with orange juice.

"Because it gets you off the guilt hook. Everybody so far has told you that Gerow finally found some happiness, which means keeping your mouth shut years ago might have been the right thing to do. If it was murder, then there's a murderer out there somewhere who's responsible, not you.''

I let Harry chew in peace for a time. After he balled up his paper napkin and dropped it on his plate, I said, ''Suppose the murder came about because of something I did ten years ago. Something I stirred up. Where does that put the guilt hook?''

Harry grimaced. ''Right through your gills. That clears up one point for me. I've been wondering why you were ignoring the juicy physical evidence Mr. Gerow handed you. The money straps, I mean. They suggest to me that your old classmate was receiving cash payments from someone. Maybe blackmail payments from one or more of the Sorrowers. Are you afraid that you set that in motion ten years ago? Maybe you jogged Gerow's memory enough to bring it all back. Maybe he's been blackmailing your old pals ever since.''

Harry picked up the reunion program. ''Let's review our principal suspects. There's Maureen McCary, first off. What's she doing now?'' He flipped through the program till he found her entry. ''She's a partner in a New York ad agency. Here's someone who doesn't want any dirty laundry on display.''

''Dirty linen,'' I said.

''Whatever. Let's see what your friend Ann Quinn's been up to. No information on her, just her name and address. Same for you. Must mean she didn't respond to the invitation either. Who else was involved in Gerow's party? Who brought the drugs?''

''Mark Plesniak.''

''Plesniak, Plesniak. Just an address. Who else was there?''

''Lucy Criscollo.''

''Ah-ha. Another success story. She works in the Justice Department now.''

''Bill Pearson.''

''Professor at Stockton State College. Down south of you at the store.''

''David Radici.''

''A small fry. He's a teacher at Hopewell Valley High School.''

''Mary Kay Ellis.''

"That's more like it. She's city editor for the *Newark Star Ledger*. Anyone else?"

"Isn't that enough?"

"Plenty. I'm seeing candidates for blackmail here, Owen. I think you are, too. I think your whole wild hunt for the heroin connection was a way of shielding your heroes. Or at least a way of avoiding an ugly possibility."

He paused to give me a chance to deny it. I couldn't. I *was* worried that I'd set something horrible in motion ten years before. And I did think that the money straps could mean blackmail. Worse than that, I was afraid that the fact they'd all come from the same Philadelphia bank might point to my one-time protector, Ann Quinn.

Harry would have that out of me and more if I left him in command of the conversation. I decided to throw up a smoke screen in the form of an unexplained detail. "Why did Ricky have the deposit tickets for this William Porter guy? How does that fit in with your blackmail theory?"

"It doesn't," Harry admitted. "It makes it seem like Gerow was the one paying out, making cash deposits to this Porter's account."

"He didn't have any money unaccounted for, according to his father."

"He was getting an extra five hundred a month."

"From whom? Are you telling me now he was blackmailing someone and being blackmailed himself, all at the same time?"

Harry smiled. "Not too likely, is it?" He gave the matter ten seconds' thought, which was an extended deliberation for him. Then he started to slide sideways out of the booth. "Let's go ask Porter. We've got his last known address."

"You're coming along? Why? Do you think I need looking after?"

"Is your last name still Keane? Relax. This will be like old times. Besides, I promised Amanda the whole story."

TEN

Harry wasn't sure how long he'd be willing to play sidekick, so we drove north to Flemington separately. Very separately, as it turned out. Harry and his sports car left me and my Cavalier in our dust at the first traffic light.

The drive took me past one notable landmark from my earlier investigation of the Sorrower: Woosamonsa Road, site of the Radicis' doomed party. I wondered as I drove past it if David and Libby and Daniel still lived in the little house in the forest, but I didn't make a side trip to find out. As Harry had guessed, I was only interested in an explanation of Gerow's death that didn't involve the Sorrowers. The mysterious William Porter was my last hope.

Flemington was an old town that was renovating itself to suit the times. Warehouses near the train station now held manufacturers' outlets, and several of the big Federal-period homes on Main Street sported bed-and-breakfast signs.

William Porter's last known address took some finding. It turned out to be in an apartment complex within earshot of the Flemington Circle. The name of the complex was Parc Bordeaux, and a Tricolor flew opposite the Stars and Stripes at the main gate. The half dozen buildings beyond the gate looked like little, prefabricated chateaux.

Harry had parked in front of the rental office. He was leaning against his car when I drove up.

"More money than taste has Mr. Porter," Harry said, looking around the complex. He kicked at some loose concrete that had tumbled like a tiny landslide from the curb near his foot. "Maybe not all that much money, either. I figured we might as well start at the office, since Mr. Gerow's letters were sent back."

One problem with having Harry as a sidekick was that he refused to act like one. Another was that a person confronted with the two of us tended to play to Harry. That was the case in the Parc Bordeaux office, which had been jammed into what was probably the living room of the standard apartment. The rental agent was a man in his twenties wearing a tie but no suit coat, the tie a bright floral print out of season on a gray November morning. He might have directed his "Can I help you?" to Harry out of kinship. They both belonged to the brotherhood of the bald spot.

"We're trying to trace a William Porter," Harry said. "We understand he was a resident here."

"Was is right," the clerk said. "We've been trying to trace him ourselves." He indicated his interest in the subject by getting up from his desk and crossing to the counter where we stood.

"Did he skip out on you?" Harry asked. Being a lawyer, he was versed in several dialects of jargon.

"Not exactly," the clerk said. "He'd been with us for three years. New tenants sign a year's lease. After that, it's month by month. Mr. Porter was paid in full at the time he left. Damage deposit and rent for April. His neighbors saw him head out on his circuit on Monday as usual. But on Friday, he didn't come back. He didn't come back the next Friday. He never came back."

"What do you mean by his circuit?" Harry asked.

"That's what he called the trips around his sales territory. He's a traveling salesman. That's what he told us. My boss, Mrs. Barth, thought he might have been in an accident. That was before we tried to get in touch with the company he said he worked for, Whirligigs. We found out there's no such company. We tried talking to the police, but we couldn't give them much to go on. Not even the license number of his car. We've been waiting to hear from him about his stuff. Or from his family or his lawyers. Which are you, family or lawyers?"

"I'm a lawyer," Harry said, shoving me further onto the periphery of the conversation.

I didn't intend to remain there for long. I was experiencing one of those moments an amateur detective lives for, when a stray point of light organizes a dozen other points of light around it, forming a constellation where there had previously been a jumble of stars.

"Porter's car was a gold Firebird, wasn't it?" I asked casually.

"Yes," the clerk said. "An old one, but a real beauty. Not the kind of car you'd want to rack up the miles on, I always thought."

This time, I'd left Harry in the dust. He shot me a look I knew well, his own special combination of irritation, incredulity, and respect. I ignored it.

"Describe Porter," I said.

The clerk tapped on the counter top with his class ring while he thought about it. "Little guy. Thin, I mean, and not real tall. Short brown hair. Clean shaven. Regular features. Very light blue eyes."

"Tattoos?" I asked.

The clerk smiled and nodded. "Right. A red and blue one of a dragon. I happened to notice it one day when Mr. Porter was washing his car. It seemed really out of character for him."

"How do you mean?" Harry asked.

"Well, he is..." The clerk paused to give us a chance to correct the tense he'd used. When we didn't, he hurried on. "He's a gentleman, I'd guess you say. Successful, well spoken, well educated. All the time quoting poetry. Shakespeare and stuff. Not the kind of guy you'd expect to have a tattoo."

The clerk was describing Richard Gerow, of course, but not the one I'd last seen outside the Build-Lite paint shop. But for the incongruous tattoo, it was Gerow as he might have turned out if he'd never run afoul of the Sorrowers.

The conversation lagged while I explored this insight. Then the clerk asked, "What about his things?"

"Where are they?" Harry asked.

"In one of our storage units."

"Let's have a look at them," Harry said. "Then we can decide." I admired the way Harry put it, as a plan of action rather than a request, which might have prompted a long-overdue demand that we properly identify ourselves.

"Sure," the clerk said. "I'll get my coat."

He stepped into a back room long enough for Harry to whisper, "So Gerow was Porter. But why?"

I was shrugging in reply when the clerk returned, tugging on a leather bomber jacket. He'd also acquired a ring of keys. He led us out of the office, past our cars, and down a road that wound through the center of the complex.

We made an interesting procession. The clerk looked back at us from time to time as though he wanted to question us but couldn't work up the nerve. Harry, next in line, directed similar, still-born inquiries toward me. I glanced behind me at one point to see if there was anyone for me to question, perhaps the ghost of Ricky Gerow. I hadn't seen his spirit on my drive through the haunted Pine Barrens, and I didn't see it now. If I had, I would have repeated Harry's "Why?"

The clerk led us to a building that looked like every other building in the complex, a parody of a French country house done in beige aluminum siding and beige brick. This color scheme was spoiled by the black shingles of the roof, which also adorned four pointy turrets, like witches' hats, one on each corner of the building.

"Mr. Porter's apartment was in here," the clerk said as he let us in through the front door. "We rerented it in July. The new tenant didn't want the basement storage area—it's an extra fifty a month—so we put Mr. Porter's furniture down there."

"Why do you still have Porter's things?" Harry asked.

"Mostly because it's a pain to get rid of them. We had to wait until a month after Mr. Porter's rent and deposit ran out before we could even reclaim the apartment. We had to do that in small claims court. We acquired the furniture at the same time to cover the month's back rent. Not that we really wanted it, but we needed a legal right to move it."

"Will you sell it?" I asked.

"Eventually, I guess. We have to run an ad in the paper giving the tenant a chance to come back and settle his debt. And if we sell the stuff, we can't get any more for it than he owes us. Like I said, it's a pain."

We descended via a metal staircase off the common laundry room. The basement was unpainted cement block that had been sectioned off into transparent rooms by chain link fencing tacked onto wooden frames. The arrangement made for very public storage. I examined bicycles, sewing machines, and even a small canoe as we made our way down the basement's center aisle.

Gerow's unit was crammed to bursting, mostly with decent, nondescript furniture. The pieces had been disassembled where possible and stacked randomly.

After unlocking a chain link door, the clerk reached in through a tangle of upended dining room chairs and pulled the string attached to an overhead light. "I've got to get back to answer the phone," he said. "Give me the nod when you're through, so I can lock up."

When he'd gone, Harry said, "Remember that kid in your will."

"Right. Who do you suppose he thinks we are?"

"FBI at least. So what are we looking for?"

"Answers," I said. "Start with these boxes. There's a desk back in the corner. I'll check it out."

I should have said I'd try to. Thin as I was, it was no easy trip. I started with a dignified approach, by which I mean an upright one, but I ended up jammed between a dresser and a mattress that was resting on its side. I backtracked and hung my trench coat on a standing lamp. Then I dropped to my hands and knees, crawling through a tunnel provided by the dining room table.

Meanwhile, Harry was rummaging noisily through the boxes. "Nothing but books in here. Not really great looking books either."

"Is there a set of O. Henry?" I asked.

"How on earth did you know that?"

"Is it complete?"

"No," Harry said after more noisy examination, "I don't think so. Why? What difference would that make?" While I was still wondering how to answer his question, he added, "Here's where Gerow got the name of the phony company his alter ego was supposed to be traveling for."

At that moment I was preoccupied with spider webs. "What are you talking about?"

"Whirligigs, remember? It's the title of one of these books by O. Henry."

I froze in the act of brushing a strand of web from my nose. Harry's discovery had switched on a light in a basement storage area inside my head. "Check and see if any of those volumes has a biographical note on O. Henry," I said.

I could no longer see Harry, but I knew he was shaking his head. "The kind of clues you work with make tea leaves seem scientific," he said.

I was lifting the last obstruction—a box of dusty bedding—onto a reclining chair when Harry spoke again, this time more respectfully. "William Sydney Porter. That was O. Henry's real name."

Gerow had found his answer in those rescued books after all, but it wasn't an answer that I understood. I put that mystery aside for the moment and finished my crawl to the desk. It was a big piece of furniture, made of dark wood and carrying enough dings and scratches to suggest that Gerow had purchased it secondhand. The back of the desk was facing me, but its large kneehole was open on both sides, giving me yet another tunnel to wiggle through.

I was in the process of wiggling when I made a discovery of my own. Taped to the bottom of the desk's center drawer—the ceiling of my tunnel—was a manila envelope the size of a dollar bill folded in half. I pulled the envelope free and stuck it in the pocket of my shirt before pushing through to the drawers.

I had a premonition that reaching them would be an anticlimax, and that proved to be true. Most of the drawers were empty. I collected a few papers and envelopes before starting the long crawl back to Harry.

While I dusted myself off, Harry summarized what he'd learned of the original William Porter's life. "This says he did time for embezzlement. He never got over the shame of that. He went to New York and wrote under the name O. Henry to hide from his past. Could Gerow have been embezzling from the factory where he worked?"

"Rust-Oleum maybe," I said. "Not money."

"How about jail? Did Gerow ever do time?"

"I don't think so," I said. "He told me a lot of things he was ashamed of. He never mentioned that."

Harry reached over to pull a bit of web from my lapel. "Did you find any lost gold mines back there when you were tunneling?"

"No." I shuffled through the papers from the desk. "Just unpaid bills, water, electric, and telephone. A copy of the lease for the apartment. And a letter from his bank." I opened that. "It's a statement for the checking account. A five hundred dollar deposit was made in April, but no checks were written. Damn, Harry, look at this. Gerow left over twenty thousand dollars behind."

"The blackmail money probably," Harry said.

"We don't know that there was any blackmail," I replied as calmly as I could. "Besides, five hundred a month wouldn't pay the rent on Porter's apartment. Gerow wouldn't have had thousands left over."

Harry tossed the book he held back into its box, raising a little mushroom cloud of dust. "Gerow only had the apartment for three years. There's no telling how long he'd been collecting five hundred a month. Maybe since just after you talked with him in seventy-eight. That would have given him six thousand a year for the better part of ten years. Sixty thousand, say. More than enough to buy all this stuff and pay the bills on the apartment for three years. About twenty thousand more than enough."

Harry surely had me where he wanted me, defending a hopeless position I'd arrived at emotionally. I was trying to figure a way out of his trap when I remembered the envelope in my shirt pocket. Its gummed flap had not been sealed. The envelope contained a small brass key, on which was stamped a number, 252.

"Safe deposit key," Harry said promptly. "Where do you suppose the box is?"

I held up the bank statement. "Here probably. The question is, what's in it?"

"Something Gerow didn't want to leave lying around an apartment that was empty five days out of seven. Evidence that backed up his blackmail play maybe."

I could have prolonged the debate between Harry and my denial by asking him what that evidence could possibly be. But I didn't need Harry's guesses. I held the answer to the mystery of the safe deposit box and perhaps to all Gerow's mysteries. I turned the key over in my hand until it caught the light cast by the storage unit's naked bulb. A piece of gold from a lost mine.

ELEVEN

WE STOPPED AT the Parc Bordeaux office long enough to say good-bye to the cooperative rental agent. Then we walked out to our cars, Harry limping slightly after so much time on his bad leg. He covered it up by lecturing me as we went.

"We'll have to get Mr. Gerow involved right away. As Gerow's next of kin, he should be able to obtain access to the box, once we've established the link between Gerow and Porter. That shouldn't take all that long."

"Could you be more specific?"

"A couple of weeks. Maybe less if we can get the cooperation of the police who investigated Gerow's death. If we can convince them that this development is a reason to reopen the case, they'll do the legwork for us."

"No police, Harry. Not yet."

"Right." Harry leaned against my car this time. It creaked as it took up the strain. "I forgot for a moment that you were still suffering from excessive school spirit. Okay then, we do it the hard way. Figure on at least a week and probably more."

"I haven't got a week, much less more. The reunion is the day after tomorrow."

Harry ran a hand through what remained of his hair. "What are you thinking, that you'll still be in the running for most successful graduate if you can drag Gerow's killer up to the podium with you?"

"Not exactly," I said.

"That reunion deadline may have some mystic significance for you, but it can't mean much to Gerow. He'll be just as dead a month from now as he is today."

"But not William Porter."

"Excuse me?"

"Nobody but us knows that Porter is dead. He could show up any time and open his box." I held up the brass key. "Today, in fact."

Harry wasn't unduly surprised. "Of course you realize that what you're proposing is against the law."

"Of course. Any serious objections?"

"Two come to mind. You must be a good half-foot taller than Gerow and your eyes are the wrong color."

"So I'll slouch and wear my private-eye sunglasses. Look, Harry, they probably don't know him by sight. For all we know, he may never have gone back after he rented the box."

"For all we know," Harry said, "he went back once a week. In fact, we know he made a deposit in that bank every month. And they don't have to remember him. They have his height and weight and the color of his eyes on his signature card. That's another thing. You'll have to duplicate Gerow's signature. Porter's, I mean."

I'd anticipated that requirement. I pulled the copy of the Parc Bordeaux lease out of the breast pocket of my suit coat and unfolded it for Harry's inspection. "Signed by William Porter in the approved Palmer Method," I said. "Even you could fake it."

"I know *I* could," Harry said. He flicked his forefinger at the signature on the lease, making the paper pop like a cap pistol. "This will be another crime, Owen. A serious one. You'd better really want to know what's in that box."

"I really want to know."

Harry shrugged and eased himself off the Chevy. "In that case, I should hit the road. It would be a real challenge to bail you out if we're sharing the same cell."

We shook hands. "Thanks for the last time you bailed me out," I said. "And the next time."

As he bent to unlock his car, Harry said, "I almost forgot. We decided to cancel our Thanksgiving trip to Cape Cod when Amanda got sick, which, incidentally, got me in solid with my dad. Amanda wanted me to tell you that we'll be home tomorrow if you'd like to have Thanksgiving dinner with us."

I directed my reply to the same intermediary that Harry had used to distance himself from the invitation. "Tell Amanda thanks, but I had to promise to work tomorrow to get this time off. I'll be on duty from eight to four."

"Maybe next year then," Harry said.

Harry had backed his car halfway from its space when he remembered something else. He lowered his window and waved at me. "There may be a code."

"A what?"

"Some banks ask box holders for an item of personal information. They use it if they're suspicious of someone trying to get into a box."

"Like what?"

"Hometown, favorite flavor of ice cream—it varies from bank to bank. You'd better have your crystal ball handy."

"Thanks," I said. "I'll bring it along."

IT MAY JUST have been my way of putting off the trip to Gerow's bank, but I suddenly wanted to make a long distance call. The urge was inspired both by the loneliness I felt as I watched Harry drive away, and by Amanda's invitation. I left the apartment complex and found a pay phone at the edge of a fast-food restaurant's parking lot. The phone box was set low enough to be accessed by someone seated in a car. Even a Chevrolet.

Directory assistance for New York City gave me the number of McGraw-Hill Incorporated. Their phone was answered by a mechanical receptionist with a dulcet voice. She invited me to enter the extension of the party I wished to reach or to press zero to talk with a human being. I pressed zero and got a human operator who sounded like she'd been out all morning hailing cabs in an acid rain shower. When I asked for Marilyn Tucci, the operator put me through without another raspy word.

I expected to deal with a secretary next, but Marilyn answered her extension herself, which meant that I didn't have time to rehearse my opening line.

"Hello," I said. "It's Owen. I'm calling from my car."

"That's funny," Marilyn said. "I don't hear any rattling. I tried to get you at home last night."

"Sorry I missed you. I was at a slumber party."

"Right," she said without missing a beat. "If you're trying to make me jealous, Keane, you'll have to do better than that. In fact, I don't think you can do that well."

That made two of us. She was the Marilyn of old for the moment at least, sure of herself and her view of the world, untroubled by fears of becoming less sure or of running out on friends who weren't sure at all.

"Why did you call last night?" I asked.

"I wanted to apologize for losing it Sunday. I've still got raw spots," she added.

The sound of Marilyn apologizing was novel enough to make me wonder if I'd gotten the right extension. It encouraged me to get to the point. "I'll be willing to forgive you if you'll come and spend Thanksgiving evening with me. I have to work till four, but we could go out after that."

"Sorry, Keane. I've made plans."

"Oh," I said.

"Maybe I could make it down this weekend if things work out." Before I could ask her what things had to work out, she mentioned item number one. "Were you able to settle your mind about that guy's death?"

"No," I said. "I've unsettled it."

"So you're still planning to make a fool of yourself at your reunion?"

"More or less."

"Well, as I said, maybe I'll see you. If not, I'll give you a call sometime. Maybe next week. What's your car phone number?"

I read off the number on the pay phone.

"'Bye, Keane," Marilyn said.

TWELVE

I GOT A HAMBURGER to go and ate it on the way to Reaville, a little town a few miles east of Flemington. I'd determined from my old friend the white pages that Reaville had a branch of the Hunterdon National Bank. I stopped by the branch long enough to open a safe deposit box. The assistant branch manager who helped me was my junior by a good ten years. I admired the earnestness with which she gave me my final instructions.

"When you sign to get into the box, your signature has to exactly match the way it appears on the card. Exactly. If you leave something off, like your middle initial, we can't prompt you. We're not allowed to."

"I wouldn't have it any other way," I said.

I went directly from the branch to another pay phone, this one in an old-fashioned booth. I now knew the item of personal information used by Hunterdon National to verify a box holder's identity. It was the maiden name of the customer's mother.

I let the phone in Mr. Gerow's apartment ring until it woke him from his latest nap. When I asked him for his wife's maiden name, he answered without hesitation.

"Toomey," he said, "like Regis Toomey."

"Who?"

"An old actor. How's it going?"

"I'll call you soon," I said.

On my drive back to Flemington, I practiced Porter's signature at every red light, signing it over and over on the blank back of the lease. It didn't take me too many tries to produce a passable imitation. I hadn't been kidding when I'd told Harry that Gerow had a schoolboy's handwriting. The capital W and P were large, faithful renderings of the standards I'd been taught and from which I'd wandered far. The small letters, over half the height of the uppercase ones, were fat and undistinguished. Gerow's script seemed frozen in time, locked in at the age he'd been when his future had been taken away from him. I wondered if that was a clue to the man himself and the mystery of his becoming William Porter. Perhaps I'd have to find a motive appropriate to a high school senior who happened to be thirty-eight years old.

The Hunterdon National Bank of Flemington was a squat pile of limestone just off the traffic circle, a block or two from the Porter apartment. I decided that the building's architectural style was early New Deal, based on its general mossiness and on a spread-wing eagle carved in the stone over the revolving front door. The worn out lobby was crowded, which pleased me. The busier the bank, the less likely they would be to remember one infrequent, blue-eyed customer.

I approached a woman whose eyes were as dark as mine and who had a hawk's profile. She looked like she dated from the same period as the building around her. The name plate on her desk identified her simply as Mrs. Nabinger, and she was speaking on the phone. She smiled briefly to acknowledge my arrival and went on talking.

That gave me a chance to case the joint over the tops of my sunglasses. A single uniformed guard stood near the revolving door, backed up by half a dozen security cameras. I realized as I looked around that I'd accidently timed my visit perfectly. The late lunchtime crowd formed a single line that wound its way back and forth across the lobby. Only four of the eight teller stations were open. While I watched, a fifth teller opened his window, and one of the original four closed hers, an action that produced an audible hiss from the serpentine line. They'd be in such a hurry to get rid of me, I told myself, they'd toss me the keys to the vault.

I wasn't taken in by my own pep talk. When Mrs. Nabinger finally got around to asking "May I help you?" I started guiltily.

I covered that reaction with a show of impatience. "I'd like to get into my safe deposit box please," I said. "It's number 252."

Mrs. Nabinger got up from her desk so quickly I almost jumped again. She led me through a swinging door in a waist-high partition of battered hardwood. Beyond the door was a wall of filing cabinets and yet another desk, behind which Mrs. Nabinger sat. She opened a drawer of the desk and flipped through the cards it contained, the charm bracelet she wore jingling away like an alarm bell. The green card she came up with looked identical to the one I'd just filled out in Reaville.

From a second drawer, Mrs. Nabinger extracted a white card and a pen, which she passed to me. The card had spaces for a signature and a date and a paragraph of fine print. I decided that the paragraph described the penalty for doing what I was doing now, so I was careful not to read it. The "William Porter" I came up with was my best to date. Or so I thought. Mrs. Nabinger only glanced at it before sliding it back across the desk to me.

"That's not right," she said.

I smiled, which was the only thing I could think to do besides standing up and running for the revolving door. "How do you mean?"

"I can't say," Mrs. Nabinger said.

That reminded me of the parting instructions I'd received from the earnest young woman in Reaville. Gerow must have used a middle initial. Luckily, Harry had read the real William Porter's middle name to me back in the storage room. I signed the card again, adding an S this time, for Sydney.

Mrs. Nabinger was satisfied with the new signature, if not with me. She had only to ask to see my eyes and I was finished. She asked instead for my mother's maiden name.

"Toomey," I said. "Like Regis Toomey."

Mrs. Nabinger smiled. "He was a favorite of mine."

"Mine, too," I said.

She stood up in her decisive way and led me down an aisle to the vault. Its massive, circular door stood open. The back panel of the door was a sheet of glass, displaying a system of brass gears controlling huge stainless steel bolts. A ramp ran from the floor of the aisle up over the lip of the door and down again onto the vault floor.

Mrs. Nabinger paused at the top of the ramp and turned to me. "Let me have your key." As I handed it to her, she said, "You can wait here."

I watched from the foot of the ramp as she used my key and a second one she took from a rack inside the vault to open a tiny stainless steel door. From the space behind the door, she extracted a long black box.

"Here you go, Mr. Porter. You know where the cubicles are."

I didn't have any idea, but I was batting a thousand on guesses that day. I hadn't seen any cubicles on our walk to the vault, and to my left were more filing cabinets. I turned to my right and started down a narrow hallway. Three doors were set in close proximity in one wall of the hallway. The arrangement reminded me of a confessional from my old parish church. I selected the center door, the priest's door, both because I liked the irony of it and because I was secretly hoping to hear Richard Gerow's posthumous confession.

A desk was built into the back wall of the cubicle. After pushing the button lock on the cubicle's door, I sat down and opened the metal box.

It contained folded papers, the topmost one being a newspaper clipping. The story concerned the rugby team at a private school, the Whitener Academy in nearby Pennington. The focus of the story was actually the team's star, whose photograph occupied the center of the clipping. The name below the photograph was Jack Quinn.

I studied the photo, trying at the same time to picture the little boy I'd met at Ann Quinn's house ten years before. My brief glimpse then had left no lasting impression, but I knew the young man in the photograph had to be him. The box contained other clippings describing Jack's sports career, which also took in baseball and swimming. Beneath the clippings were copies of his records from a Catholic grammar school, Little Flower. These told me that Jack was a scholar as well as an athlete. The oldest sheet was a grainy gray photocopy dated 1979. Jack had been in the third grade that year. He'd gotten all A's and B's and won an award for perfect attendance. The quality of the photocopies improved with each passing grade. So had Jack's performance. He'd been a straight A student in eighty-four, his last year at Little Flower, and president of his class.

I sat back in my chair and stared at the wall in front of me. A yellowed card was thumbtacked on it at the level of my nose. It told me what to do in case of fire. The four wordy steps could have been distilled into four words: get the hell out.

"I wish I could," I said aloud.

THIRTEEN

THE DRIVE SOUTH from Flemington to Pennington should have taken me fifteen minutes at most, but I was an hour making the trip. I spent the first forty minutes or so sitting in my car outside the Hunterdon National Bank, paging through the papers I'd taken from box 252. I think I was giving the bank guard one last chance to retract his parting wish that I have a good day and arrest me. He'd come out of the bank about ten ten minutes into my reverie and raised my hopes. But after sniffing the air, he'd smoked a quick cigarette and gone back inside.

To pass the time until his next break, I tried to organize what I'd learned so far that day. I now knew that Richard Gerow had established a weekend identity as William Porter, financed by cash payments from an unknown source. As Harry had observed, the extent of the Porter setup suggested that the money had been coming in for some time. The little physical evidence I had regarding the payments—the money straps—pointed to a Philadelphia bank, and that, in turn, pointed to Ann Quinn. Despite her involvement in the Sorrowers' poisoning of Gerow in sixty-eight, I'd been able to persuade myself that Ann couldn't be mixed up in Gerow's death. I still wanted to believe that.

But now I'd tripped over Quinn again, or rather, her son Jack. Gerow had been keeping tabs on Jack over a period of years, perhaps since seventy-nine, the year after I had shown up at the Build-Lite plant. Gerow had established his new identity close by Jack's second school, the Whitener Academy, and at about the same time Jack had arrived there in 1985. Gerow had treated his file on Jack with extreme care, not leaving it in his Flemington hideaway, but locking it instead in a safe deposit box. Worthless pieces of paper treated as valuables. Why?

The answer that came to me scared me enough to make my second arrest in two days seem like an attractive out. Gerow could have been planning to revenge himself on Quinn through Jack. Jack was almost the age Gerow had been at the time of the secret graduation party. Jack's life was as full of promise now as Gerow's had been then. Jack's mother had been a member of the group responsible for snuffing out Gerow's promise. Gerow had made the connection between Ann Quinn and his nightmares, if I was reading the evidence of the money straps correctly. All of which meant that, if Gerow's death was murder, Ann was surely involved.

The bank guard didn't reappear with his revolver drawn, so I put the Chevy in gear and headed south. I wasn't exactly sure where the Whitener Academy was located, but I didn't expect to have any trouble finding it. Pennington was in the part of New Jersey that knew more about zoning than Einstein knew about bad-hair days. It remained stubbornly little and unchanged, not so much a town as an exclusive club with a waiting list for membership. Pennington's homes weren't grandiose or its businesses chic, so it might have been its ordinariness as much as its zoning that had spared it from Princeton's choking growth.

I made a left off Route 31 at the traffic light next to the town's only supermarket. As I topped the bridge that carried the road over some railroad tracks, I spotted the Whitener Academy. From my vantage point, I could see two large buildings with mansard roofs of slate, like huge brick barns whose sides were doted with dozens of small-paned windows. Around this pair were trees and open spaces and other, smaller buildings. The whole collection was surrounded by a matching brick wall.

I drove down from the bridge and along the brick wall until I came to a gate. I was wondering how I would misrepresent myself this time until I noticed that the gate was open and unmanned. The Chevy and I ascended a drive whose gutters were filled with dead oak leaves. I spotted a sign marked "visitor parking" and pulled in there, honest citizen that I was. A bigger sign on the lawn in front of me told me that I'd found the administration offices. The flagstone walk beside the sign led me to an unmarked double door.

On the other side of the door, I found myself in something very like a doctor's waiting room. Comfortable-looking living room furniture was arranged around a coffee table that held two parallel rows of magazines. On a sea foam green wall next to a door marked "employees only," was a window with a circular hole cut in its glass. Behind the window, somebody's grandmother was eyeing me expectantly. I crossed the room to her, feeling the weight of my shoes each time I lifted one clear of the plush carpet. I decided that my fatigue was psychological, that I was tired of pretending to be someone else.

"Good afternoon," I said through the hole in the glass. "I'd like to speak with one of your students, please. Jack Quinn. My name is Owen Keane."

"Are you a relative?" the woman asked.

"No," I said. "A friend of the family."

Her grandmotherly smile slowly disappeared, and I felt my new-found scruples fading in direct proportion. "Ann, Jack's mother, asked me to stop by and see the boy. To pass on a message," I added for good measure.

My audience was actually frowning now. "It's still class time, you see," she said. "Jack won't be free to talk with you for the better part of an hour."

"No problem," I said. "I'll wait."

I'd spent the previous night in a strange cell and I'd been on the move ever since, so an hour's downtime sounded great. I settled into an easy chair that felt like a feather bed after the Chevy's bucket seat. In addition to magazines, the waiting room's coffee table offered little pamphlets describing the history of the school. I picked one up and read that the academy had been founded in 1845 by a Presbyterian minister and his wife, who had abandoned their home in Virginia over the issue of slavery. As the school had grown, it had lost touch with its religious roots and was now "aggressively humanistic."

Happens to the best of us, I thought just before I fell asleep.

I awoke to the sound of my name spoken softly. There was a young man in front of my easy chair, dressed in a gray sweat suit and a blue nylon warm-up jacket. He had a pink, broad face, eyes the color of his jacket, and short, curly brown hair that was a shade away from being blond.

He also seemed unusually tall. Then I realized that I'd slipped down into the chair while I'd slept. The collar of my trench coat was up around my ears. I struggled to right myself in the coat and the chair.

"They said you wanted to talk with me," Jack said with unnecessary force. Then he whispered, "Do I know you?"

Before I could decide whether I was supposed to shout my reply or whisper it, Jack spoke again, projecting from his diaphragm. "Something about a message from my mom." I was expecting the whispered aside this time, and it followed immediately. "What do you want?"

It finally dawned on me that the spoken statements were made for the benefit of the receptionist, who had cocked an ear toward the hole in her front window. The whispered questions were meant for me alone. Jack had no idea who I was, but he accepted the premise that we had some business to conduct. More than that, he had somehow concluded that it had to be conducted secretly. The secrecy angle reminded me of the phantom I'd been chasing all morning.

"I want to talk about William Porter," I said.

Jack's blue eyes lit up, but his junior G-man training held him in check. "I'd like to show you the rugby field," he said. "We can talk on the way."

Outside, the afternoon had gotten colder. At least it felt that way after the nap I'd taken in my topcoat cocoon. I cinched up the coat's belt and pulled the lapels together across my chest. Jack strode along beside me, the wind billowing the back of his open jacket like a sail.

"Do you really know my mother?" he asked when we were out on the drive and well clear of the building.

"Yes," I said. "You and I have met before, too. I came by your house one night about ten years ago."

He looked me over again out of courtesy. "Sorry. I don't remember."

"Does your mother still have that Dutch wallpaper in her breakfast nook?"

Jack smiled. "The windmill stuff? No. That is, it's still there, but we painted over it. I did, I mean. Mom said we'd never get the paper off if we painted it, but I figure that's the next guy's problem."

We left the drive and cut across an empty ball diamond, Jack pausing briefly on the pitcher's mound to stare down an imaginary batter. Ahead of us, on a flat, featureless field, a half dozen boys were wrestling for an overweight football.

"Is that rugby?" I asked.

"Not really," Jack said. "They're just goofing around."

He was tall enough to look me in the eye when he faced me, which he did now. "Where is Mr. Porter?" he asked. "What's happened to him?"

"He's disappeared," I said. "I'm trying to trace him."

"Who are you?"

"A friend of his, from a long time back." I decided that I'd better start asking the questions before I ran out of half-truths. "How do you happen to know Porter?"

"I met him over there," Jack said, pointing past my shoulder to the baseball diamond. "He came up after a game one day and introduced himself. It was a year ago last spring. A year and a half ago now. He said he'd been to a lot of our games. I hadn't noticed him before, but I don't pay attention to the stands too much, unless Mom comes up for a game, which isn't often.

"Anyway, Mr. Porter said he knew Mom from way back, that they'd grown up together. Is that true?"

"What else did you talk about?"

"He asked about my dad." Jack broke eye contact with me then, looking out toward the struggles on the rugby field. "I told him that I didn't know much about my father. Just that he and Mom never actually got married." He said that in an offhand way that was studied but admirable. "A lot of people didn't get married back then. They didn't believe in it.

"That's just about all I know about my father, except that he was killed in Vietnam. Mr. Porter asked me if I wanted to know more."

"What did you say to that?"

"Are you kidding? I said sure I would. I was dying to know more. I've tried asking Mom about a million times, but she won't talk about it. I can't blame her," he added protectively. "He hurt her a lot."

"What did Porter tell you?"

"Nothing at first. He asked if he could come back some weekend and talk. We set it up. On that first real visit, he talked a lot but didn't say much. Not about my father. Mostly he talked about Mom, what she was like when she was younger. Made her sound like a pretty free spirit. She's a lot more serious now."

"I know," I said.

"He asked if he could come back again, and I said okay, 'cause I was still hoping to hear something about my father. We walked out here the next time. To this spot." Jack looked back to me, remembering Porter in the same place.

"He told me that my dad had come back from Vietnam alive. I looked into his eyes. They were kind of washed out and they were surrounded by all these real fine lines. I thought, this guy's been looking into the sun, you know? He's stared straight into some really hard things. So I said, 'Were you in Vietnam?' And he just nodded and started to cry. So I said, 'Are you my father?' And he hugged me. And he was really crying then and I was crying, too. It was really awesome. I was blown away."

I felt the same way about it. I took a turn watching the scrimmage to hide my reaction. I needn't have bothered. Jack was rushing on, oblivious of me.

"He didn't blame Mom for telling me that he was dead. He said he'd deserted her and had no right to call himself my father. He said he didn't want anything from me. Except that he wanted to come by and see me once in a while."

"Did you agree to that?"

"Sure. I wanted to know about him. I think I've got a right to know. Is that wrong?"

"What did you find out?"

"Nothing really. I mean, I found out that he was a nice guy and that he cared about me. But I didn't find out a lot about his past. Just the Vietnam stuff. He'd talk about that. And about drugs.''

The lapels of my coat had blown open. I drew them together again. "What about drugs, Jack?"

"He told me he'd used them in 'Nam and that they'd almost ruined his life. They had ruined it for a while, I guess, but he fought his way back.''

"Did he say anything to you about using drugs?"

"He told me I'd better never do it. He got majorly worked up about it. It's the only preaching he ever did. Only it wasn't preaching coming from him, 'cause he'd been there himself.''

"So he never offered you anything? Not even a beer?"

Jack's indignation made him formal. "Mr. Porter? No way. What did I just get through telling you?"

"How about money? Did he ever offer you that?"

"No. He asked if I needed anything. Told me to let him know if I did." Jack hesitated for as long as it took his eyes to move from my face to my shoes and back again. "I told him that Mom took care of everything.''

"You had something in mind though," I said. "What was it?"

Jack nodded. "It was his car. He drives this neat old Firebird. I asked him if I could borrow it sometime. I thought it'd be a great car to drive to the prom.''

So much for Jack's dark, secret desires. "What did he say?"

"That we'd have to see. The kind of answer my mom likes to use. Just after that, he stopped coming by. No calls or letters or anything.''

"When was that?" I knew the answer, but it didn't hurt to double-check.

"Early last spring. We'd just started spring training for baseball. I looked for him at all our home games, but he never showed. I was thinking he might come by for my birthday in October—my eighteenth—but he didn't.''

Jack took a step closer to me. "What's happened to him?"

I noted that Jack had squared his shoulders and clenched his hands into fists. He was steeling himself for the worst. Or so he imagined. The news I carried was more terrible than any possibility he'd been beating himself up with. Not just that his self-proclaimed father was dead. That his death had been a suicide. That the preacher of abstinence had died of a drug overdose.

I had no intention of telling Jack any of that. Not until I'd had a chance to check out Gerow's claims. There was only one way to check. "What about your mother? Did you tell her about Porter?"

"No. He asked me not to. It's been tough keeping that promise. I'll have to ask her sooner or later. Unless you'll tell me something."

"I will," I said. "When I've done some more digging. I'll come back and talk to you. I promise."

Jack let me off with that. As much as he wanted to know the single answer, he also wanted to live in the land of possibility a little longer. I knew that dilemma.

As we walked back toward my car, I asked a casual question. "Is your mom still in nursing?"

"Yes," Jack said. "At Mercy General in Philly."

WHEN I APPROACHED my parked car, I saw a uniformed figure standing behind it. The uniform was too fancy to be a policeman's, and the man who was wearing it was too overweight to pass a physical. When I drew closer, I read the name of the school on a patch on the fat man's shoulder. I also noted that he was writing my license number down in a small notebook.

"Help you?" I asked.

"Security," the man said. He turned so I could see that the word was embroidered on the front of his jacket. "Just keeping tabs on our visitors." His hairless face was pink like Jack's, except for the extremities the cold had reddened.

"And their license numbers?" I asked.

"You can't be too careful."

"That's been my experience," I said.

FOURTEEN

MERCY GENERAL HOSPITAL was on the northern edge of Philadelphia proper, not far from Brookshire, the suburb containing the Quinn cottage. I'd stopped by Brookshire on my drive in, hoping that Ann would be available for a quiet, private talk. She hadn't been home, so I'd driven from gas station to gas station until the directions I'd received at the last one had taken me to Mercy General. It was a big place made shapeless by years of adding on. In that respect, it reminded me of Our Lady of Sorrows High School, not so much a building as an ongoing attempt at one.

The second thing that reminded me of Our Lady was the presence of nuns. One came to my rescue in the lobby after the volunteer behind the reception desk drew a blank when I asked for Nurse Quinn. The nun was dressed like any lay administrator in any hospital, except for a blue, vestigial veil pinned to the back of her hair.

She had touches of red on her cheeks, like an incipient rash, which gave her a jolly look. "Have a seat, Mr. . . . ."

"Keane," I said.

"Mr. Keane. I'll give Annie a call. Maybe she'll have a minute free."

The lobby was fitted out with rows of vinyl chairs joined at the armrest. The rows hid most of an elaborate design that had been worked into the marble floor, leading me to surmise that the space had been drafted into its present role of waiting area. The acoustics backed up this guess, the high ceiling making the lobby a place where you could hear everyone and no one.

The waiting area reminded me of a gate in a busy airline terminal and, more specifically, of a particular gate in a particular airport where I'd said one of the most important good-byes of my life to Mary Fitzgerald. She'd told me there of her intention to become Mary Ohlman, a plan I'd accepted without protest, even though it had changed the course of my life. The memory made the Mercy General lobby seem like a bad place for my reunion with Ann Quinn, a setting for inaction and defeat.

The lobby ended in a short, broad flight of marble steps leading up to a bank of elevators. When I first saw Ann, she was standing at the top of the stairs, her hands resting on the topmost support of the handrail that divided the staircase traffic into two lanes, one heading up and the other down. We watched each other for a while over a sea of strangers' heads, Ann so immobile that she looked like a statue of a nurse placed at the edge of the landing as a tribute, a pale figure in a white cap and dress and a cardigan sweater the same blue as the jolly nun's veil. I couldn't tell if Ann had cut her hair or had only pinned it up. Her hand went up to her hair as I watched. Then she started down the stairs.

I stood up, but didn't move to meet her. There was an empty chair next to mine, and two together were valuable real estate in the crowded waiting area. Ann finally smiled when she was a few steps from me, by which time the gesture seemed pointedly empty.

"Owen," she said. "Hello."

Instead of saying hello back, I thanked her for taking the time to see me.

"I was due for a break," she said. "Everybody in this place has a few coming. They owe me some from last year." It was the theme song of the unappreciated, burned-out professional, but that wasn't at all how Ann looked. She looked good, not thoroughly rested but not pushed to her limit either. An athlete who had found her stride in the event she'd been born for.

I'd spent much of my two days in greater Trenton noting how people had changed or failed to change since I'd last seen them. Ann no longer seemed to have a lead on me in the aging race. Her pale face was fuller and the lines around her eyes had begun to cross one another and deepen. Overall, though, she seemed to have skipped at least half of the years I'd wandered through since our last meeting.

Her thoughts were running along similar lines. "Your hair's getting gray, Owen." After a pause she added, "It's distinguished."

"Yes," I said. "It distinguishes me from young people."

Ann's smile became less rigid for a moment. "Did you come in for the reunion?" she asked.

"Sort of. Someone sent me free tickets. Any chance it was you?"

"No," she said almost before I'd gotten the question out. "I didn't even open my invitation."

"So you won't be there to look after me."

I was trying to make another joke, but Ann shook her head without smiling. "I suppose you know about Ricky," she said.

"Not as much as I'd like to."

"He died last spring. Of a drug overdose. It might have been an accident."

"It might not have been," I said. "How did you find out about it?"

"Mary Kay called me."

"Is she still hyphenated? I mean, married?"

"Yes. She'd heard about Ricky through the alumni grapevine. Is that all you wanted to know?"

"Not exactly." We had to stand close together to hear one another in the echoing lobby. I could see now that Ann hadn't cut her hair. It had a wavy quality that was new, though. It looked like a mass of tiny springs drawn taut and gathered at the base of her cap. "How's Jack?" I asked.

"He's fine," Ann said briefly.

She looked over my shoulder then and nodded to someone. I turned and saw a white-haired couple loaded down with mismatched shopping bags. They were eyeing our unused chairs through the upper halves of their bifocals.

"These are free," Ann called to them. To me, she said, "Come upstairs. I shouldn't be off the floor too long."

As we climbed the stairs to the elevators, Ann worked at changing the subject. "So what have you been doing, Owen? Nobody's heard from you."

Her question reminded me of my parting promise to her in seventy-eight that I would accomplish something by the next reunion. I'd accomplished a variety of things, but I couldn't think of a good way to sum up my decade. I needed Harry there to recount my exploits, as he had for the Trenton police force that morning. He could make a proper job of it, because he had the advantage of distance. My adventures followed a recognizable pattern for him. To me, my career seemed like the design in the floor of the hospital's lobby, a thing made unintelligible by proximity and by the layers of meaningless activity that overlaid it.

"I've been searching," I finally said.

"For what?" Ann asked.

I could have bailed out then with a punch line: the perfect woman, an honest man, the great white whale. I decided not to make the joke at my expense. "For lost things, people, answers."

"Found any?"

"I've done okay with the things and the people," I said. "Not so good with the answers."

"People are the answers, Owen. That's what I think."

The elevator that carried us up into the hospital was long enough to accommodate gurneys, but it was still crowded. Its passengers were silent, as people tend to be in elevators, our only interaction a communal swaying to the car's rhythm. Ann shared a corner with a man in a bathrobe. He was leaning on a tall stainless steel pole, like a shepherd's staff on wheels. Hanging from the crook of the staff was a plastic bag of clear liquid. A tube from the bag disappeared into the sleeve of the man's robe. Ann made him the gift of a beautiful smile.

The woman next to me carried a potted plant, some kind of fleshy succulent, like a spineless cactus. The Owen Keane plant, it might have been called. I'd already backed down from my plan to be tough with Ann. I'd surrendered the initiative, letting her take me from the almost neutral ground of the lobby and into her own domain. There she would have access to cases of hypodermic needles like the one that had been used on Gerow. I found I couldn't picture that particular needle in

Ann's hand. Not while she was looking up in friendly support at the patient beside her.

We got off on the sixth floor, where it was dinnertime. I had a brief glimpse of a busy hallway, of aides pushing tall carts stacked with covered trays, of patients moving back to their rooms, of visitors seizing the excuse to scurry away. Ann waved to a nurse behind a central counter and pointed to an unmarked door across from the elevators. The room was fitted out with a large stainless steel bathtub, racks of towels, and a Rube Goldberg affair that looked like a child's swing crossed with a block and tackle. For lifting wheel-chair-bound patients into the tub, I decided.

Ann closed the door behind us and leaned against it. Her uniform was made of some cheap, synthetic material that was textured like a paper towel. It was cut along straight, one-size-fits-all lines that suited Ann not one bit. It was an ugly dress in fact, but somehow it reminded me of a long lost prom.

"What is it, Owen?" Ann asked. "What do you want?"

"I want to know about payments made to Ricky Gerow. Cash payments of five hundred dollars a month."

"Why ask me?"

"The money straps Gerow left behind were stamped with the name First Penn. There's a branch of that bank about a block from here."

"So you're still a frustrated detective. Who told you about these straps?"

"Gerow's father. I'm looking into this for him. He doesn't believe Ricky was a suicide. He thinks his son was murdered."

Ann was as pale as I'd ever seen her, the blue veins in her temples standing out clearly. "Why would anyone murder Ricky?" she asked.

"Maybe because he was blackmailing someone."

"That five hundred dollars a month wasn't blackmail money, Owen. It was conscience money. Ricky didn't even want to take it at first. I had to twist his arm."

"Tell me about it."

"After that night you came to my house and told me what Ricky's life was like, I knew that whatever we were doing to atone for hurting him wasn't enough. We were never going to work out our own problems until we helped him. So I got in touch with the Sorrowers who had been at the party at Ricky's. Some of us decided to try to make his life better. We were hoping we might even get him to go back to college.

"I went to that factory where Ricky worked to talk with him. Seeing him there was a shock, Owen. After hearing your story, I was ready for it, but it was still a shock. I told him that some of us wanted to help him get his life back on track. I offered him the first five hundred dollars."

"Did you tell him why the Sorrowers were interested?"

"I couldn't. That was part of the deal I made with them. I told Ricky that we wanted to help him because he'd been in the war."

"Did he buy that?"

"Yes," she said while she was still trying to decide. "I don't know. He seemed to. He took the money finally, just when I was ready to give up and go home.

"After that, I got together with him once a month at a little diner on Parkway Avenue. On Saturday mornings. We'd eat something and talk for a while and then I'd give him the money.

"Those meetings got to be like dates. Or what I remember dates being like in high school. A lot of awkwardness followed by a lot of talking."

"What did you talk about?"

"Books he'd read. He was always reading. I tried to encourage that. I told him about work."

"And about Jack?"

"Yes," Ann said after a second's hesitation. "It's an effort for me not to talk about Jack. He's my life. Ricky took an interest in him. He always wanted to see the latest picture and hear how Jack was doing at school."

"Why didn't you just mail him the money? Why did you go on meeting him?"

"Because Ricky would only take the money that way. And because he'd been a drug addict. Some of us were afraid he would use the money for drugs. I was supposed to be watching for that. There was never any sign of it though. Ricky seemed

better and better year after year. Happier and more contented.
I also wanted to keep encouraging him about college. I gave up
on that after a while."

"But you kept paying him."

"He deserved that little bit, Owen, after all we'd put him
through. He was barely getting by on what he made in that
awful factory. There were five of us chipping in most of the
time, so it wasn't so bad. It got easier as the years went by and
we were all doing better.

"Then last May Ricky didn't show up for our meeting. The
first time he'd ever missed. I called the factory and found out
that he'd died. Mary Kay did some checking for me. She's an
editor now with the *Star Ledger*. She found out that Ricky had
committed suicide. That's the whole story. That's all there is to
it."

"Why did the number of contributors change?"

"One of the guys was having problems. He got divorced and
couldn't come up with the money. Later, though, he started
again."

"Who were the five?"

"I can't tell you, Owen. That was part of the deal I made."

"Was Maureen McCary one of them?"

Ann tried to stare me down. When that didn't work, she said,
"No. Maureen wouldn't even talk about it. That's not important. The important thing is that nobody was being blackmailed. If you think Ricky was murdered, you'll have to find
another motive."

Unfortunately for Ann, I already had another one waiting in
the winds. "Have you ever heard of William Porter?"

Ann thought about it, pushing a few golden brown cork-
screws of hair back from her pale forehead while she pon-
dered. "No," she finally said. "I haven't. Who is he?"

"No one now. He used to be Richard Gerow. William Porter was an alias he used. He had an apartment in Flemington
under that name. Paid for with your conscience money."

If Ann had already known that, she was great at feigning
surprise. Surprise with a undercurrent of alarm. "Why Flemington?" she asked.

"Because it was far enough away from West Trenton for Gerow to feel safe passing himself off as someone else. And because it was close to the Whitener Academy."

Throughout our conversation, Ann had been pressed against the door, unwilling to be any closer to me than was absolutely necessary. Now she sprang off the door as though pushed from behind, her momentum almost carrying her into me. She tried to speak twice, but never got past opening her mouth. Then she whispered one word that contained all her questions. "Jack?"

I nodded. "Gerow visited him as Porter for about a year. Right up to the time he died. He had copies of Jack's school records going back to seventy-nine."

"I don't believe you." Ann's pale face was suddenly as lifeless and hard as a porcelain mask. "Leave my son out of this."

"I can't."

"You can," Ann fired back. "You're not a policeman. You're not even a detective. You're just a compulsive busybody. You could go away and mind your own business."

"This is my business. You would never have gone to see Gerow if I hadn't stuck my nose in. There would never have been a William Porter. Gerow would never have heard about Jack. Jack wouldn't be involved somehow in his death."

"Jack's not involved. He would have told me if he'd been seeing a stranger."

"He wants to tell you, badly. He wants to ask you some questions, too. You're not going to like them."

"What questions?"

I'd never get a better opening, or have less to lose by using it. Ann was looking at me now with open contempt. "Who is Jack's father?"

"Jack's father is dead. I told you that ten years ago."

"I know," I said. "Now I'm wondering if he was really dead back then or if he just obliged recently."

"What do you mean by that?"

She knew what I meant, but our ritual dance required me to ask the question point-blank. "Was Richard Gerow Jack's father?"

"No," Ann said. "You're the only man I ever slept with out of sympathy."

I watched her jaw muscles tighten while I waited for the rejoinder that would never come to me. After a time, the line of her jaw and her eyes softened together, slowly. "Is that all?" she asked.

"Not quite." I reached inside the breast pocket of my jacket and produced my spare ticket to the reunion. I handed it to Ann. "I think you should change your mind about staying home Friday night. And you can pass on the same advice to any of the Sorrowers you happen to talk to. Tell them that the Owen Keane detective agency is back in business. I'll be at the reunion, looking for a murderer. They won't want to miss it."

FIFTEEN

THE NEXT MORNING, bright and early, I traded in my finger-print kit and magnifying glass for a shot glass and blender. Thanksgiving should have been a quiet day in a casino bar, with everyone at home eating too much, counting their blessings, and complaining about the calls in the Lions game. It should have been quiet, but it wasn't. There seemed to be a significant number of people in New Jersey who didn't have homes or families or things to be thankful for. They'd all come to the casino, hoping to win a few blessings before the holiday dead-line passed.

Three of us were jammed in a little satellite bar where I of-ten worked alone. Donna and Eve kept up a steady, combative banter that I enjoyed overhearing. Donna was from Edison, in north Jersey, while Eve hailed from Brooklyn, which, to their thinking, was the equivalent of having been born on separate, warring continents. This was despite the fact that ninety-eight percent of their fellow citizens would have guessed they were first cousins.

Manny, our supervisor, came by every hour or so to heighten our sense of urgency with his own personal aura of impending doom. During one of these visits, I watched out of the corner of my eye while Manny fixed a Long Island iced tea. He poured the ingredients into a tall glass half filled with ice and then mixed the drink by throwing it into the air and catching it in a stainless steel cup. He reversed the process and handed the glass to a waitress. I'd tried the trick myself, and it had never failed to result in two or three escaped ice cubes sliding across the bar floor. It was yet another faith thing, I decided.

Casino drinkers seldom sit down at a bar. Not early in the day anyway. Not with millions to be won on the floor and an army of cocktail waitresses to bring them any drink they choose. One exception that day was an older lady in a cloth coat trimmed in fur. She had thinning hair, big, friendly eyes, and an endless supply of red lipstick, which she smeared on the series of glasses I brought her. She was drinking very sweet Manhattans and looking around the casino wistfully. "Lose something?" I finally asked her.

"My family," she said, smiling politely.

There was a story there, but I never got it. Manny called the bartenders together at that moment to identify a drink left in one of the blenders. I'd never seen it before, and Eve and Donna pointed at each other, so Manny poured the mixture down the sink. When I turned back to the Manhattan lady, her stool was empty. I checked the soggy dollar she'd left behind for clues, but old George was, as ever, tight lipped.

It was just as well that my day was busy. The time passed quickly, and I got a break from thinking about Ricky and Ann and the Sorrowers. At four o'clock, I turned down Manny's offer of overtime and hit the road for Mystic Island. My back ached, and there was a faint answering pain in my head, as though I'd been sampling my wares all day. I was just as glad that Marilyn had turned down my invitation.

At least I felt that way until I neared home. The lights were coming on in Mystic Island when the Chevy and I pulled in. These included the town's Christmas decorations, which had been put up during my sojourn on Jersey's west coast. The decorations consisted of metal frames bent into appropriate holiday shapes: stars, bells, fir trees, Santa Clauses. These were wrapped in lights and plastic garland and bolted to telephone poles in front of the bait shops and liquor stores that made up the town's business district. It wasn't much of a display, but it was enough to make a lonely man feel a little lonelier. I thought of the old lady in the fur-trimmed coat, scanning the casino crowd for a friendly face. Like her, I seemed to have been extremely careless with my relations.

My house was the only dark one on Lake Champlain Drive. I let myself in with the hidden key and sat down at the kitchen table, still wearing my top coat. I sat for some time, watching the gray light fade over the lagoon. My straight-backed kitchen chair was nowhere near as comfortable as the one I'd napped

in at the Whitener Academy, but I was preparing to make do
when a knock sounded on my front door.

It was Harry and his daughter Amanda, loaded down with
aluminum trays covered in foil.

"Happy Thanksgiving," Amanda said. "I like your bow
tie." She was a fair-haired seven-year-old whose face had a
tendency to dimple.

"We were getting takeout anyway," Harry said. "Amanda
thought we might as well heat it up over here."

"Might as well," I said.

While Harry and Amanda took over my kitchen, I sat down
in the living room feeling out of the loop, a guest in my own
house. I was even dressed like one. When Amanda came in to
keep me company—walking stiff legged with arms outstretched like Frankenstein's monster—she tugged at the belt of
my trench coat.

"Take off your coat and stay awhile," she said.

As she helped me out of it, she told me about the parade
she'd watched that morning. Every few words, her eyes would
stray from mine and over to the portrait of her mother that
hung on the wall behind me. Harry gave it a long look, too,
when he finally joined us. He'd drawn it during the dark time
when he'd been cut off from his dead wife, when he'd been
alone in the universe, to use the tipsy Don Cranny's haunting
phrase. Harry had given the portrait to me when he'd ceased to
be alone, an achievement I had yet to equal.

Harry was carrying three mismatched glasses of eggnog.
"You don't have any nutmeg," he said to me.

"There's a shock," I replied.

Amanda laughed and lighted on the arm of my chair.

"Yours is the blue glass, Owen," Harry said. "It's fortified.
You look like you could use a little pepping up."

"What's it fortified with?" I asked.

"Scotch. It's all I could find in there."

"There's a shock," Amanda said.

While our turkey was reheating, I told Harry and Amanda
of my adventure in the Hunterdon National Bank. Amanda,
who was an Owen Keane fan, patted my shoulder when I re-

lated how I'd figured out the problem with William Porter's signature. Harry just shook his head. They were both quietly attentive as I described my visits to the Whitener Academy and Mercy Hospital.

When I'd finished, I sat waiting for Harry's cross-examination, but it was Amanda who asked the first question. "If his mom works in Pennsylvania, why does Jack go to school in New Jersey?"

"I don't know," I said. "I never thought to ask."

"Good one, A," Harry said.

I tried to work out the answer, but Harry and Amanda were exchanging high fives, which made thinking difficult. "Someday I'll get a step ahead of you Ohlmans," I told Amanda.

She patted my shoulder again. "Yeah, right," she said. She then filled the time until the oven buzzer went off demonstrating her new talent for turning cartwheels.

We ate in the living room so Harry could watch the end of the late football game. That ran right up to the start of *Mary Poppins,* which pleased Amanda. She lay on the floor in front of the set while Harry and I poked at rubbery pumpkin pie on the sofa. I was still waiting for Harry's criticism of my investigation's most recent phase, and he was still oddly silent. Finally, the suspense got to be too much for me.

"So how am I screwing up now?" I asked.

"Who says you are?" Harry replied quickly enough to tell me he'd been thinking about it, too. "You're following your clues now, at least, instead of dragging them in the direction you want to go."

That modest compliment might have been inspired by the number Julie Andrews had just finished singing, which was about a spoon full of sugar helping medicine go down. Harry's medicine followed directly.

"You're doing what you always do, though, which is identifying emotionally with the people you're supposed to be investigating. It makes you lose perspective. I'm talking about the Quinns, mother and son. And, of course, Ricky Gerow."

"Two of whom I haven't seen in ten years and one I'd never really met before yesterday," I said in my defense.

"As though that matters. I've seen you start siding with people who died before you were born. All I'm saying is that you should keep a little distance. Whenever you mention Ann Quinn, you sound like you're still carrying the torch she lit back in your sophomore year."

"Freshman year," I said.

"And you talk about Jack like he's Amanda's age and you're hoping he'll end up calling you Uncle Owen. The kid's eighteen, for God's sake, which means he's very nearly an adult, which means he's capable of anything."

"What's my blind spot with Gerow supposed to be? Guilt?"

"Guilt's always a safe bet with you, Owen. In Gerow's case, it has more layers than an onion. You feel bad because you didn't try to help him ten years ago. You feel worse about the possibility that he'd be alive today if you hadn't dug around in that old scandal. Then there's Vietnam."

"I had nothing to do with that," I said.

"Exactly. Men our age who didn't have to go over there have a load of guilt about Vietnam. Especially when we're dealing with someone who did go over, like Gerow."

"Cut to the summation," I said.

"Okay. My summation is don't be afraid to ask the tough questions about these people."

"For example?"

"For example, would this Ann Quinn kill to protect her son?"

"In a minute. She wanted to drown me in a bathtub yesterday."

"Seriously, Owen."

"Seriously, I think she would do anything to protect her son. But she didn't kill Gerow."

"What makes you so sure?"

"She didn't know about William Porter till I told her, which means she didn't know about the threat to Jack, which means she had no motive."

"Assuming she told you the truth about the payments."

"Assuming she did," I said. Harry was right. It was too much to take on faith. So was Ann's statement that Gerow was not Jack's father.

"Those payments are cockamamy anyway," Harry said. "You screw up a guy's life, so you pay him a monthly stipend? Does that make sense?"

"Yes," I said. "It's the way people get involved without getting involved. We send money. It's harder to understand why Gerow took it."

"Maybe he really knew what the Sorrowers had done to him. Maybe he'd always known."

"Maybe he just wanted to have breakfast with Ann once a month," I said. "I'd compromise my principles for that."

It was the glimmer of a real idea, but Harry mistook it for a wisecrack and shifted the subject. "You never did let me in on the business of the O. Henry books. What was that all about?"

I told him how Gerow had saved the books from the Build-Lite pulping machine and how he'd searched them for answers.

Harry was smiling at me when I finished. "If only he'd known that the answers are in mystery stories."

"Very funny," I said.

"So why did he use the name William Porter? What does that mean?"

I thought about it while Ms. Andrews and Dick Van Dyke raced merry-go-round horses. Gerow's choice of alias could mean that he'd found in O. Henry's life story instructions for starting over again, moving to another town, finding a new life. Only Gerow hadn't moved, not really, and his new life was a sham, a façade propped up with two-by-fours like a movie set. I thought again of my recent cell mate. The double life of Ricky Gerow reminded me of Cranny's take on Don Quixote, that his fantasy world had been created to sustain an impossible belief. It was an insight at odds with the sinister role in which I'd cast Gerow, so I put it out of my mind.

"And what happened to Maureen McCary?" Harry asked. "She was your archenemy ten years ago. Twenty years ago she cooked up the whole damn party at Gerow's. Now she seems like an innocent bystander. How did she get out of the picture?''

"I don't know," I said.

It wasn't the best time for deep thinking. When the movie was on, someone was always singing. When the commercials came on, Amanda would treat us to her own rendition of the most recent number.

Finally, Harry looked at his watch and sat up. "We're out of here, A," he said. "It's late and Uncle Owen needs to be fresh tomorrow for his big reunion."

"Tomorrow you solve the case, right?" Amanda asked.

"Right," I said.

She kissed me on the cheek. "You feel hot," she told me When she put her hand on my forehead, her little fingers were ominously cool. "Yep," she said, "You're coming down with something."

It was easy to dismiss a seven-year-old's diagnosis, even one couched in the correct, adult terms. "I can't get sick now," I said. "It would be bad timing."

SIXTEEN

I WOKE UP at two on Friday morning after what seemed like a thousand repetitions of the same feverish dream. In the dream, I was trying to board a merry-go-round that wouldn't stop for me. I never did manage to get on, despite a steady stream of people from my past—Maureen McCary, David Radici, Lucy Criscollo, Bill Pearson—who brushed past me and mounted the painted wooden animals without effort. Ann Quinn was part of this parade, as was Ricky Gerow. Ann selected a yellow charger with a flowing white mane, while Poor Ricky ended up on a dragon.

I got up at two to be sick, an event I tried to blame on Harry and his misbegotten eggnog. After suffering through three additional attacks spaced out through the early morning, I had to admit that Dr. Amanda had been right. I'd chosen the worst possible moment to be tripped up by a germ.

I'd planned to work the early shift at the casino before heading up to Trenton, so I had to call Manny at dawn to tell him I wouldn't be in. There was a twenty-four-hour bug going around, Manny told me. I wasn't sure if he was trying to make me feel better or just putting an expiration date on my excuse. If his motive was consolation, he was wasting his time. A twenty-four-hour illness would be more than enough to mess up my showdown with the Sorrowers.

I spent most of the day flat on my back, catching up on the sleep I'd missed with a series of short, fretful naps. I tried eating a couple of times, but those experiments ended disastrously.

At four, I forced myself to get dressed. My current "good" suit was a dark one, a charcoal gray that was almost black. It accentuated my pallor nicely, I decided as I looked myself over in the bathroom mirror. I place my hands across my chest to complete the effect. "Rest in peace," I told my reflection.

My drive through the Pines was uneventful. For once, I was content to be part of a line of traffic snaking its way through the haunted forest. I picked up I-95 outside of Allentown and took it to the first exit for Hamilton, another of Trenton's prosperous, ungrateful suburbs. I planned to ask for directions to Angelo's, the site of the reunion, but I put it off so long I ended up spotting the restaurant's neon sign unassisted.

I parked the Chevy in a large lot next to what looked like a bowling alley. The lot was crowded, too crowded for one high school class reunion. That mystery was solved for me when I made it through the building's heavy, Mediterranean-style doors. Angelo's was hosting three functions that night. A black velvet sign with white plastic lettering told me that Our Lady of Sorrows High School Class of 1968 was gathering in the Michelangelo Room.

I weaved my way down a carpeted hallway past the da Vinci Room and the Botticelli Room. In each, a noisy gathering was already in progress. I was sorely tempted to join one of them, to pick up some stranger's name tag and lie my way into a safe hiding place. I might have tried it, if I'd felt better. As it was, I wasn't sure I'd be able to pass myself off as Owen Keane.

A whimsical doctor once told me that a reunion was a chance to shake hands with the mistakes of your youth. A big mistake from my youth greeted me outside the Michelangelo Room. Maureen McCary by name. She was dressed in blue again, sans sequins this time. Her outfit was a blue satin jacket over a low-cut dress of the same material. The jacket had shoulder pads fit for a linebacker, intended to disguise a general widening of McCary's figure. To complement this effect, her golden hair was teased out almost to the width of her shoulders, making her face seem small and a little lost. That was only until she spotted me. Then her oversize smile flashed on. It was a rerun of her television ads: a smile as unrestrained and sincere as a skeleton's.

"Well, well," she said, "if it isn't the ghost at the feast."

"That would be Ricky Gerow," I said.

McCary put a long, vermilion-tipped finger to my lips. "No lines for you, Owen. You're a bit player, and bit players don't get lines."

She patted my cheek as she drew her hand away. Then she swept past me, a tall ship leaving a dingy in its wake.

A rudderless dingy. Here was my old opponent, taunting me with the bravado of a Hollywood villain. Not so much as a phony tear for Gerow or an empty apology to me for the joke of ten years ago. And yet, as Harry had pointed out, I couldn't pull McCary into the puzzle of Gerow's death. She had nothing to do with his pursuit of Jack, and she hadn't been chipping in on his monthly allowance. Why then the show of defiance?

The question reminded me of the mysterious reunion program I'd been sent and one of my pet theories about it. Namely, that it had been a challenge to me from someone involved in Gerow's death. The program suddenly seemed to be the missing connection to McCary. It had been mailed from New York City, where McCary worked. She'd sent it to me as her invitation to Game Two of the match we'd begun ten years before. I didn't pause to ask myself why she would take the risk. I wanted to follow up the lead while I was still on my feet.

The woman seated behind the reception table told me I was getting too much sun and then laughed extravagantly. I asked her about the program.

"They're on the tables," she said. "Every place has one."

I stole a glance at her name tag when she gestured toward the tables behind her. "Thanks, Patrice," I said. "What I'd like to know is who had access to the programs a week or two ago?"

"Access to them?" Patrice's laugh bubbled up again. "They're not classified documents, Owen. We only got them from the printer about two weeks ago. That is, the program person on the committee did."

"Maureen McCary?"

That guess produced another chorus of laughter, and I felt McCary slipping from my hook. "Her majesty volunteer? No way. It was Mary Kay Ellis-something."

"Humphrey," I said. I would have slapped the side of my head in disgust, but I didn't think I'd survive the gesture. Mary Kay, journalist, was the obvious draftee for the program editor's job, and I'd been told by Ann that Mary Kay had looked into Gerow's death. I set out to find her.

The room was big and dark with a gray ceiling so heavily textured that it looked like the roof of a cave. The faces that floated past me seemed too old to be my classmates, even though they were also vaguely familiar. They were the parents of the kids from Our Lady, I decided. One of the faces stepped forward to speak to me. It was David Radici, the aging flower child. His hairline was moving backward in the direction of his pony tail, but the eyes behind the wire rims were still as frank and open as a baby's. He wore a canvas double-breasted jacket over a black shirt, the sleeves of the jacket pushed up almost to his elbows. I knew there were jeans below the jacket without even looking.

"God, Owen, I'm glad to see you," Radici said. "I've been waiting a long time to apologize for that joke we pulled at the last reunion." Radici spoke with the urgency of someone seeking the forgiveness of a dying man. I had to look even worse than I felt.

"What about Gerow?" I asked. "Did you ever apologize to him?"

"No. What would I have said to him? I kept up with him through Ann though. She's turned out to be the conscience of the Sorrowers, Owen. She really has. She helped me see what a terrible thing we'd done to Gerow. And she set up a fund for him. I kicked into it every month. The sin tax, Libby called it. It wasn't easy to find the money, but I wish to God we were still paying it."

"Who's we?"

Radici looked down at his deck shoes. "I can't tell you, Owen."

"Where's Libby?" I asked, looking around for her. She was someone I could talk to, someone who didn't respect Sorrower vows of silence.

"She didn't come," Radici said. "She still has a sour taste in her mouth from the last reunion. And it's tough to get a baby-sitter for three kids."

He grinned proudly as he said that. In another second, he would have been showing me the latest photos. I sidestepped the distraction. "Are you still living outside Pennington?"

"Yep," Radici said. "Same mansion."

"Did you know that Ann Quinn's son goes to school at the Whitener Academy?"

"No, I didn't. Ann must be doing great. That place costs a fortune."

I assayed his reaction and came up with only genuine sur-prise and trace elements of envy. Before I could pursue the subject of Jack, we were joined by Bill Pearson. Radici gave Pearson a look to match the sour taste in Libby's mouth, pat-ted me on the shoulder, and left.

Pearson didn't seem to notice the slight. My old teammate had changed a lot since the last reunion. He sported a full beard, shot through with gray. The jacket of his wrinkled khaki suit hung open to accommodate a modest paunch.

Pearson's big right hand held a full glass of bourbon col-ored liquor in which a single ice cube was dying happy. He waved the glass under my nose. "What are you drinking, Owen?"

I could barely stand the fumes, so I tried to pass on the of-fer. Pearson wasn't having any of that. His free hand clamped onto my elbow and guided me toward the bar. There I ordered a club soda.

"What's the matter?" Pearson asked. "You still hung over from the last reunion? God, you put enough away that night."

He appeared to be going after my record. He ordered an-other double bourbon and then finished off its predecessor. I thought of what Ann had once told me about Pearson, that he was a man slowly crumbling under the unseen pressures of his life. When our drinks arrived, he raised his in a toast. "De-parted friends," he said.

I drank to that, tentatively. The club soda went down and stayed down. Pearson finished half his drink in his first attempt. Then he said, "Whoever got the idea of calling dead people the departed had no real insight into them. The problem with dead people is that they don't depart. Not really."

I didn't have time for any sour mash philosophy just then. During Pearson's speech, I'd spotted Mary Kay talking with a disc jockey who had set up shop on the bandstand. I looked around for someone on whom I could unload Pearson. His wife's name escaped me, so I asked for her generically.

"My wife?" Pearson repeated. "I haven't got one. Patty left me years ago. She's not dead, but she's departed." So Pearson was the contributor to the Gerow fund who had dropped out and then returned. It was another bit of confirmation for Ann's story.

I snuck away when Pearson turned to look for a bartender. Mary Kay smiled as I walked up to her.

"Owen, I'm glad you came."

"You sent me an invitation I couldn't refuse," I said.

"Figured that out, did you? Yes, I'm the culprit."

"Why?"

Mary Kay said good-bye to the deejay and drew me out onto the empty dance floor. "A few month's ago, Ann Quinn asked me to find out all I could about Richard Gerow's death. I didn't like what I found out, Owen. It's bothered me ever since. I decided I needed a crack investigator, so I hired you."

"Why didn't you just call me?"

"After that fiasco at the tenth reunion, I wasn't sure you'd talk to me. And I wasn't sure you'd give a damn about my worries. I wanted to play on your curiosity. So I sent you an invitation right out of those paperback mysteries we wasted our younger days reading."

I was wasting my middle age on them, too, but I hadn't come to Hamilton to compare bad habits. "Since I'm working for you, maybe you'll be willing to answer some questions."

"Such as?"

"Was Ricky Gerow Jack Quinn's father?"

Mary Kay was confused enough to lower her left for a moment. "No. Why would you think that?"

"I got it from Gerow, secondhand. If Gerow wasn't the father, who was?"

"Owen, I can't talk about this. Really. I'd tell you if I could."

Mary Kay was a client right out of a detective story. She held things back. Dangerous, important things. I indulged in the paperback private eye's prerogative and told my client off. "Don't give me any of that crossed-my-heart-and-hoped-to-die nonsense. Ricky Gerow is dead. You don't think he was a suicide and neither do I. Jack Quinn is mixed up in this. You're the only person who can tell me how."

Mary Kay looked past me toward the reception table. "There's the person you have to ask," she said.

I followed her gaze in time to see Ann Quinn make the entrance of the evening. She'd traded in her nurse's uniform for a black cocktail dress under a short, embroidered jacket of reds and blues. Her hair was a Pre-Raphaelite mantel of soft curls that caught the light from the bright hallway behind her and drew it into the dark room. Or so it seemed to my fevered eye.

Ann stood scanning the crowd, oblivious to the stir her entrance had created. The first woman of her class, I thought, still turning heads after twenty years. Then her unsmiling gaze came to rest on me, or rather it ran me through, fixing me to the dance floor like a pin holding a butterfly to a card. I could only stand there as she crossed the room to me. I couldn't so much as look toward Mary Kay, but I knew without looking that my client had deserted me.

Ann's porcelain mask softened slightly when she drew close enough to recognize my symptoms. "Are you okay?" she asked.

"One of your patients must have breathed on me," I said.

I was hoping to solicit Ann's beside manner, but she'd left it in her other suit. "Serves you right," she said, "for nosing around where you weren't wanted. I went through hell yesterday because of you."

"Jack?"

"Yes, Jack. Full of questions you and Ricky Gerow put into his head."

"Those questions would have come along without us, Ann. Sooner or later."

"I was counting on later, Owen. When Jack was old enough not to be damaged by the answers. He's such a sweet kid. Ricky couldn't have wanted to hurt him. You couldn't want to hurt him." The porcelain was definitely cracking. Ann looked close to tears.

"I don't want to hurt Jack," I said. "I don't want to hurt you either. I know now that you were telling me the truth about those payments to Ricky. I'm sorry I didn't have more faith in you."

We were looking into each other's eyes, and the connection seemed as real as an embrace. For a moment, it was 1978, and we were swaying to the music in the Lawrenceville firehouse. Then Ann reached out to steady me, and I realized that I had been swaying alone, from hunger and fatigue.

"Everyone's sitting down," Ann said. "Who are you sitting with?"

"You?" I asked, still knee-deep in déjà vu.

Ann broke that spell by rewriting the dialogue. "Not this time, Owen. I need some space. There are people I want to talk to."

"We'll talk to them together."

When Ann saw that I wasn't going away, she shrugged. "Pick a table," she said.

SEVENTEEN

I SELECTED A TABLE at the back of the room. It turned out to be a gathering place for disaffected Sorrowers. Mary Kay joined us, dragging along a tall, thin man she introduced as George Humphrey, her husband. Humphrey was a stockbroker who worked in New York City, which explained how Mary Kay's mailing to me had acquired its postmark. The happy couple was followed by David Radici. I expected Bill Pearson to stagger in next, but he never did.

Radici opened the dinner conversation, his subject being his three boys. Humphrey saw Radici and raised him, chipping in his own experiences as a father and then topping those stories by describing his career as a Little League coach. I had nothing to contribute on either subject, which didn't cheer me up. Mary Kay watched Ann and me and said little. Ann watched her plate and said nothing.

Across the room, Maureen McCary was holding court with the faithful remnants of our old group. I spotted Pearson there, sitting next to Lucy Criscollo. A familiar figure held the place of honor next to McCary. It was Roland of the white disco suit. He was still dressed in the fashion of the moment, this moment's choice being a silken suit a size too big for him. At the tenth reunion, Roland had seemed no more than an accessory to McCary's outfit, so I was surprised to see that he had survived the decade.

Encouraged by my success with the club soda, I ate a little dry salad. Marilyn had been wrong about the entrée. Instead of chicken and pencil points, we were served cubes of beef on a mound of rice. I dug tunnels in the rice and waited for someone to remember my name.

Mary Kay eventually did. "Owen, do you remember telling me once that I should read Dorothy L. Sayers?"

"Yes," I said.

"I took your advice in a big way. I read all her mysteries. I liked them so much, I also read her biography."

"Huh," I said.

Mary Kay looked from me to Ann as she rattled on. "Dorothy was one strange lady. What I mean is, her life was as strange as any of her stories."

"Do you know her life story?" Mary Kay asked.

"Better than my own," I said. At least I knew how Sayer's had ended.

By then it had dawned on me that sticking close to Ann had been the wrong play. I should have given her some line and then kept an eye on her. She was the old Ann Quinn once again, distant and detached, no more aware of my presence than she was of Radici and Humphrey's admiring glances. It was an indication of how much we'd hurt her, the Sorrowers and I, that we'd driven her back to that old line of defense.

Shortly after dinner, Ann and Mary Kay excused themselves and went out together. I left the proud fathers alone and wandered over to the bar, which felt a little like home, God help me. From that safe vantage point, I surveyed the crowd, both the surviving Sorrowers and the less destructive majority of the class. The mood of the evening was entirely different from that of our last gathering. It was quieter, sadder. There wasn't the same feeling of lives blossoming and possibilities opening up. For the class of sixty-eight, the cement seemed definitely to have set.

Mary Kay and Ann were gone a long time. Long enough for my attention to wander. I fell into a couple of restful conversations with people who had never come within a mile of the Sorrowers. I watched brave souls out on the dance floor trying to move to our old music, which was as out-of-date now as the big-band hits I'd heard in Mrs. Nix's laundromat. Then the deejay got around to playing "Lighter Shade of Pale," and the tables really emptied.

It was the song I'd danced to at the last reunion with Ann Quinn, the woman I was supposed to be keeping an eye on. She still hadn't come back into the room as far as I could tell. I didn't panic until I spotted Mary Kay out on the dance floor

with her husband. I went out belatedly to check the hallway
outside the banquet room and found only outcast smokers, one
of them a bored-looking Bill Pearson.

George Humphrey went off happily enough when I cut in.
His wife was considerably less pleased with the transaction.

"Where's Ann?" I asked while she was still looking after her
husband's retreating back.

She put her hand on my shoulder reluctantly. "She left,
Owen. Don't ask me where she's gone, because I don't know."
A few revolutions later, she added, "I asked her to trust you,
but she wouldn't. I'm afraid of what might happen."

"Take your own advice then and trust me. Tell me what you
know."

It was a song that dragged on forever, luckily for me. It took
almost that long for Mary Kay to decide to talk again. "I've
already told you all I can tell you."

I almost lost my temper at yet another evasion. At the last
second, I realized that Mary Kay's tone was not evasive. She
was as nervous and hesitant as someone parting with a secret.

"I've already told you," she repeated as the dance ended.

"Already told me what?" I asked the dark room after she'd
left me. I wandered back to the bar, trying to remember the
snatches of conversation I'd had with Mary Kay. Prior to Ann's
entrance, she'd refused point blank to answer questions about
Jack. At dinner our only exchange had been about mystery
stories.

"Dorothy Sayers," I said aloud to the amusement of the
bartender.

He was a thin man with the aggressively greased black hair
of a fifties hood. "Don't tell me," he said, "she was the girl
you took to the junior prom." He followed that bon mot with
a very professional "What'll it be?"

"Scotch," I said from old habit. I was finally feeling better.
I sipped the liquor and thought back. Mary Kay and I hadn't
talked about Sayers. She'd talked and I'd failed to listen. The
clue, if there was one, wasn't in one of Sayers's plots. Mary Kay
hadn't mentioned a single title. She'd said that she'd read a life

of Sayers. And that Sayers had been one strange woman. What had she meant by that?

The bartender seemed to be waiting for the answer, too. When it came to me, I shared it with him. "Sayers had a baby. A baby boy. She gave the baby away to a friend."

"Wish I'd thought of that," the bartender said. "Does it work with teenagers?"

I let him daydream about it alone. Mary Kay had been hinting that Ann Quinn was not Jack's mother. Hinting and not telling to honor some old promise she'd made, probably to Ann herself. I remembered then how Mary Kay had studied Ann's face as she'd told me, looking for the least sign that Quinn herself knew Sayers's story.

I scanned the crowd for Mary Kay and her husband without spotting them. I did see David Radici, standing next to our table with his hands sunk in his pockets.

"Pretty dead group, Owen," he said as I walked up. "You'd think this was our fiftieth reunion." When I asked for Mary Kay, he shook his head. "She and George hit the road. Something about having to drive to New Brunswick. Like that's in Tibet."

I'd have to work the rest out on my own. Jack had told me that his eighteenth birthday had been in October. So he'd been born when all the Sorrowers but Gerow had been juniors in college.

"Ann went to some Philadelphia school, didn't she?" I asked Radici.

"LaSalle," Radici said.

"I need to talk to somebody else who went there. Somebody who's here tonight."

"You just missed one. But you wouldn't have gotten the time of day from her."

"Who?"

"Maureen McCary," Radici said. "Or, as Libby calls her, Bitch Queen of the Universe."

"Who else went there?"

"Damn, Owen, I don't know. Is this important?"

"Think of it as one last payment to Ricky Gerow."

Several questions passed through Radici's eyes, but he didn't waste my time with them. "We can ask around," he said.

We split up and worked different sides of the dwindling crowd. I was at my third table when I saw Radici waving to me from across the room. When I reached him, he was standing next to a woman in an untucked black dress shirt over black stirrup pants. Her ash blond hair was spiked up like a frozen wave.

"Still playing the trumpet?" she asked me.

"Every day," I said, wondering who I was supposed to be this time. I was too tired to care.

"You remember Sharon," Radici said. "She went to La-Salle."

"Correct," Sharon said.

"With Ann Quinn?" I asked.

"Hell, yes," Sharon said. "Where is Annie? I haven't talked with her yet."

"Ann didn't graduate with you though," I said. "She took some time off, didn't she?"

"What are you talking about?" Sharon asked. She thought about it. "Annie was at graduation. I'm sure of it. I remember being pissed off at how good she looked in that dammed cap and gown." She turned to Radici. "Where's Annie hiding?"

"Sorry," I said. "I'm mixed up. I was thinking of Maureen McCary. She took time off."

"Correct," Sharon said. "Maureen took a year off and did Europe. Her folks had the bucks. Where is old Maureen? I want to talk to her, too."

So did I.

EIGHTEEN

RADICI DIDN'T KNOW where McCary had gone, so I thanked him for his help and left him. Bill Pearson was still leaning on a hallway wall outside the Michelangelo Room. He held an empty glass in one hand and an unlit cigarette in the other, both items looking unnaturally pristine, like props for a dress rehearsal. Remarkably, Pearson didn't seem to be any more drunk now than he'd been before dinner.

"Keane," he said. "Got a match?"

"No," I said.

Pearson shook his head. "The correct answer is, 'No, mine died on the cross.'"

"It isn't correct for me," I said.

Pearson shrugged. "You'd know best."

"I'm trying to find McCary."

He waved his glass toward the exit. "Too late. She and her inflatable date went thataway."

"I know," I said. "Do you happen to know where they went?"

Pearson stuck with the cowboy dialogue. "Stay clear of her. She's a rattler."

"Sidewinder, you mean," I said.

"That would've worked, too. I know that she could chew you up and spit you out, pardner. Don't give her the chance."

"You were sitting at her table. Did she say where she was staying? Was it her mother's place in Bucks County?"

"Nope."

"Where then?"

"You ask too many questions, Keane. You always did."

"I'm asking them for Ricky Gerow now, Bill. I want to know why he died. I think McCary can tell me."

Pearson scratched at his beard with the edge of his empty glass. The operation produced a sound like the rustling of dead leaves. "For Ricky?" he asked.

"Where did she go?"

"She's staying at one of the new hotels up on Route 1 outside of Princeton."

"Which one?"

"Don't say I didn't give you fair warning."

"I won't, pardner."

"The Omni-Sevren, then. And watch your back."

I didn't trust my memory of the surface roads in Hamilton, so I doubled back to the interstate. It crossed Route 1, I knew, just south of the state vehicle inspection station where my old Ghia used to fail its emissions test every year. I was surprised to see that the mall north of the station had empty parking lots. I checked my watch and found that it was already ten thirty. Time flies when you're screwing up.

The name Omni-Sevren was familiar. I was sure I'd seen it on my drive south from Mr. Gerow's place earlier in the week. I wondered, belatedly, how the old man's Thanksgiving had been, knowing in my heart that the answer was long and lonely. Then I wondered how he would feel if I pulled a grandson out of my hat for him. I didn't like my chances of carrying off that trick. Ricky and McCary were an even less likely couple than Ricky and Ann. And Mary Kay, my secretive client, had flatly dismissed Ricky's claim to be Jack's father. But did she really even know? There was nothing to build on in a case where everyone was swearing everyone else to secrecy. Where everyone was lying. That seemed too harsh a judgment, so I amended it. It was a case where everyone believed the thing they most wanted to be true.

I remembered then how I'd tried to twist the facts to fit a solution I'd wanted, an exercise that had landed me in jail. That led to thoughts of O. Henry and breakfasts with Ann Quinn and the empty feeling I'd had at the reunion table listening to other men talk about their sons.

The Omni-Sevren's grounds were surprisingly large, given the property values in its neighborhood. It was a hotel and conference center according to the long, low sign at the entrance, which accounted for the two buildings that flanked the entry road and were unlit on this Friday night. The center building, at which the drive ended, was lit inside and out. The building was three stories in some places and two in others, with the shallow roof and the clean lines of a Prairie School mansion from the early years of the century. A glass entrance displayed the lobby, which had as its centerpiece a rock garden complete with a waterfall and a pond. There were ducks in the pond, tiny gray and green ones with impeccable manners. A pair of them paddled around at my end of the pool, not so much panhandling as entertaining me.

I was still communing with nature when an elevator opened at the far end of the lobby. Ann Quinn rushed out of it, her cheeks bright with anger. I dodged behind the centerpiece garden before she had a chance to spot me. The move was instinctive and the instinct was self-preservation. The emotion on Ann's face was almost dehumanizing, making her seem less a person than a dangerous natural phenomenon, a tidal wave or a forest fire.

She passed the front desk attendant without a word and exited through the automatic doors. When she was out of sight, I approached the desk. The young man behind it wore a uniform of the same green and gray as the lobby ducks, and I wondered who had been dyed to match whom. The clerk also shared the ducks' gentle breeding.

"How may I help you?" he asked.

"I need the room number of one of your guests," I said.

The clerk raised his hands above the keyboard of a small computer terminal and awaited my downbeat. When I gave him McCary's name, he dropped his hands to his sides, glancing at the same time toward the exit Ann had just used.

"That would be 217," the clerk said. "May I announce you?"

"You may not," I replied.

Ann's elevator opened when I pushed the call button. I thought I could smell her perfume as the silent doors shut me in, but that was probably just my imagination going for time and a half. The second floor, when I arrived, was quiet. I followed engraved brass signs to Room 217 and knocked.

Roland answered the door. He remembered me, which I didn't expect. Perhaps McCary had pointed me out during a lull in the dinner conversation. His wide-eyed expression segued smoothly into a grin that was too bright for the hour. "What do you want, Mr. Keane?"

I was still deep in the evening's fog of memories. "I have an appointment to see a woman about some nude photographs. I'm a little late."

Roland nodded. "Ten years late." It would have been a good line to slam the door on. He opened it wide instead.

The Omni-Sevren was a step up from our old Howard Johnson. A whole flight of steps up, in fact. I entered the sitting room of a suite decorated in mauves and greens and lit by a single fat lamp. There was a small bar in one corner and a tall television cabinet in another. Between them was a coffee table, a sofa, and an easy chair. McCary was on the sofa in a heavy white robe, her long legs stretched out beside her. Her hair was pulled back from her face and held in place by a cloth band that matched her robe. She held a tall glass tilted at a dangerous angle, and her gaze was fixed on the empty chair. The bottle of Stolichnaya on the table beside her was down by about a third.

My exchange with Roland should have spoiled the surprise of my arrival, but McCary seemed not to have heard it. She spilled a little vodka from her tilted glass when she finally got around to noticing me.

"Who invited you?"

She looked from me to Roland, who was now standing behind the bar, his white grin floating in the dark corner. I wondered if I was just a break in the monotony for him or a chance to score some points in his own ongoing contest with McCary.

"Your date did the honors," I said, nodding toward Roland. "How about sending him out for ice? Or does he already know where the bodies are buried?"

"He knows more than you do," McCary said, "which is nothing." She didn't even believe that herself. She looked over at the grin in the corner and then gestured toward the door with her glass. Roland shrugged and went out the way I'd come in, nodding to me as he passed.

When the door shut behind him, McCary said, "He's not my date."

"What is he then? Your best friend?"

"My business partner."

"With a weakness for other people's class reunions, I suppose."

"With a financial interest in keeping me happy," McCary said, "which tonight meant keeping me company."

The admission didn't soften me up. "You've had all kinds of company tonight. Ann Quinn, for instance. Was she here to give you a progress report on your son?"

The onetime actress swept her legs off the sofa and planted her bare feet on the carpet. It was the preamble for a lunge at me, but she didn't follow through. She sat leaning forward with her weight on the balls of her feet, a diver who didn't like the looks of the water.

"Who told you that?" she demanded.

"Nobody. I deduced it." That was true enough, although it would have embarrassed me to describe the clues Mary Kay had given me. "Jack Quinn is your son, and Ricky Gerow was killed for getting too close to him."

McCary sank back onto the sofa. "Jack couldn't be involved," she said. The reply was intended for me, but McCary addressed it to the empty chair she'd been staring at when I'd first come in. It was the chair Ann had used, I decided, the space she'd occupied when she'd confronted McCary with the connection between Jack and Gerow.

I walked over behind the chair and rested my weight on its rounded back, a move intended to align me with Ann's continuing aura. "Start at the beginning," I said. "Tell me how you and Ann came to be joined at the womb."

McCary tossed back the swallow of vodka that hadn't spilled from her glass and then refilled it. "I got pregnant in college," she said.

"Who was the father?"

"I never knew. There were a number of candidates at the time. You remember how it was back then." She took a long drink. "Or maybe you don't."

"Was one of the candidates Gerow?"

"No way on earth," McCary said.

"Go on."

"I had the baby. I didn't have to, but I did." She looked up at me for approval and then took another drink. "An aunt of mine in Doylestown kept him while I finished school. By the time I graduated, I'd made up my mind to put him up for adoption. I had a chance to go to New York. I had my whole life ahead of me."

"Where did Ann come in?"

"She'd been in all along. In on the secret. She was the only one at LaSalle I could trust. You could always trust Annie, because she just didn't give a damn. Not back then. I never expected her to really get involved. That wasn't her style. She always kept her distance from anything messy."

"Unlike you," I said.

"Fuck you, Keane. Some people make messes. Some people clean them up. Annie just looked on from the sidelines."

"That was her deficiency," I said, remembering Ann's own assessment.

McCary nodded. "Out of the blue, Ann said she wanted to adopt Jack. It wasn't easy to work out, with Ann being single, but we finally got it done."

"Why did she do it?"

McCary spilled more vodka with a sweeping shrug. "Maybe so she wouldn't have to deal with you anymore. Men, I mean. She was sick of being a goddess by then."

"Did you see Jack after that?"

"Only in photographs. Ann wanted it that way, so don't look down your nose at me. When I started to make some real money, I helped Ann out. I got her to take Jack out of the crummy Catholic schools she had him in. I'm the one paying for the Whitener Academy, if you haven't already guessed. You've been there. You know it's a first class operation."

"How do you know I've been there?"

McCary started as though I'd cleverly maneuvered her into a confession. Then the wheels inside her head began to turn. They turned in slow motion, as the works were flooded with vodka. I could see every step from her initial shock to the eventual relief when she came up with a plausible explanation. "Ann told me."

My own wheels were finally in motion. "Are you sure it wasn't an overweight guard who likes to collect license plate numbers? Someone you're paying to keep an eye on Jack behind Ann's back? He would have told you about Jack's regular visits with William Porter of Flemington. Only when he checked on Porter's license number—or you did—it turned out to belong to Ricky Gerow."

"You're crazy," McCary said.

"You found out that Gerow was visiting your son under an assumed name. Ricky Gerow, a man whose life you'd ruined, showing up at the same crucial moment in Jack's life. How did you react?"

"You know everything. You surely know that."

"I should. I jumped to the same wrong conclusion. When I first tracked Gerow to the school, I thought he'd meant to take his revenge out on Jack. To do to Jack what you and the Sorrowers had done to him."

"Who says you were wrong?"

I had to think about that. I'd glimpsed Gerow's real motive on the drive to McCary's hotel, but I hadn't fit it into the puzzle. I did that now for both of us. "Gerow didn't want to hurt anybody. He only wanted to get his future back. He wanted to live a dream of what his life might have been like."

McCary turned the answer against me. "Then he woke up from his dream and saw that his life was nothing. He couldn't take that, so he killed himself."

"I think he had help."

McCary smiled her trademark smile. "Think it then, if it makes you happy. If it makes your own stupid life easier to take. But leave me out of it. I haven't seen Gerow or spoken to him in twenty years. Not you or all the cops in the world can prove I did."

I'd counted too heavily on McCary's drinking. She seemed so sober now that I wondered if she'd been putting on a show earlier for my benefit.

"You're harmless, Keane. You can't tie me in with Gerow's death because I wasn't in the same state. And you can't involve Jack without hurting Ann, which means you can't do it period. You're still one of those puppies who lope along after her with your tongue hanging out. You always will be."

My big scene wasn't supposed to play out this way. McCary was supposed to crack and confess or make some careless reference to the color of Gerow's sheets or the weather on the day he died. Some silly clue I could use to tie it all together. If the missing piece was there, I'd overlooked it. Without it, I was nothing more than the bit player McCary had pegged me for back at the reunion. Out of guesses and out of lines.

"Work on it, Owen," McCary said. "And get back to me in ten years."

NINETEEN

To JUDGE FROM the length of my drive home, someone had moved Mystic Island a hundred miles or so farther east while I'd been away chasing shadows. As I passed through endless miles of black pine forest, I scanned the radio dial, looking for the song that would drown out McCary's parting laughter. They hadn't recorded that one yet, so I settled for a late night call-in show out of Philly hosted by a financial wizard. His first caller was worried about being too heavily invested in municipal bonds. It was a nice worry to have.

If I'd had a car phone, I could have called in and asked the host what to do about a misdirected life. I'd invested too much in my ability to solve mysteries and gotten too little return on it. Worse, I'd squandered other people's peace of mind. Ann Quinn's for example. I'd disrupted her life again for no good reason. If I kept at it, I might destroy her altogether. McCary had guessed correctly that I had no room to maneuver in the Quinn's direction, showing that her old talent for spotting weakness was alive and well.

I switched off the radio and tried to work out the puzzle of McCary's relationship with Ann and Jack. I could now answer the question Amanda had put to me about Jack attending school so far from his mother. The Whitener Academy had been McCary's idea. It was second nature for me now to scrap her stated motive—a sense of obligation—and look for a secret one. She'd chosen the Pennington school to move Jack a little farther from Ann's influence and a little closer to her own. McCary could talk Ann into anything with the trump card she held: the ability to step forward at any time and announce her existence to the boy.

Poor Jack was first prize in contests he couldn't even imagine, but prize wasn't the image that really fit the case. He was more of a key, a passport to a specific kind of life. According to McCary, he'd offered Ann an escape from a brief unhappy career as a goddess. For McCary herself, he was a second shot at possibilities she'd turned her back on years before, a way out of the empty, lonely life she'd made for herself. And for Gerow, what?

If I'd been guessing right back at the Omni-Sevren, Jack Quinn had been the key to a new life for Gerow, too, a life from which the damaged man had thought himself cut off. Jack had been the one real thing in the cardboard world of William Porter, the final ingredient that had made the rest seem real.

I finally spotted the overpass for the Garden State Parkway, which marked the eastern edge of the forest. At that same second, a deer bounded from the pine trees to my right. I locked the Chevy's wheels and shot forward into my shoulder harness. The doe leapt to safety, but its place was taken by a second, smaller one that froze in my headlights. I'd braced myself to hit the deer when it, too, disappeared in one, unreal bound.

I sat in the darkness in the motionless car for a time, thinking not of the deer or of our mutual narrow escape. I thought instead of Ricky Gerow, seeing him on the road before me, frozen in the light. He'd been caught just that way, blinded and frozen and then killed by something he'd understood no better than a deer understood an automobile. Something that had broken into his dream world and shocked him so thoroughly that he'd been unable to save himself. What had that thing been?

Headlights appeared in my rearview mirror, and I realized that I was still stopped on the highway. I got the Chevy going just in time to avoid a rear-end collision. The car that came up behind me chased me all the way to the Tuckerton intersection. Its high beams lit up the inside of my car and bounced back at me from my mirrors, giving me a taste of the deers' point of view.

I made a right at the light and my pursuer went straight, returning me to the peace of darkness. Mystic Island was awash in that kind of peace. Even the town's cheesy Christmas decorations had called it quits. The stars I could see through the

Chevy's windows were winter stars, sharp little pinpoints of comfortless light.

I spotted Marilyn's car as soon as I turned onto Lake Champlain, but I didn't allow myself to react until I'd drawn close enough to confirm that the little wagon had New York plates. She'd come after all to surprise me, knowing, perhaps, that I'd be in need of a friendly shoulder. Marilyn had parked at the curb, saving the driveway for me. As I pulled into it, I noted that there were no lights on in the house. She'd given up on me and gone to bed, I decided. That would make for an interesting reception.

I was still wondering what line I'd take with her as I patted the Chevy's hood good night. When I was halfway to the front door, I saw someone step from the black gap between my house and the neighbor's. I thought first of Marilyn, then, when I saw that it was a man, of Roland, McCary's all-purpose business partner. Finally, I recognized Bill Pearson. Despite the cold, he wore only his rumpled suit from the reunion. He hadn't bothered to button his jacket, but he had buried his hands in its pockets. He stopped some distance away from me, staying in the darkest corner of the carport.

"Owen," Pearson said. "We have to talk." His frozen breath was a passing shadow in the darkness.

"What about, Bill?"

"Ricky Gerow. I need you to understand how it was."

Pearson's tone was calm and reasonable, as though our coming together in the darkness at midnight was the most natural thing in the world. I had to work to keep my own voice steady. "How what was?"

"His death. How that was. You need to understand."

I thought I did, now that it was too late. I thought I could finally put a name to the nameless force that had taken Gerow by surprise and run him down.

"Let's go inside," Pearson said.

It was the last place I wanted to go, as Marilyn was surely there. "I'm tired, Bill," I said. "Come back in the morning."

In reply, Pearson pulled his right hand from its pocket. In his big fist was a gun. It was the kind of long, black automatic that

Bogart used to wave at people in the good old days. Pearson carried his with equal ease, not quite dangling it at his side and not quite pointing it at me either.

I fell back into the cowboy talk of our most recent conversation. "What's with the shooting iron, Bill?"

"It's just so you'll listen to what I have to say." He gestured toward the house with the gun.

I stole a glance toward my bedroom as I turned for the door and saw that the window I'd left closed was now open a crack. Marilyn was on the other side, perhaps already awake. If I gave her enough time, she might make it out the sliding doors to some hiding place near the lagoon. On her way, she might even have time to call the police.

I opened the bidding high to guarantee Pearson's attention, and Marilyn's. "So you killed Ricky."

"He killed himself," Pearson said. "I just sat by and watched."

"With your friend there pointed at his head?"

Pearson looked down at the gun absentmindedly. "Yes," he said in his dead calm voice. "But I didn't really need it. Gerow did it willingly enough. He was nothing but a stinking junkie in the end. An evil thing, Owen. Not a person we ever knew. Not the old Ricky Gerow. That's what I want to tell you about."

The smart play was agreeing with everything Pearson had to say. I argued with him. "Ricky wasn't evil. He wasn't all he'd been, but what was left was good."

Pearson's voice came alive now with steadily rising pain. "You're wrong. Nothing good could survive what we did to Gerow. I've had that beaten into me for twenty years, till there wasn't a good thing left in my life. There couldn't have been any good in his. There wasn't. There was only this rotten thing that wouldn't go away. That I could never get clear of."

He fell over against the house, and I took a half step toward him. "Why you, Bill? Of all the Sorrowers, why are you the damned one? You were there when Gerow took the LSD, but you didn't give it to him. McCary did. You didn't even bring it, Plesniak did."

Pearson pushed himself off the house, the movement carrying him out of the shadows. His wild eyes seemed to have a light of their own. "Who told you that?"

I thought back. Ann Quinn had told me, but her source had been an unreliable one. McCary.

"You brought the LSD?"

"My brother had smuggled it home from Brown. Just to show it off. I brought it that night for the same stupid reason. I was the one who made Gerow what he was. I made that evil and I had to take care of it."

"To end his misery or your own?"

"To keep the evil from spreading. I'll tell you about it inside."

"I already know about it. I know McCary put you up to it. You used to moon after her in the old days, like the rest of us followed Ann. Only you must have done more than follow her around, at least after we all got into college. When she called you about Ricky, she was able to convince you that you were the father of her child."

"I am Jack's father," Pearson said.

It was the detail I'd overlooked in McCary's parlor. I'd let her finesse me with her claim not to know who Jack's father was. When she'd seen that I hadn't worked out that one link, she'd felt safe. She'd laughed me out of the room.

"McCary told you that Gerow was after Jack. That he meant to get his revenge on her by ruining Jack's life."

"He did mean to do it."

"Did he admit it? You were going to kill him anyway. Did Gerow admit that he meant to hurt Jack?"

Pearson's features faded away behind another cloud of frozen breath. "No."

"He never would have," I said.

"Wrong, Keane. All wrong. That little shit meant to hurt my son. I didn't take Maureen's word for it. I know better than that. Yes, she put me onto him, but I checked it out for myself. The William Porter setup was just like she said. A way for Gerow to get to Jack without being traced."

"A blind man could have traced Gerow to Porter," I said. "I did it in an afternoon."

Pearson pointed the gun at me for the first time. "Shut up," he said, loudly enough to wake the people across the street. "I searched Gerow's apartment. I found the heroin he meant to use on Jack. I found the needle. They were together in a box wrapped up with yellow ribbon like a goddamn present. I knew then that Maureen was right."

I felt the knob of the front door hit my spine as I swayed backward.

"I went to visit Gerow. Late, so no one would see me. He was happy enough to let me in, like I was some kind of old pal. Then I told him I knew everything. That he'd figured out what we'd done to him in sixty-eight. That he was onto the truth about Jack's mother. That he'd set up the William Porter scam. That he planned to screw up Jack's life as a way of hitting back at us. I pulled the heroin out of its hiding place and held it under his nose."

"What did he say?"

"Nothing. He cried a little." The memory stopped Pearson for a second. "He never said a thing. I told him he was going to get what he'd saved for Jack. He sat down on his bed and mixed up enough of that poison to kill anything."

"He never said another word?"

Pearson had to be honest to maintain his illusion of righteousness. "Just after he shot himself up, he said Jack's name."

Before I could react, Pearson stepped toward me and touched my chest with the barrel of the gun. "Now get inside. I'm not going to tell you again."

Marilyn had put the front door key back in its hiding place, which was a mixed blessing. It bought a little more time for me, but it put her in a bad spot if she was still inside the house. I told myself that she was surely long gone as I unlocked the door.

I stepped up into the doorway, then turned to face Pearson. I wasn't stalling this time. I was making one last try for the truth.

"You're wrong about Ricky. He never did figure out that McCary was Jack's mother. There was no clue to that in the research he'd done on the boy. And he kept that heroin for himself, not Jack. It was a symbol of the addiction he could never escape. That's what the yellow ribbon meant. Jack was part of what kept him from using it. Jack and Ann.

"Ann thought Ricky was meeting her once a month to collect the money she'd squeezed out of you Sorrowers. But he was just taking the money for the chance to see her. She called those meetings high school dates, and that's what they were. Dates between Ricky and his fantasies. Dates with a life he might have had.

"When he found out that Ann had a son, he latched onto him, too. Not because he wanted to hurt him later. Jack was another part of his fantasy life. The best part. A son."

"My son," Pearson said, stepping up into the doorway. I fell back a step, but kept on pitching. "After a while, Ricky figured out how he could use the conscience money that had been piling up. He found the idea while reading about a writer who had made a new life for himself in a new city under a new name. He picked a place close to his fantasy son and, when he got up enough nerve, he approached him. He found that Jack wanted a father as badly as he wanted his new life. And Ricky tried to be a good father. He got a happy year out of it. Before you killed him."

"He killed himself." Pearson spoke uncertainly, as though it was an effort to remember.

"When he saw the mess his fantasies had created for Jack. The danger he'd put him in."

"What danger?" Pearson pushed me a step deeper into the room. "What danger was there if Gerow didn't intend to hurt him?"

"The danger of losing the only mother he'd ever known. The danger of finding out that his father was a murderer. Gerow went along with you to keep that from happening. He died to protect *his* son."

I expected Pearson's answer to come in the form of a muzzle flash. I couldn't see his expression in the darkness, but his big outline in the open doorway seemed to grow smaller. The barrel of the gun moved away from me slightly.

Then we both heard a sound from the darkness behind and to the left of me. A jingling of keys. It was followed by another sound, a whoosh like soda escaping from a shaken bottle. I turned in time to see Marilyn, a pale figure with wild eyes, her right arm outstretched.

Pearson roared in pain, waving his free hand in front of his face. The automatic was pointing at Marilyn now. I grabbed it with my left hand and Pearson's forearm with my right and pushed the gun toward the wall. I raised my left knee and tried to bring his wrist down on it. At the last second, he pulled back, and I hit my leg with the butt of the gun. The blow sent a numbing pain down as far as my ankle. I fell toward the pain, pulling Pearson with me, but he fought against the movement, yanking me upright again. I added my weight to his and sent us both crashing into the door frame, his gun hand leading the way. The forty-five dropped with a flat thud.

That freed up his right for a swing at my head, but blind as he was, he couldn't see to land it. I threw a right of my own, catching him on the ear. My follow through put my weight on my left leg, which was still missing in action. I went on over onto the floor, and my chin found the automatic.

I struggled up on my good leg with the gun in my hand, just in time to see Pearson stumble out through the door. He had both hands to his face, and he caromed off my car and into the side of the carport as he ran. Then he was gone.

My own eyes were burning now, and my jaw was as numb as my knee. I felt myself sliding down the living room wall. Marilyn was at my side before I quite made it to the floor. She was barefoot and shivering. Perhaps from the cold.

The sound of a car starting came into us. I limped to the door in time to see Pearson's tail lights disappearing around a bend in the street.

"You'd better check the expiration date on your tear gas," I said in a voice that was fairly close to my own.

Marilyn came up beside me. "You had the gun," she said. "You could have..." She rested her head against my shoulder. "Look who I'm talking to about guns."

I put my arm around her. "Thanks for sticking by me," I said.

Her eyes were tearing now, making it unanimous. "Damned if I didn't," she said.

TWENTY

MARILYN AND I spent a restless night on the living room sofa. My rescuer was curled up under a blanket. I thought for a long time that she was asleep, but when one of my neighbors drove up Lake Champlain Drive around three, she raised her head immediately. I sat beside her, alternately nursing a tall scotch, neat, and dozing. On the table near my left hand was Pearson's gun, pointed toward the front door.

We'd had an argument prior to settling down. Marilyn had wanted me to call the police, and I had refused. She hadn't called them herself during my heart-to-heart with Pearson, because she hadn't been able to find the phone in the dark house. When she abandoned the pretense of sleep around six, her first words were "Call the damn cops."

"I can't," I said. "Everything would come out." That answer hadn't satisfied her before. Now it wouldn't even quiet her.

"There's a nut out there wandering around loose who wants you dead."

"The nut has a son who's better off not knowing about all of this. Ricky Gerow felt that way, and he was right."

That got Marilyn upright on the sofa in a hurry. "You were serious about that? I thought you were making it up for that lunatic's benefit. You really think that Gerow killed himself to protect the boy?"

"It's what I'd like to think happened." It was a whimsical justification, but that seemed appropriate for this case, which had been brim full of hopeless dreaming. Marilyn wasn't given to that weakness, though, so I took a more reasonable line. "Maybe that wasn't why Gerow did it. Maybe it was an effort for him not to do it, and Pearson gave him an excuse to give up the fight. Maybe the shock of finally knowing what the Sorrowers had done to him was enough to shove him over the edge. Gerow might not have known the real reason himself.''

"Which means there's no excuse for you putting yourself in danger so this kid can grow up happy.''

There wasn't, of course. Not when the thing was considered Marilyn's way, rationally. "He's a nice kid though," I said.

Marilyn kicked the blanket onto the floor. "You men need keepers. You spend the first half of your lives searching for fathers and the second half looking for sons."

"Must mean I'm in the second half," I said.

"With no time-outs remaining," Marilyn added. She picked up the blanket and stomped away as far as the doorway to the dining room. Then she came back, to kiss me, I thought. Instead, she hit me with the blanket.

Just after Pearson had gone, I'd placed a call to the Omni-Sevren in Princeton to warn McCary that he might be headed her way. I thought she might be a candidate for successor to Gerow as Pearson's symbol of all the pain and frustration in his life. I'd gotten the desk clerk who had helped me earlier, or so I'd judged from his general politeness. He'd regretted to inform me that McCary had checked out.

As I listened to the restful sound of Marilyn running the shower, I realized that I'd come very close to not solving the mystery when I'd decided to trace Gerow's drug connection. I might actually have stumbled on the person who'd sold him his secret, symbolic heroin supply, which he'd modeled after Minerva Fine's pint of whiskey. I wondered if we all wouldn't have been better off if I had followed through on that mistake.

Marilyn came out into the kitchen in my old plaid bathrobe and began to search for the makings of breakfast. I pointed out the Cheerios and some white bread so stale it constituted instant toast. Wet, Marilyn's wild hair was almost demure. It had time to dry while we ate and I told her what I'd been up to all week. As it dried, her hair regained its natural character, creating the flattering false impression that the telling of my adventures was making it stand on end.

After breakfast, Marilyn brought a hairbrush in from the bedroom and struggled to create order out of chaos. At the same time, she scared me with a story of her own.

"He knocked on the door when he first showed up. Pearson, I mean. Maybe half an hour before you got here."

"But you didn't answer it."

"I don't open my own door at night, never mind one out here in the wilds. Besides, I'd gotten here bushed and put my head down right away. I just peeked out to make sure it wasn't you, too drunk to find the key. After a little bit, he gave up. I thought he'd gone away. Now I'm wondering why he didn't try to break in."

"He wasn't good enough at breaking and entering to do it without leaving a trace. He wanted me to invite him in like Gerow did."

"So you could kill yourself the way Gerow did? What was he planning to do? He can't have counted on your having a secret heroin stash."

"Bill was way past planning by last night. He was just bouncing off things in the dark."

Marilyn shook her head, undoing all her brushing.

"Thanks again for staying last night," I said. "In the old days, you would have let me face my troubles alone."

Marilyn had had time to think about what had happened and to question the stand she'd made. "Last night wasn't like the old days. It wasn't you being chased by some bogeyman out of your own imagination. It wasn't like me running out on Tony, either. You were up against something real, a man with a gun. I'm okay with things you can see and touch and spray Mace on."

"There was a lot going on last night that you couldn't see or touch. You faced it all."

Marilyn stood up and walked toward the sliding doors, forcing the brush through her hair as she went. "It may be the age of miracles after all," she said.

I left her to stand guard and took a shower myself. Afterward, I felt better than I had in days. I recognized the old high that always came from solving a mystery, and the recognition made me feel dishonest. I hadn't really accomplished anything to feel good about. And I was stuck for my next move.

Luckily, I had Marilyn around to prod me on. "You should do something, Keane," she said.

She was still in my kitchen and still in my bathrobe, more or less. "We should do something together," I countered. "I haven't made the bed yet."

She smiled. "That sounds a little sick, considering that we narrowly avoided getting killed not too long ago."

"It's a natural reaction," I said, "like pinecones opening up after a forest fire."

"You can explain that one to me later."

She hadn't quite stood up before the phone rang. It was my client, Mary Kay Ellis-Humphrey.

"I'm calling from the office," she said, a little out of breath. "I was scrolling the AP wire for our deathwatch story..."

"What?"

"Sorry. I was using our computer to check wire stories on automobile accidents. We're keeping a running total because it's a holiday weekend."

"Okay," I said. "I'm with you."

"I found a mention of a one-car accident that happened early this morning near Smithtown."

"In the Pine Barrens," I said.

"Right. A car went into a ditch at high speed and flipped over. Several times, I guess. The driver was killed. Owen, it was Bill Pearson."

During the silence that followed, I looked at Marilyn and she looked at me. I don't know what Mary Kay was looking at.

Then she said, "The state police are guessing that he swerved to avoid a deer."

"Or a ghost," I said.

"What?"

"Nothing." Pearson had found one last symbol of evil to wrestle with, and it hadn't been McCary or me.

"Owen, does this have anything to do with what we talked about last night? Please tell me that I'm not responsible somehow."

If the Sorrowers ever got around to selecting a motto, my vote would go to Mary Kay's hushed appeal. "Tell me I'm not responsible."

"It was just an accident," I said. "Take care of that family of yours."

Mary Kay wasn't buying. "So long, Owen," she said.

"You can stop worrying about Pearson," I told Marilyn as I dropped the handset back onto its cradle. "He cleaned up his own mess." I told her about the accident.

I was afraid she might blame herself and her handy Mace, but she was too busy reading my mind. "Now I suppose you think he drove into the ditch to protect this Jack kid, too. Or was it just his bad conscience?"

"Just a bad road," I said.

"That still leaves Maureen McCary," Marilyn said. "What are you going to do about her?"

"I don't know." The news about Pearson had brought me down to earth, hard. I would have been content to leave McCary to her own ghosts, if it hadn't been for her continuing influence over the Quinns. "I should do something," I said.

Marilyn decided to take pity on a poor, confused detective. "Yeah," she said. She hooked a hand around my belt. "You should try your pinecone line on me again."

TWENTY-ONE

FOR ME, solving a mystery always meant telling stories, sharing all or part of what I'd learned with the people who had helped me learn it. There was an unusually large number of those debts to pay off in the Gerow case. I drove up to Trenton on the first Saturday of December to balance the books.

I talked first with Minerva Fine. I could be frank with her, and telling the whole story through from beginning to end gave me the chance to mentally edit it for my next audience, Mr. Gerow. The version I told him began with the Sorrowers' LSD experiment of 1968, although I was careful to omit names. I told him that Ricky had been murdered by one of his old persecutors who had been unbalanced by his guilt and that the murderer had later taken his own life. I told the old man the truth about the money straps and William Porter and who he could talk to in Flemington to claim his son's things. I told him about Jack Quinn and what he had meant to Ricky, without mentioning Jack's extra mother or that Jack had been involved, unknowingly, in Ricky's murder. Mr. Gerow didn't press me for specifics. I was also relieved to find that he wasn't interested in any public, official clearing of his son's name. He seemed content to be reassured that Ricky had been in the end the same son in whom he had never lost faith.

The Whitener Academy was my next stop. I was late for an appointment there, and the man I had the appointment with, Harry Ohlman, was not pleased. He sat in his Porsche with the windows rolled up until I tapped on the glass. Then he climbed out stiffly.

"Sorry," I said. "I was a long time breaking everything to Mr. Gerow. I don't know how much good I did."

"More than we'll accomplish with this, I bet," Harry said. He handed me a white business envelope. "You were right about the guard. He did tip McCary to William Porter's visits.

He made the connection between Porter and Gerow for her, too. Seems he's a frustrated detective.''

"A dangerous type," I said.

"It's all in his deposition," Harry added, nodding toward the envelope.

"You work fast. I hope you didn't break too many of his fingers."

"Threatening to have him canned was enough. Little does he know we can never go through with it for fear of publicity."

I took two folded pieces of paper from my pocket and put them into the white envelope. They were my statement and Marilyn's, both describing Pearson's rambling confession in which he'd named McCary as an accessory in the murder of Richard Gerow.

I handed the envelope back to Harry. He let it dangle between his thumb and forefinger, like a fish he was thinking of throwing back. "I'd hate to go near a court of law with this 'evidence' of yours, Owen."

"It won't come to that," I said. "Tell Ann she has to make McCary believe that she'd rather have the truth come out than lose Jack."

"I have a grasp of the basic situation," Harry said dryly. "What I don't understand is, why aren't you delivering this stuff yourself? Ms. Quinn is going to want to talk with you. To thank you, if nothing else."

"If she finds out I've been to see Jack again," I said, "she'll be the next one after me with a gun."

"Why do it, then?"

"I promised him I'd come back."

I said good-bye to Harry and went off to make good on my promise. It was a bright, cold morning and a steady wind was blowing in from the northwest. The still-green grass had had a recent growth spurt. It was tall enough to ripple in the wind.

I headed for the rugby field, hoping to find Jack or some teammate I could send off in search of him. Instead, I found Ann Quinn. She was standing on the far sidelines, wrapped in a stadium coat, and she was staring at the field as though reliving some big game from years ago.

She wasn't surprised to see me, which answered the question of how she came to be there. Harry Ohlman, my reluctant sidekick, had exceeded his instructions yet again. He'd wanted me to have one last scene with Ann, so he'd arranged one.

"Hello, Owen," Ann said. "I know about what happened with Bill. Your Mr. Ohlman told me. I'm sorry. I had no idea that Bill had been to see Ricky. Or that he was so dangerous. I'm glad you came through it okay."

I decided that her statement of fact was really a question and answered it. "I'm fine," I said. "Are you here to keep me from talking to Jack?"

"Tell me what you were planning to say to him."

She was standing with her back to the wind. I looked over her blowing hair and studied the blank blue sky while I thought about it. "I was going to tell him that Porter wasn't his father. He was someone who had known you years ago and had loved you, in a quiet, unrequited away. He'd gone to Vietnam and come back damaged. After that he'd made a life for himself, but only a fragmented one, as incomplete as he was himself. He'd found out you had a son and that your son didn't have a father. And he'd wanted to be that father very badly—not to hurt Jack—to fill a void in Jack's life and maybe find a missing piece of his own."

"Is that all true?" Ann asked.

"Yes."

Ann turned to face the wind, which put her back to me. "Poor Ricky. Poor Bill. Was there anything else?"

"I was going to tell Jack to trust you."

She started to turn her head toward me and then thought better of it. "What about Maureen? What were you going to tell Jack about her?"

"Nothing. I think I've figured out a way to get her out of your life and away from Jack for good." I reached into my pocket for the depositions that were now in Harry's pocket.

"Mr. Ohlman told me," Ann said. "Thanks for trying, Owen. But I can't threaten Maureen."

"Why not?"

"Because she's not the devil incarnate. She's a person who's made mistakes. She didn't know what she was setting loose when she sent Bill after Ricky. I'm sure of that. I can't make my life—or Jack's—better by blaming everything on her. Or by hurting her. That's the solution Bill Pearson tried to work with Ricky and it only made things worse for him."

"So you're going to go on as though nothing's happened?"

"No," Ann said. "I can't do that, either. I don't want to be like Ricky, using Jack to live out a fantasy."

She turned back to face me. I expected to see that she'd been crying, but her eyes were as dry as mine. "Did Maureen tell you why I adopted Jack?"

"She didn't seem to understand it completely. She had some idea that it was a way of escaping from men."

Ann shook her head. "I did it to save him, Owen. I didn't save Ricky because I was afraid of getting involved. I didn't want to fail like that again. And Jack saved me in return. He saved me from living my life alone."

"You, alone?" I asked.

"I'd always been alone, Owen. That's what happens when you let people treat you like you're better than they are. Jack saved me from that. I owe him a lot. I owe him the whole truth. I want you to help me pay that debt."

"How?"

"By being there when I talk to him. By telling him all you know about the Sorrowers and Ricky and me."

I thought it over and decided that Ann's request was really a gesture, that she was including me in her grand scheme to reconcile all the scattered pieces of her life. It was a tempting offer, but I stepped back from it, figuratively and literally.

"Thanks," I said. "But you'll do a better job without me around. Besides, Jack might ask you to explain me. Then you'd be stuck."

"No, I wouldn't," Ann said.

I took another step away from her, afraid that she'd share her explanation of Owen Keane. Afraid of being summed up, as the dead Gerow and Pearson now could be.

"Don't give up, Owen," Ann said.

"I won't."

I was almost across the field when I caught sight of Jack running toward Ann. When he drew within a few yards of her, his momentum dropped away to nothing, as though he'd gone from dry, hard ground to a stretch of sand. They stood looking at each other for a time across the rippling grass. Then Jack held out his hand to her.

I watched from the safety of a grove of trees until Ann stepped over and took Jack's hand. Then I addressed her softly. "See you in ten years," I said.

ALASKA GRAY

SUSAN FROETSCHEL

A Jane McBride Mystery

NEW BEGINNINGS, DEADLY ENDINGS

Jane McBride is a woman with secrets and sadness—and Alaska seems just about as far away as she can get from her past.

Her big welcome comes in the form of an anonymous phone call telling her to leave. Then Jane learns that the finance job she left Boston for has been eliminated. But the beauty of Sitka lures her, and she is determined to stay— even after she surprises an intruder ransacking her room.

The death of a young local woman has no connection to her…or does it? Soon Jane is trapped in the middle of a very sophisticated evil in the small town….

"A page-turner…"—*Pittsburgh Advertiser*

Available in July at your favorite retail stores.

Down Among The DEAD Men

GERALDINE EVANS

An Inspector Rafferty/Sergeant Llewellyn Mystery

A FAMILY AFFAIR

When rich and beautiful Barbara Longman is found dead among the meadow flowers, Inspector Rafferty doesn't believe it's the latest grisly offering by the Suffolk killer—though he believes her killer would like him to think so.

Rafferty and Llewellyn suspect someone close to home—someone among the descendants of the family's long-dead patriarch, Maximillian Shore. Everyone, it seems, had a motive: Barbara's weak, ineffectual husband; Henry, her ruthless brother-in-law; as well as Henry's bitter ex-wife. And the police duo discover that Maximillian Shore can wield his influence even from the grave—in a twisted legacy of murder.

"Competent…"—*Kirkus Reviews*

Available in July at your favorite retail stores.

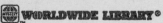

REGINALD HILL
BLOOD SYMPATHY

First Time in Paperback

A Joe Sixsmith Mystery

ALL THIS AND A MATCHMAKING AUNT, TOO...

It is feast or famine for ex-machinist turned private investigator Joe Sixsmith. One minute he's dozing in his office, the next he's been hired by a self-proclaimed dabbler in the dark arts to retrieve a stolen locket. There's also a man who dreams he has murdered his entire family and two thugs who seem to think Joe's in possession of several kilos of heroin. Add to that a meddlesome aunt who wants to fix him up with marriage candidates.

Things are sticky at best. But for a private eye with admittedly more wits than guts, and an alcoholic cat as partner, a bit of luck may just keep him single— and alive.

"Sumptuously plotted..."—*Kirkus Reviews*

Available in August at your favorite retail stores.

 **WORLDWIDE LIBRARY** ®

BLOOD

Jeanne McCafferty

A MacKenzie Griffin Mystery

CLIMBING THE CHARTS IS MURDER...

Murder scenes aren't supposed to look this good. The lighting, the staging, the arrangement of the body, even the clothes are eerie recreations of pop superstar Peter Rossellini's hot music videos. In fact, each victim resembles the sexy singer.

Clearly, the killer is obsessed. But is Peter the next intended victim? Criminologist MacKenzie Griffin fears just that. Mac has no shortage of suspects. And one is setting the stage for a hit that's to die for.

"A highly recommended first novel."

—Susan Rogers Cooper, author of
Dead Moon on the Rise

Available in August at your favorite retail stores.

 **WORLDWIDE LIBRARY®**

STAR